DIAMONDS
IN THE
WATER

BY MARY ANN JENKINS

BOOKS BY MARY ANN JENKINS

Diamonds in the Water
Dreams Return to Rivers Run (*The Sequel to Diamonds in the Water*)
The Witch's Journal
The Journal Reopened (*The Sequel to the Witch's Journal*)
The Cardboard Box (*Co-authored with Mary Anne Enslow*)

1. Fiction/Family Life 2. Fiction/Romance 3. Fiction/Suspense
4. Fiction/Drama

Book is set in Garamond
Interior layout and design by Mary Barrows

Majenkins@earthlink.net

Paperback - ISBN 978-0-9993064-1-3

DIAMONDS
IN THE
WATER

CHAPTER ONE

In school that morning I had no idea that my life was about to change. It was October 20, 1971, and I was seven years old.

In class I had been joking and laughing with a bunch of friends. Then the principal came into my classroom and talked with my teacher and the teacher called my name.

"Jennette Fiona Walters!"

I raised my hand, and the principal took me out of the class. By the look she gave me I just knew I was going to be punished for all the laughing I was causing in the classroom, but it had been fun. I did it all the time and never got called about it before.

In her office there was an officer in a uniform and a lady in a bright red coat she introduced as Miss Tammy. They sat me down and told me there had been an accident and my mother and father had died and I wouldn't be going home.

I couldn't believe it at first and yelled and screamed. When my crying changed to sobs, Miss Tammy held me close and said that everything would be different now, but they would take care of me. I didn't understand and don't remember much after that except that I continued to cry.

Miss Tammy helped me put on my coat, wiped my face, and hugged me. The principal told me everything would be okay as I left with Miss Tammy.

Miss Tammy also said, "Everything would be okay," and drove to a big, tall red brick building and parked in front of it. She explained that it was where other children lived. She took me to an office on the first floor where I met Miss Hannity.

Miss Hannity sat with me and told me I would live with other children for a while until they could locate a family member. Eventually I was taken upstairs to a big room where there were many other children. I was assigned a bed and Miss Hannity talked to the other children and introduced me to them. I only remember that I didn't feel like eating at dinnertime and many days after that passed in a blur. I cried myself to sleep every night for days missing my mom and dad. In the mornings I would constantly picture the last images I had of them when they kissed me goodbye before I went into school.

I was very unhappy at the orphanage. The other girls in my room were often mean and liked to pick on me. My cot was not soft and I was often cold.

Several weeks later I was told that they had not located any relatives. My dad's father and mother had died before I was born, and my mother's parents were also gone. I knew I had never met any other family members. My friends had aunts, uncles, and cousins. I remembered when I asked my mom about that one day, she said my dad had no relatives like aunts and uncles and she was an only child. Several of my dad's great uncles had died in the First World War when they were very young, and in the Second World War he had lost an uncle and his older brother.

One day followed another and months went by. I felt abandoned and mistreated, being shuffled from the orphanage to foster homes. Many nights I looked through small windows at the stars in unfamiliar beds, wondering what happened to the place I called "home." Miss Hannity had been right—it was different, but she was wrong—I never felt cared for again and knew I was alone in my misery.

That was when I started having marvelous dreams. I would fall asleep and suddenly be on a wonderful farm with children and servants, often sleeping in a soft bed in a lovely big place with many rooms.

In those dreams I was with a little girl, Kathleen, and a little boy, Junior, as we laughed and played together. Both were about my size and I began to love them. Every night when I went to bed in the orphanage, I would look forward to a dream with them again, but it didn't happen every night.

Kathleen had long reddish blonde curls, creamy looking skin, blue eyes, and a beautiful smile, always in lovely dresses with big bows in the back.

Junior was taller than both of us, and would tap me on my head, laughing about how short I was. He had reddish blonde hair and blue eyes too, and ran around us all the time, pulling at Kathleen's bows. He would tell me I looked like Kathleen, laugh and call me fatty, pulling at my hair. Being with them in those dreams kept me going through tough times, especially after a bad day in a foster home.

Kathleen and I always tried to hide from Junior and his dog, Princess, but they found us no matter where we hid in the big place. One night when we were hiding from Junior, Kathleen and I sneaked into her father's library. She said they were never allowed in there and it would be a good place to hide.

When she opened the door, her father was behind a big desk, leaning down under it. He jumped up with a bag in his hand, and jerked to hide it behind his back. He told Kathleen to leave and never play in there, and Kathleen and I ran out quickly. I always wondered if that bag had a gift in it for Kathleen.

Some of those dreams had another little boy in them. He didn't talk very much and when he did I could not understand him very well. He was about my size with dark hair and blue eyes, and Kathleen called him Marty. He smiled, but I could tell he was sad like me.

I tried to get Marty to run and play with us. He seemed very somber when left alone, and I tried to comfort him. I would laugh at things he did, and get him interested in things we were doing.

Kathleen's mother was beautiful and dressed in long flowing gowns. Whenever her mother was there with us, Kathleen would tell her that she and Junior were playing with her friends, Jenny and Marty. Her mother would just smile and say, "That's nice, dear." She was very nice but I don't think she could see us.

As the years went by in the orphanage, I learned to cope very easily, making fun of everything I didn't understand, knowing that I was older and capable of handling myself. That's when my dreams with Kathleen and Junior stopped.

I loved school because it got me away from the foster home or the orphanage for a time. In high school I found myself volunteering to take charge and enjoying difficult assignments from the teachers, graduating with honors and many friends.

After graduation, Miss Brewster from the county office settled me into an apartment and a job at Amy's Gift Shop located in our town of Shadyside, Virginia. I also found time to take classes at night in a local college preparatory school.

After I moved into my apartment she brought me two small boxes of things that had belonged to my mother and father.

When alone, I lifted a few things from the first box—a shirt of my father's and a blouse of my mother's. I embedded my face in the folds and cried. The other box had their wallets, pictures, mementos and souvenirs of trips we had taken. I just couldn't bear to look at all of them and closed the boxes, putting them in my closet.

There I go again remembering happenings in my young life. I've awakened early and soon my alarm clock will announce another day in May 1985. Once again as I wait for it to tell me to get up, I tend to bring those days back in my thoughts.

When my clock sounds, I sit up quickly, thinking about the date. Last week on May 12th, I had my twenty-first birthday and I should be happy. My small apartment is nice, and I like my job at the gift shop in Shadyside, Virginia. It is enough to bring a smile but only for a moment, because I am very much aware that no one knows what will happen today that may drastically change lives. I also try to make life better, and usually strive to make it fun when I'm with others.

I look at the clock, bury those childhood memories in my mind once again, jump out of bed and get dressed. Before I leave the apartment, there's a mirror in the hall and I look to make sure I'm presentable. My long, slightly curly auburn hair has a nice shine to it and my hazel eyes look blue with my blue blouse and skirt. My costume jewelry earrings are silver and go well with the blouse. I have lost weight and look thinner since I am in charge of what I eat. I am not very tall so any extra weight always makes me look pudgy.

I close the door and step out into the sunshine, hurrying along the small neighborhood to the busy part of town and Amy's Gift Shop. A soft spring breeze greets me, bringing sweet smells of new, early flowers in the gardens.

When I get there the bell on the door announces my arrival. Amy Forrester comes out immediately from the backroom. "Hello, Jenny, how are you today?" She quickly turns and goes back into the backroom before I can answer.

Anyway, I say loudly, "Just fine."

Then she appears again and says, "Put your purse away and help me with this box, will you? I have a box of things from Gifts, Inc. that has been delivered, and I am rewrapping it to send back. I didn't like their attitude when I ordered. I think that is one supplier I can get along without." Then she disappears.

That's Mrs. Forrester for you. She very seldom finds things acceptable.

Mrs. Forrester is a young, 28-year-old widow who owns the little shop. She's taller than me by a few inches, has a nice figure, blue eyes, and lovely blonde hair that she wears in a short style that complements her round face. She is a nice person but moody and pessimistic, often making comments about how things could be better.

I never agree with her because then life would be disgusting.

I have learned she lost her husband four years ago from cancer after the shop had opened. She has kept running the place, but doesn't seem happy about anything, blaming God for the circumstances. She never talks about her family or her husband's family except that they live on the West Coast.

I hurry over to help with the box but then the bell on the door announces an arrival. I quickly go back, and standing at the door is a tall, large built, middle-aged man. His mixed-gray, thinning hair emerges as he takes off a dark blue hat, which matches his business suit.

Amy appears behind me, goes over to the counter, and says, "May I help you."

The tall man advances into the shop looking around. I notice his deep brown eyes that look at me in a way that makes me uneasy. His face is clean-shaven but he looks clumsy and out of place in his clothes, carrying too much weight. As he steps uneasily to the counter adjusting his suit coat, he fiddles with his hat before he speaks.

"Mrs. Forrester?"

Amy goes closer to the counter. "Yes."

"I'm Jerry Whitaker from a Law Office in Richmond, Virginia." Then he brings out his business card. "The County Office told me Miss Jennette Fiona Walters works here, and I talked with you about her on the telephone last evening."

Amy turns to me and introduces us. I go over and shake hands with Mr. Whitaker. He says, "This is a pleasure, my dear."

He continues to look me over while talking to Amy. "Mrs. Forrester, if Miss Walters is available, I need to discuss something with her privately."

I am surprised, and first I raise my eyebrows in disbelief, but nod my head at Amy. I feel protected and comfortable with Amy here.

The County Office probably has a person to share my apartment and I will have to sign more papers. I wonder if it will be someone I can have fun with?

Amy starts walking toward a room in the back. "Come this way— there's a room we use for lunch. It will be private."

The lawyer and I follow along as Amy takes us to the lunch table. *Amy leaves us there and I'm glad she keeps the door open.*

The lawyer places a folder on the table and says, "Miss Walters, my law office has been looking for you for some time. We finally traced your lineage with the Walters family from England in the late 1800's, and you are the only living heir to the property. You, having been in an orphanage for years, did not help us in the search."

I stare at him confused because I was told that I had no living relatives after my father and mother were killed. He must have the wrong person!

He looks at me, sighs, and says, "I can see this will take a little time." He gets up, takes off his suit coat and puts it on the back of his chair, revealing a tight white shirt with buttons that are clearly on their last stretch.

He said he was with a law office from Richmond, but to me I wonder if I am having dreams again. Could he be a figment of my crazy imagination that took me to a great house with children when I was an orphan and now he wants to take me back?

CHAPTER TWO

Mr. Whitaker grunts, sits back down and continues, "We have proof that in 1867, after the Civil War, Donald Andrew Rivers, an only son of Martin Stephen Rivers, a banker in Richmond, bought property in Opal, Virginia, and named it Rivers Run. It consists of 300 acres of farmland that Mr. Rivers began farming with sharecroppers. While his house was being built on the property he took a trip to England, married Helen Marie Walters, and brought her back to Rivers Run with him in December of that year."

I watch as he sighs, wipes his brow, spreading out documents. "Miss Walters, this case has been investigated thoroughly. Helen Marie Walters, born in England in 1849, married Donald Andrew Rivers when she was 18 years old. She had a brother, Harrison Tomas Walters, your great-great-grandfather who also came to America."

Then Mr. Whitaker shows me a faded copy of the Rivers' marriage document.

He clears his throat, gets up and paces, talking about the children, Kathleen and Donald Junior and when they were born.

Did he say the children were Kathleen and Junior?

He then tells me that Helen Marie Rivers died in 1904 and her husband had the town of Opal renamed "Helen" in honor of her.

Walking back and forth the lawyer tries to explain further. "The last member of the Rivers family, John Matthew Rivers, died two years ago at the age of 90. His body is buried in the family cemetery. The Rivers Run manor house has been vacant since then. We were not able to find a legitimate heir—until now." The lawyer stares at me for a response.

I am trying hard to focus but my mind is repeating the names Kathleen and Junior. I can see them so well and also the beautiful place where my dreams put me.

Then he says, "Miss Walters, according to the records you are the only one left in the Walters' or the Rivers' families. I traced Helen Marie Walters Rivers to your father and mother, Samuel and Lisa Walters, who died when you were seven, and John Matthew Rivers was the last heir on the Rivers' side."

Mr. Whitaker sits back in his chair, looking over the documents, and says, "John Matthew Rivers had come back to Rivers Run after college, stayed on the property and never married, renting the property to farmers to raise crops. He died two years ago."

Nothing he says is making any sense. I have a connection with the Walters family ancestry? It can't be possible, can it?

I feel faint, "You can't be serious—this is very hard to believe! Say it again only slower!"

Mr. Whitaker sighs and stands up, moving papers around. "Well, Miss Walters, I assure you these documents will prove that you have inherited Rivers Run. I only need your signature on a few papers that stipulate you will live there and take care of the place. Once you sign, you will have the estate, plus money from the farmers who have rented the grounds for farming. If we hadn't found you, according to Virginia law, the farm and money would have been turned over to the State of Virginia."

The lawyer places the pages in front of me that I am to sign and looks at me again for a response.

I'm breathing but I don't seem able to express myself. My energy has escaped me and the facts are getting mixed with the names of Kathleen and Junior, and several wonderful escapades with them running around in my brain.

I look at the lawyer who has just told me a story that seems outrageous. I sit back in the chair holding the pages I am to sign and burst out laughing because I think I'm dreaming again.

From the worried look on Mr. Whitaker's face he apparently senses something is wrong, and asks, "Would you like some water?"

"Yes please."

Maybe this dream with this man will fade away if he leaves.

He hurries out, and minutes later Amy comes in behind him carrying a glass of water. She sets the glass down, puts her arm around my shoulders and says, "Are you all right? What's happened?"

That's Mrs. Forrester. Gosh, maybe this isn't a dream!

With the lawyer's words about the Rivers family still taking center stage in my mind, I say, "I think so. Just give me a minute." Hoping it will help me swallow this story about my inheritance, I take a drink of water and breathe deeply.

I'm thinking of all those dreams I have had throughout my young days in the orphanage, about a beautiful home with people on a farm. They were always so real and I felt during those dreams that I was taking part in their lives, running with them through those lovely rooms. It seemed to get me through the nights when I was so distraught and unhappy—but those were just dreams! Now, according to Mr. Whitaker, Kathleen and Donald Junior were born in the 1800's! I would have had to go back in time to be with them!

I gradually realize the lawyer is talking to Amy and he says, "Mrs. Forrester, it's as I told you briefly last evening."

Amy says, "Mr. Whitaker, I really did not pay attention. It was late and I was tired. Could you please tell me again with details this time?" Then I notice there are definite questions in Amy's eyes. I am so glad because I haven't really listened, and I need to hear everything again.

After the lawyer gives a short detailed explanation, Amy puts her hand on my shoulder and says, "Jenny, this could be a good thing for you."

Then Amy frowns at the lawyer and says, "Would it be all right if I look over the papers?"

He looks over at me. "As long as Miss Walters is in agreement." I nod my head and Amy sits down to read the documents. I decide I had better read them carefully too, and I sit down beside her as she passes them to me after her review.

When she passes the last page, I look with awe at the stack of papers that represent my ancestry and inheritance.

All those years when I didn't think I belonged to anyone or anything—it is truly astonishing to read that my ancestors came from England so long ago.

Amy says, "Mr. Whitaker, could you explain to Jenny just exactly what to expect at this place in Helen, Virginia?"

"Of course." He rubs his hand over his forehead. "Rivers Run Estate consists of a manor house and stables on 300 acres of land. It was John Matthew Rivers' wish that the farmers continue renting the property for farming while he was alive, and he signed a letter to that effect. I would recommend you do the same as it has brought a considerable amount of money to the estate."

Mr. Whitaker stands and walks back and forth. "John Matthew Rivers had a Will with a request that all heirs be found. The court assigned our law office to find out if a rightful owner existed, and left us in charge until the inheritance could be settled. We have continued to rent the property for farming, the rent money being kept in escrow. Of course we've had permission to use some of the money for necessary expenses and for hired help as needed."

Then he sighs and sits down again. "Mr. and Mrs. Waller have been hired as caretakers to manage the property. I also hired an accountant, Bob Humphrey, to take care of the financial needs and the bank statements. He goes to the manor house once a month to write checks for the caretakers and for the other bills, and provides cash to be used for food and other incidentals. Their contracts are good for a year or until you get settled."

He hands me a copy of each contract. "I will contact Mr. Humphrey as soon as the court approval is received concerning your inheritance. I recommend that you continue his services."

I sign the papers because they are in front of me, and because he says I should. Then he puts them in his briefcase.

"Well, that's that," and he stands. "I am very happy for you, Miss Walters. I will notify you as soon as the firm has this approved in court. It shouldn't take more than a few days after I return to Richmond. It will just be a formality since you are of legal age to take on this responsibility."

He sighs and says, "The rent from the farmers' properties and other monies are in the Community Bank in Helen and we will put that account in your name. If you have a bank account here in Shadyside, remember to transfer those assets when you get there."

I still feel in a dreamlike state and just thank him.

Putting on his suit coat he says, "The house needs someone to care for it, Miss Walters, but I think you will find it rewarding."

Going out the door he hesitates and says, "Just let us know when you feel you can manage without the caretakers and I will cancel their contract. They can continue with you as servants, but you must arrange that with them. Their salaries and duties will be your responsibility—you won't need a contract."

Amy and I are watching him go like we have nothing else to do. I stand there dumbfounded. She pats me on the back and says, "Jenny, I can't believe it—this is a big responsibility for you. I hope you will be able to meet the challenges you will face."

I'm speechless. I had not thought of that and take a deep breath.

Amy takes me by the hand, directing me into the backroom to sit and drink tea. The rest of the day I work around the shop in a trance. We have customers, and Amy takes care of most of them. I try to help, but my situation has changed and I walk around the shop lightheaded, feeling abandoned by gravity, still thinking about Kathleen and Junior, my two dream playmates.

That night, I try to sleep. The moon is shining into my window and all I can think of is the large farm I have inherited.

What will I do with such a place? I don't remember my dad ever telling me about his father, his grandfather, his great-grandfather or his great-great-grandfather, but I was very young. It's almost morning and I am exhausted.

I close my eyes and finally drift off thinking about the wonderful dreams I had with Kathleen and Junior. Could the children Mr. Whitaker talked about be the same ones I knew in my childhood dreams? This whole thing seems outrageously funny to me and I have to laugh again.

The next morning I get into my clothes and look into the mirror. *Who am I? My ancestry goes back into the 1800's—to a Helen Marie Walters, who married Donald Andrew Rivers, and she had a brother, Harrison Tomas Walters.*

I go into my tiny kitchen and pour a glass of milk, reaching for the bread to make toast. My favorite thing is peanut butter on toast every morning, and I always asked for it when I was fostered.

I laugh, remembering the oatmeal the county orphanage cooked that stayed on my teeth and tasted like school paste.

I hurry over to Amy's Gift Shop. The air still has the fragrances of spring flowers, but I think I am more aware this morning because it smells so much sweeter.

When I walk in, Amy is behind the counter struggling with the cash register that seems to give her trouble from time to time. Then she gives the register drawer a good shove with a curse or two, and it finally closes.

She looks up. "Hi there, Jenny. How are you this morning after all that excitement yesterday?"

"Oh, I still can't believe this is happening to me."

"Well, it's true and not at a bad time for you either."

I go over closer and look at her. She seems upset. "Why—what's going on?"

"Oh nothing much. Just that I have decided it is the right time to close the shop. I have tried everything to make it work and last night I went over all my bills again—the money I take in is not enough. Ever since the factory closed last June the town has been losing people, and sales have gone down. Besides that, you'll be leaving soon. It's almost the end of May, and I'm going to give my notice. June will be my last month here. I will notify the owner today."

What? All of a sudden she's closing the store?

CHAPTER THREE

The news that Amy is really going to close her shop stuns me. I slowly sit down on a small, decorated old bench we've tried to sell and think about what this means.

When she talked about closing the shop, Amy's face had taken on a different look. I have never seen her so disgruntled, and that says a lot. Suddenly I need to know more.

Watching her try to open the register again to add money for today's business, I say, "Where will you go?"

"Well, I have a little money saved. I really have no plans. Maybe I'll go to New York. The big city might be a place to find employment and start over. I definitely don't want to go back home—I've never liked Eddy's family, and my mom and I have never gotten along."

Sitting there on the bench I think about her going to New York without a plan and me going to Virginia not knowing what I'll find, and it doesn't seem right. Scratching my head over the details I wonder how good my situation really is—me going off to find that place.

I get busy arranging gifts and all afternoon listen to Amy as she sputters to herself about what she will be faced with now. Under her breath she is talking to her husband about him leaving her with this shop when she needed him most.

She'll be closing the shop and going alone to New York City.

I look out the window at two women walking along smiling. They have no idea of our problems. I am sure they have problems too, but they're together!

Then, without really thinking of what it will be like living with Amy, so close and personal, I suddenly blurt out, "Mrs. Forrester, would you like to go with me?"

She shuts the register, comes around the counter smiling and staring at me as if I am a new item in the shop. "Do you mean that? You want me to go with you?"

"Sure I mean it. I have no idea what I'll find, and frankly, I feel lost already. If you don't like it there, you can still go to New York, but to have you with me at first would give me a better feeling about the whole thing."

"Let me think about this," and she walks back and forth for several minutes. "Would you help me with the shop until I can close it next month?"

I think about that for a moment. Rivers Run will still be there no matter when I get there.

"Of course, Mrs. Forrester. It might take that long for Mr. Whitaker to settle this thing anyway."

"Jenny, if you really mean it, I would love to see Rivers Run, and if it will give you a better feeling about going, I'll do it!"

We hug and she stands back and says, "I think this will be good for both of us!"

Amy seems fired up and goes around the shop in a different mood, and I start dusting items with new energy.

Amy comes over to me. "I will rearrange the window, give a discount, and perhaps we can push some of these nice gifts."

"That sounds great, Mrs. Forrester."

"Jenny, please call me Amy. We'll just be friends from now on."

As I think of my future with Amy, I hope I have done the right thing.

Later that day in the gift shop, I listen as Amy calls the owner of the shop and her landlady at her apartment informing them of her plans— she will close the end of June. She also calls The Shadyside Sentinel, the local paper, informing them about the shop closing and discounts, surprising me when she tells them about my inheritance.

The next day, I read the story on the front page about me, a poor orphan girl inheriting property in Helen, Virginia. As I spread the peanut butter on my toast, I can just imagine that news will spread just as quickly.

When I get to the shop it is already busy with customers who have come to take advantage of the reduced prices.

One evening I get a visit from Miss Brewster from the county program for orphans. "Hello, Jenny. I'm glad Mr. Whitaker found you. He did not tell us all the details, so I didn't know about your inheritance until I read the papers." I thank her, and tell her about Amy Forrester going with me.

She frowns and says, "Jenny, I don't know her very well. I know you are a strong capable person, but this world is full of people who will take advantage of you. Try to be vigilant."

Before she goes she says, "I wish you well, Jenny," and gives me a hug.

Amy's intolerant nature is bothersome, but I might need her support in this unknown world I'm about to step into.

On June 15th I receive an insured package enclosing the court notification with documents I signed, the deed to the property, and a key to the Rivers Run manor house. A statement from the Community Bank in Helen, Virginia, shows an astounding balance in that checking account that makes my totals in the Shadyside bank seem pitiful.

By the end of June we have sold more than half of the things in the gift shop, and Amy is going to rent a storage unit for the items that remain. I have mailed the box of my family things to Rivers Run.

After closing the store on June 29th, Amy and I sit at the backroom table.

Amy says, "The money from the sales will sustain me until I decide what I'm going to do in the future. Maybe in your little town in Virginia there is a gift shop that will need some gifts and I can supply them with the things here in storage."

"Sounds good, Amy—we'll wait and see."

On July 3rd, a taxi takes us to the bus station and we are told it will take about two hours to get to Richmond. We climb aboard the bus while the driver puts our suitcases in a storage compartment. Amy has two suitcases and I have one and we settled down for the long trip.

At the Richmond bus terminal, we climb aboard another bus that will take us to the town of Helen that is in the western hills not far from

Richmond. We sit in front seats and I watch the busy shopping district of Richmond and the heavy traffic. I'm hoping the town of Helen will have the "country" look as we begin to go through that very populated town.

As Richmond fades from sight and things quiet down, the bus driver looks at us and says, "So, you're going to Helen. That's a nice town."

I tell the bus driver that we are going to Rivers Run. He looks surprised and asks, "Are you the new owners?"

Amy quickly says, "Yes."

Is she already claiming to be more than an invited friend?

I speak up then and say, "Yes, I am Jenny Walters and this is a friend, Mrs. Amy Forrester."

"Welcome. I'm Leo Henderson. I have been expecting you. This is my regular route from Richmond through several towns, and the people that ride this bus, to and from Helen, have been telling me that the owner of Rivers Run had been located, and they have been waiting. Your arrival will be a nice surprise for the town."

The ride is comfortable and soon we get the first glimpse of the town of Helen. As we ride along I see a town hall in the square, a library, an occasional dress shop, two restaurants, a drug store, and several variety shops. Flowers of many colors are hanging in pots everywhere, attached to street lamps, fences, window boxes, and shop fronts. It all looks so clean and beautiful.

The bus turns a corner and stops at a Rivers Run sign stuck in a garden of mixed flowers. Leo unloads our suitcases, telling us it's not far—just over a rise in the road. We thank him with suitcases in hand, and watch the bus disappear.

Ahead, I see a stone embankment deeply engraved with the Rivers Run name, and I notice the road from there is gravel covered. Walking slowly, we look beyond us but can't see very much for the trees and bushes with fencing on both sides. We stop to rest as the gravel makes walking difficult, and in the distant fields I notice rows of growing plants that I can't identify.

Walking along another few minutes on the gravel I finally see a big house that looks very familiar! I stop to stare!

Amy looks over at me. "Are you okay?"

"Oh yes," *I stammer, wondering how this can be.* "I guess it's just the heat."

I plop down on my suitcase unable to walk any farther until I grasp the situation. I think I have been here before, but everything was beautiful then. I am overwhelmed! Can this be the beautiful house in my dreams that Kathleen, Junior, and I ran and played around? I gasp thinking about it!

There are wild, straggly-looking flowers and tall weeds around a circular gravel driveway, also surrounding the far corners and up the sides of the house. In the center of the circular driveway is what looks like a weed garden with rose bushes that you can barely see among the tall, wild flowers that hang over old rough wooden benches.

In my dreams there were always smiling people in long dresses sitting there with the lovely flowers behind them as Kathleen, Junior and I ran around the circle.

The place is a big, old, two-story white house with a large porch extending around the sides and big pillars supporting the roof. There are huge trees on both corners with large limbs hanging over the roof. They look as if they are trying to hold the house from falling. It's hard to believe that this huge, tired-looking house is still standing. I stand there in the heat, staring in awe for several minutes. Pieces of wood are loose on the siding and a coat of paint is needed on the entire outside. From the looks of it I can believe it is a hundred years old.

It stops me for another moment, remembering.

In one of my dreams, as I stood at the door, Kathleen, dressed in a lovely pleated pink dress, went running out of the house to say goodbye to her daddy who was on horseback. At that time the house looked very majestic.

I sigh with grief, as I look at this rundown place, comparing it to how it was in my dreams.

Looking over at Amy it makes me laugh though, because she is sitting on one of her suitcases and looks as exhausted as the house at this moment. Her hair looks damp, and she wipes her forehead with a look of frustration.

She says with a sigh, "This place looks pretty bad, Jenny—should we try to go in?"

"Yes, the lawyer gave me a key. I hope it works. However, he mentioned caretakers that should be in charge here."

It had been a longer walk than anticipated and I am uncomfortably warm but I don't think the inside of this house will be much cooler. I'm wondering if it will look the same. In my dreams the house was always beautiful, and bustling with adults and children. I'm still wondering how I can be standing here!

Bushes on both sides of the steps are trying to reach across to each other. We push them aside as we go carefully up the six rickety steps lifting our suitcases onto a large porch, which continues around both sides of the house.

I step to the big double door, which surprisingly is the only thing on the house that doesn't look like it needs replacing, and ring the bell even though I have a key. Then I put the large key in the slot and turn it. I feel a sense of wonder as I step in cautiously with Amy following.

Closing the door, I step on a round, royal blue rug on wooden flooring in a circular foyer and then enter into a huge, poorly lit room with a high ceiling and stairs to my right, curving up to a top floor.

I stand there and focus on how grand a place it was in my dreams and how it looks now—suffering in a state of disrepair. I feel like crying. It's not at all like the place I remember—with joy and happiness in the air.

Suddenly, and shockingly, even though this place resembles a lost cause, I feel a sense of belonging come over me and want to shout to my ancestors that I am here.

I sigh from the importance of the moment while, behind me, Amy is complaining about being tired and sweaty, bringing me back to the Twentieth Century and the ache in my heart about the precarious condition of this Nineteenth Century place.

CHAPTER FOUR

From the foyer of the house I try to see good things and focus on the large royal-blue scatter rugs and runners that paint a picture of color.

Amy says, "It could definitely use some polish on the wooden floors and the rugs are too faded." Looking up over my head she blinks disapproval, "and that chandelier needs some serious cleaning."

The air feels cooler to my sun-heated body and that is a surprise. Putting down my suitcase I see Amy has plopped hers down at the door. I breathe a sigh of relief and say, "Well, here we are," and look around cautiously at several closed doors, somehow knowing that I have been in some of them, but I don't want to tell Amy just yet, until I can cope with the bizarre possibility myself.

At that moment, a woman appears from a door behind the stairs. She is small, slightly overweight, middle-aged with graying hair, wearing a blue uniform. She rushes forward very excitedly. "I'm sorry, the house isn't available for visitors. The door should have been locked."

I look at the woman, and for a moment the words don't come. Then I hold the key up in front of me, "I'm Miss Jenny Walters. I'm going to live here. This is Mrs. Forrester. She is my guest. Didn't Mr. Whitaker inform you we were coming?"

The woman's mouth drops open in surprise. "Oh, I'm sorry, Miss Walters. Yes, he did tell us but I didn't expect you for several days. I'm Grace Waller. Just call me Gracie. My husband, Bill, and I are caretakers of the house and property. We have been managing the property and getting the house in order for you. We've been here only since January ourselves."

Coming closer, Gracie gives us a smile. She says, "I thought you were visitors. We have turned away many people who have come to see the house since word about an heir has gotten around. They are naturally curious and want to meet the new owner. We also had several people who wanted to buy Rivers Run. When I saw you here, I thought perhaps Bill had left the door unlocked."

Amy makes "tsking" sounds with her tongue and says, "The lawyer should have called ahead and had someone meet us at the bus stop!"

Then Gracie says, "I'm sorry. We could have arranged it if we had known. Leave your suitcases there in the foyer and my husband will put them in your rooms upstairs. Please come into the parlor."

Amy and I follow Gracie into a large room with sofas and chairs around a fireplace of stone.

It looks familiar, and once again I remember Kathleen and Junior running around me and I gasp, but Amy and Gracie don't notice. I quickly sit in one of the chairs as my strength escapes me from my awareness of the place and the strange circumstances.

Gracie says, "After your trip you may want to relax and have some refreshments. I'll prepare tea or coffee and snacks."

As the images of the past fade from my mind, I look at Gracie. "Thank you, ice tea will be nice."

She says, "Make yourselves comfortable. I'll prepare your rooms upstairs if you will give me a little more time. Feel free to look around while I get the snacks." She points to a door in the back of the room and says, "If you need to freshen up, this parlor has a small bathroom."

Before Gracie leaves she says, "Oh, Miss Walters, a big box came for you, and I'll have it brought up to your room later."

"Thank you. That's the box I sent here last week with family mementos."

After we use the small bathroom in the parlor, Amy walks around the room commenting about what's wrong with the couches, chairs, and tables.

I am actually admiring all the antiques.

While waiting for refreshments, Amy walks over to a small bookcase. She looks at several book titles. "I love to read but these books are really old."

I am never interested in books and wouldn't know about them if she told me the titles and the authors, which she starts to do as I walk around. I hear her say something about "Moby Dick," but I am focusing on the fireplace. It is made of beautiful stone, the colors of gray, pink, and amber. I think it will be lovely when it is cleaned of smoke residue from years of use.

Above the fireplace there is a large painting of a woman and her two children. One child is a little girl about three years old with reddish-brown curls and beside her is a boy a bit older with blonde hair. They look familiar!

I sit down in awe—They must be Kathleen and Junior, but in my dreams they were my age—about seven or eight.

The woman has reddish-blonde hair matching the girl's, and a lovely smile with dimples. She is looking down at the children with tenderness and devotion in her eyes. It definitely brings forgotten feelings of love from my own mother.

If that is Kathleen and Junior then the mother is Helen Marie Rivers, my great-great aunt.

"Amy, come look at this painting. It is so beautiful!"

Amy comes over, sighs, and looks up at it with a nonchalant attitude. "The colors are a bit faded. It's probably some of your ancient family members." Then she quickly goes back to checking everything.

It is obvious she didn't get the same feelings I did, but has much to say about the old furniture that doesn't quite meet her standards but looks wonderful to me.

While Amy is criticizing the decor in the parlor, Gracie comes into the room rolling a cart with a pitcher of ice tea, a platter of cheese, deli meat and crackers.

Gracie smiles and her eyes seem to sparkle. "If there is anything else you would like, I'll be happy to get it for you."

I smile and say, "These snacks are very welcomed after the bus trip."

Amy says, "It seems very comfortable in the house."

Gracie responds, "Yes Ma'am. It's the air-conditioning. We were told the late Mr. Rivers had heat and air-conditioning added about six years ago. We have shut down the air in some of the rooms but I will turn it on again in several of them now that you are here."

Looking up at the painting of the mother and children, I ask, "Gracie, Do you know anything about the painting above the fireplace?"

"Yes, Miss. I'm told that's the first mistress and her children. You might find out more from Ward Wendell, a gentleman in town. He's a young historian who teaches at the local college. He has grown up in Helen, and spends time in the town library."

"Thank you, Gracie. I may check with him."

Gracie turns to go and I say, "Oh, Gracie, I understand your contract is good until I feel comfortable here."

"Yes Ma'am. We will be leaving after you get settled."

Then Gracie says, "To celebrate your first evening here, how does a steak dinner sound for tonight?"

Amy looks over at me, "I think that's good, don't you, Jenny?" I agree.

Amy and I sit and enjoy the snacks in the parlor and as she talks about how bad things look, I am momentarily distracted.

To have a real home that my people lived in all those years is awesome even though repairs need to be done to the house, and I suddenly feel grateful.

It isn't long before Gracie comes to escort us to the rooms upstairs. The stairway to the second floor looks like a small replica of the one from Tara in "Gone With the Wind." The blue rugs covering each step match the blue area rugs in the foyer but show worn spots. As I step on the worn places in the carpet it makes me think of the last heir who made the trip up the stairs.

I do recall a dream where I was running up these stairs with Kathleen and Junior. They had been sent to their rooms for trying to ride the bannister down, and were laughing on the way back up like they didn't care.

On the wall next to me, as I take the stairs, are two large paintings of young and old men and women that I assume are family in different stages of their lives. One painting appears to be of two young adults and they look like Kathleen and Junior in their teens. I never had dreams with them at that time in my life.

I feel very blessed to be an heir and put a smile on my face. Halfway up the wide stairway, I look at Amy and she looks at me and smirks. She says, "You look so out of place, Jenny." I just laugh.

I want to tell her that only my timing is wrong, thinking that I should have lived back then.

When we get to the landing at the top, Gracie turns to the right and says, "I have prepared two bedrooms across the hall from each other. The rooms each have a bathroom and a sitting area away from the bed. The room to the right of the stairs overlooks the front flower gardens. From the one across the hall you can see the hills and the river out back. You will have other choices once we get the other six suites made ready, but the front gardens will soon be pretty because Bill has been working on them."

I look at Amy and know she likes flowers so I say, "Amy, why don't you take the one overlooking the front gardens. I know you'll enjoy the view once we get nice flowers growing, and I'll enjoy the hill country." Amy nods in agreement.

I follow Amy to her room on the right, into a large area with antique furnishings. Her room is decorated in colors of blue, with a mixture of blue, yellow, and white on the drapes and bed linens. The floors are hardwood with large heavy area rugs of mixed colors. The rugs are a bit frayed and worn, but I notice that the room is nice and cool.

Bill Waller comes in with Amy's luggage, and we are introduced. Bill is very nice looking with graying hair and a muscular build. He gives Gracie a smile when she says they have been married for thirty years, so I assume they are about fifty.

They soon leave us to get ourselves settled into our rooms. Amy and I leave our doors open and go back and forth, checking the rooms together. My suite is almost identical but decorated with colors of green, yellow, and white. My view from the back of the house is magnificent with the sun disappearing behind the various colors of trees in the distant hills and valleys.

Amy goes back to her room to unpack. She wants to wash up, change clothes and rest. I think that is a good idea.

My bathroom has all the necessary items, complete with a small tub and shower. As I shower, dress, and unpack, everything seems adequate. I'm very glad bathrooms were added over the years.

I decide to rest by the window in a chaise lounge and look out at the dim shades of pink in the sky. There is only a hint of color left anywhere, barely implying that the sun has been there. I lean back in the soft lounge chair, look around at the old furnishings and decor, rest my eyes, and sigh…

Suddenly I am in a big bedroom with a man and woman dressed in colonial clothes. The man is young and goes close to a young woman by the fireplace and I feel the warmth from the fire, but as I walk around I realize they don't see me.

The man says, "Helen, I think I will have to go to Richmond and get the doctor. The sharecroppers are coming down with that terrible illness that has been spreading throughout our town."

The woman looks unhappy and moves her handkerchief to her eyes. "If you think you must go, Donald, please be careful. The weather has been frightful! I don't want you to come down with this illness or bring it back to us here at home." She wipes her eyes again and they embrace. *I stand there realizing that these people must be Helen and Donald Rivers in their early days at rivers run.*

Then Donald says, "Helen, remember when we sat by the river in the summer and I compared life to the way the river was performing for us?"

Helen says, "Yes, I do. You told me about the diamonds in the water with the sun shining on the ripples. You mentioned there is also dark, rough water there too, and you compared life like that—good times and bad."

"Well then, Helen, this is only a bad time. We'll get past this bad time, and hopefully Rivers Run will never run out of diamonds or, like you say your ancestors tell you, we'll never run out of heirs." Then he hugs her and says goodbye.…

CHAPTER FIVE

I cough and sit up stunned. I think I had a dream! I was there with them but they didn't see me like Kathleen and Junior did in my dreams with them!

The bedroom looked very similar to mine with the same furniture and the dream was so real. Their names were Helen and Donald, and I think I recognized them but my dreams with Kathleen and Junior happened when I was just a child. I am amazed but I'm sure that was my great-great aunt, Helen Marie Walters Rivers and Donald Andrew Rivers Senior. He was going to Richmond for a doctor and Helen was not too happy about it because of the danger that he faced by the epidemic!

Donald was trying to console her. I think it is so sweet how he compared the good times with the "diamonds" in the water from the sun and the bad times with rough and dark water. He also said Rivers Run would never run out of diamonds or heirs. That is interesting--a glimpse of their life long ago.

When Amy knocks on my door I'm still thinking about the dream and feel so blessed, but confused.

I wonder whether or not there will be more dreams. I don't think I will tell Amy about the dream or any with Kathleen and Junior that I recall, or the fact that I was in them. I can just imagine her response.

Amy comes in and says, "Hey, everything is very old. Did you try out the bed? It is not as soft as the one I had in Shadyside."

"No, I didn't. I suppose it will be all right. As an orphan I had to adjust to old cots and small uncomfortable beds."

Amy looks at her watch as she approaches my side. "Well, it's dinner time I think."

"I am ready for dinner too, but look at this view would you? Isn't it lovely?"

She comes over to see. "Yes it is, and look, there's a river beyond the property too." Then she pats her stomach, "I'm hungry though, let's go see what's cooking!"

We go down the stairs together and meet Gracie in the hall. She nods her head in greeting and with a very lighthearted tone of voice she says, "I have dinner prepared. Come with me to the dining room." She turns and goes through a door on the left of the stairs and we walk through another hallway.

The dining room is large and has a long table in the center. It is set for us to eat dinner on one end of it with lit candles and a small vase of roses.

Strangely this trip to the dining room is very familiar. I recall that in a dream I had gone with Kathleen to the back of the house. I don't remember a kitchen. There was nothing beyond the dining room but what they called a cookhouse connected to the back door area.

We sit down and Gracie rolls a cart of food in. She serves sliced tomatoes on lettuce and a dinner of steak with mashed potatoes, gravy, green beans, along with baked cornbread and ice tea. The food is delicious and I think it is wonderful being waited on and I can see Amy thinks so too.

During dinner Amy suggests that I talk with Gracie about what time we will have breakfast in the morning.

She says, "I usually get up early and she needs to know that."

"I will ask Gracie when breakfast will be served. They are caretakers not servants to us you know, and I think they are very nice. I plan on talking with them tomorrow about staying here as servants once I'm comfortable managing the place."

After dinner Gracie takes us through a door to a sitting room from the dining area that Gracie calls the small parlor, and she suggests a glass of orange liqueur for us to enjoy. I take a sip and it is a delight. It seems Amy is enjoying it too.

Gracie says, "Mr. Rivers left several types of liqueurs in the pantry and this is one of them."

Before she leaves, she says, "We get up early and breakfast will be served anytime after 9:00, if that meets with your approval."

I answer, "Certainly, Gracie." Then I tell her that I would like to meet with her and Bill after breakfast tomorrow in this small parlor. She agrees.

Amy is smiling after she leaves. "Gracie must have heard me about breakfast," and she laughs.

Amy's voice of authority is irritating. Actually, I'm scared beyond thinking straight. I feel I should pinch myself every second to get back to reality. I am so glad that Gracie and Bill are here, and already I wonder if Amy is going to stay very long.

I rub my head trying to make sense of what is happening to me.

I'm really thinking that nothing looks like it did in my younger dreams. There were more people around us and it seemed joyful, not gloomy and depressing in such rundown conditions.

I say to Amy, "What am I doing here? All this is so strange."

Amy says, "Well, I'll help you all I can." I don't comment.

I wonder about her help. In my anxiety about my situation I had forgotten that she has a tendency to find fault with everything and everyone.

While Amy and I sit here in the small parlor, I think about the manor house and what has been added through the years. "I need to have a tour of the house, but I know they are still working to get all the rooms cleaned. Maybe Bill could show us the grounds. I'll need to know about the farmers who rent the property too."

Amy sips the liqueur. "Nice idea. I wonder about the stables. Do you have horses? If you do, Bill probably handles them."

I shrug my shoulders. "I think the lawyer said there are horses."

Gracie comes in and asks if we need anything else and I tell her no. She says, "All the doors are locked for the night. Bill and I will be retiring to our quarters above the kitchen."

I give her a smile. "Thank you, Gracie. We will see you in the morning. Tonight we may walk around—maybe into the kitchen, so if you hear anything it will probably be us."

Gracie nods, "I'll tell Bill. I'll be glad to give you a tour whenever you wish. Have a restful night." We both thank her as she leaves.

Amy and I stay seated in our soft, comfortable chairs in front of the fireplace, which looks cold and empty this time of year. I just imagine how nice it will be with the fire going. This parlor, off the dining room, is cozy and smaller than the parlor we went to when we arrived. The windows face an area of the side yard.

Above this fireplace is a faded portrait of a rather handsome young man with blonde hair and piercing blue eyes. I wonder if it is the last heir, John Matthew Rivers. He was never in my dreams with Kathleen and Junior.

Then I imagine being alone here and I think of Amy. "Amy, I just thought about the winter time here. Will you stay until then?"

"I guess so. I'm glad to be here as long as you want me. I have no other place to go at the moment and it is lovely being waited on."

That's what I thought might keep her here, but it's nice for me too.

After we finish our liqueur Amy wants to check out the rooms on the first floor and I follow her into the large corridor to the entryway. There are three doors to our right and Amy goes over and opens the first one. It is a small dark stairway.

I recall from my hide-and-seek escapades with Kathleen that it is another way to the upper rooms.

"Amy, let's tour that later before we go up to our rooms for the night." Amy agrees.

The next door near the foyer is a large, walk-in closet for coats, hats, umbrellas, etc. We go down the hall past the big parlor that we had seen this morning.

Amy opens a door, steps in and says, "Wow!" I follow behind and see it is a library with an old antique desk in a corner.

It's the one that Kathleen and I tried to sneak into when we were hiding from Junior, but her father caught us. I remember well the scolding she received when he reminded Kathleen not to ever play in there.

Behind the desk there are shelves full of books. These shelves extend around several walls. One wall has floor to ceiling windows with heavy maroon drapes and a fireplace next to the desk. The wooden floor has a round, maroon area rug in the center. There are several soft chairs with tables and lamps.

It seems very cozy, and I can see Amy's eyes have a look of wonder and joy as her hands lightly touch the books on one shelf. I know she wants to stay here, but I take her arm and lead her out quickly with a suggestion that we come back tomorrow when we have more time.

Reluctantly she comes along and says, "I love to read and will definitely want to spend time in here, but it needs to be aired out—it has an old musty smell."

We continue our exploration to a door farther down the corridor in the other direction that opens into a dark room. I see a panel of switches on the wall next to us and turn on the lights. Immediately I see many small light fixtures light up on the walls all around a large room displaying many paintings. There is a huge chandelier in the very center of the ceiling that is dark. I reach for another switch that is round and I push it in and the ceiling chandelier turns on but it isn't very bright. Amy says it's a dimmer light and tells me to turn the switch all the way around. As I turn the knob the chandelier gets brighter and brighter. The hanging cut glass reflects the light beautifully in all directions.

We walk in and are amazed at the size of the room. It has stately wooden chairs and sofas next to the walls. There's a wooden floor that I can see needs scrubbing and polishing and rugs under the furniture along the sides of the room. It is definitely a ballroom with plenty of floor space for dancing.

I think this was the room that was always locked when Kathleen, Junior, Marty, and I played in the house.

On one side of the room are floor to ceiling windows covered in heavy, dark blue drapes.

I say, "Amy, this is perfect for parties and dancing."

Amy nods her head in agreement. "I'm sure it was used for just that." Then she goes over to the windows to feel the heavy drapes.

I walk over to the large paintings on the walls. The chairs have beautifully carved wooden backs and legs. The tapestry on the chairs and sofas need recovering.

I am sure Amy will tell me about that.

This huge room is like the ones I've seen in old movies. It has many landscape paintings on the walls that I admire and I go over to get a closer look at some of them.

When I look back to tell Amy about a painting, I don't see her anywhere. She has disappeared!

CHAPTER SIX

I look all around the big room but Amy is nowhere in sight! I call her name and go over to where she had been. I feel a breeze and the heavy drape flutters with a cloud of dust escaping. I pull the drape away and find that there is an opening to the porch. Amy is standing there looking up and is completely decorated with lights from a bright, gorgeous moon.

I step out onto the porch and stand behind Amy. Surprisingly, I am on a side porch with steps to the grounds that are also bright from the moon.

"Hey, I didn't know where you were! How did you get through the window?"

"It was easy. The bottom panel slides across into an opening in the wood and I just raised the large window. I have read about them in historical magazines. Your relatives must have held dances here and the open window panels gave their guests access to the outside porch and the grounds."

Amazed, I look at the opening again and try to slide the panel. It moves back and forth from the wall enclosure.

It's a lovely warm night with a breeze, and the moon gives a bright view of our surroundings. The moonlight exposes tall plants growing in the middle of a pathway where they are not wanted, and areas with old benches among Weeping Willow trees.

I never had a dream in this room but I close my eyes imagining a night like this long ago with music playing and women in lovely long gowns.

Amy says, "It must have been lovely when it was maintained with flowers and shrubs but now you can't see anything but tall weeds. This whole place is in such rundown shape, Jenny."

I quickly check myself because I almost blurt out that she should have seen it in the old days, the grounds and pathways were beautiful with flowering bushes.

After her discouraging words I look over and see an ornamental garden statue of an angel that needs to be cleaned.

I remember Kathleen and I hiding in the flowers and bushes there.

I give Amy a look of joy. "I'm convinced! We need to have a dance here for the people in Helen to come and get acquainted with us."

Amy gives me a thoughtful look. "Maybe after you get used to the place and get things cleaned, repaired, and flowers planted."

She is right about that.

It has been a long day and even though it is a lovely night, Amy looks as tired as I feel. She turns to go back in and I don't object. She closes and locks the access panels, and straightens the drapes with a look of disgust from the dust that is heavy in the air around us.

We get back to the hall and Amy goes to the door that has a stairway going up. I sigh, feeling like I have had enough intrigue with those ballroom windows that suddenly became doors to the outside porch.

"Amy, let's leave this for now, but how about a snack before bedtime?"

She raises her eyebrows. "Maybe another piece of that cornbread with butter and a little milk?" I agree, and we go in the direction of the kitchen area behind the stairway. Amy turns on the light and we step in cautiously. There is a large center counter with stools on one side, and on the other side I see a large stove with ten burners and two ovens.

There are several refrigerators, a freezer and two deep sinks directly across from the stove next to a pantry, with a back door to the outside. To my right is a small dining area for the workers, I imagine, and a small stairway to the servants' rooms upstairs over the kitchen. Everything looks like it has seen better days.

Amy says, "I've read about these old places. The kitchen area and additional rooms were built onto the back of the house in modern times."

I know she's right because I never saw a kitchen in my dreams with Kathleen and Junior, and I remember Junior used to run out to the cookhouse and come back with cookies that I never could hold or put my teeth into.

I look around amazed. "Well, it sure has everything a cook would need as long as the appliances still function."

We find the cornbread and I fix a couple pieces. Amy pours the milk and we start back to the stairs.

Upstairs, we go to my room, sit in the two wing-backed chairs by the small fireplace and enjoy our cornbread and milk, talking about our first day here. Soon, Amy says she's going to try out her bed and we say goodnight.

For me there's a great deal to think about, but exhaustion takes over and I get ready for bed.

The bit of exploring we did has emphasized the needs of the house and the burden I am going to have in this place. I crawl into my sheets, thanking John Matthew Rivers for functioning electricity, air-conditioning, and heat. I close my eyes, wondering if I will have another dream and what tomorrow will bring. I feel my tired body start to relax....

Suddenly I am in the large parlor downstairs with an aging decrepit man with white hair and blue eyes, holding on to his cane, looking up at the painting over the fireplace of Helen Rivers with her two children that are Kathleen and Junior. There is a fire going in the great fireplace and he's alone.

I listen as he turns to look up at the painting and speaks, "Grandma, I am alone without anyone left in the family. The place needs repairs that I can't do anymore. The gardens look awful and the servants are soon to retire and leave. I should sell the place and leave as well." *He must be the last heir, John Matthew Rivers.*

He wipes his brow and says, "You have told me in a dream that when I die, they will need to find all the heirs and if they are not found, those with your family bloodline will not rest in peace and that includes me. Your deception in England may make it difficult to find a relative to inherit Rivers Run, but I should have searched. I'm also sorry about Lia and her child, and Margaret and her daughter in Richmond. I should have been truthful but it would have done damage. I feel terrible because you have told me that my bloodline is responsible for the dreams."

He rubs his chin and looks up. "Grandma, I have been foolish. Perhaps I should write the truth about everything. Surely someone needs to know our connection in Richmond that Grandfather got us involved in. I should at least leave some note for an heir to find, but I'm afraid it is too late, and I don't want just anyone to find it." Then he covers his face with his hands and seems distressed. I want to reach out and console him...

I awaken with noises outside my window—and realize that once again I have had an unusual dream with a Rivers' family member! Why? This is shocking—and unbelievable! My heart is beating fast now as I remember the dream, and I get up and wash my face with cold water.

Still hearing a commotion outside my windows, I look out and see Bill in the back courtyard fussing with a dog about something as he waters the plants. The dog, cowering behind a bush, is medium-sized and brown with touches of white on the face and body. Bill says, "Get on with you now, you mangy pup. You have done your damage!"

I watch the little dog run and hide behind a large clay pot of flowers. I open the window and call out, "Bill, what's the matter?"

He looks up at the window shaking his head. "Oh, Miss, this pup keeps coming here. I don't know what she wants. We don't feed her and she shouldn't stay. She keeps digging up my plants though and I want her gone."

"Leave her there and I'll come down as soon as I get dressed." Bill just shrugs his shoulders and continues watering around the bushes.

Putting finishing touches on my face I think of the dream. It was so real just like the others. John Rivers was speaking to Helen in the painting over the fireplace as if she was right there. He talked about things I cannot understand. The odd thing is that I felt at peace there with him. I thought he could see me, but he didn't speak to me, only to Helen in the painting.

I realize I'll forget many of the things he said so I get my journal and write down the names he mentioned—Lia and Margaret—and what he said about his grandmother's family bloodline, the dreams he had, and leaving behind the truth somewhere about the Richmond connection.

Gosh, what does her bloodline have to do with it—and what is the Richmond connection?

When I go to the kitchen, I greet Gracie and quickly go outside to see the pup. Bill has her in his arms and says, "Well, Miss, she let me pick her up and she isn't so bad really. I have to go to the store, I'll take her with me and ask around to see if she has run away from someone."

He looks at the kitchen window because Gracie is motioning to him about something. Then he says, "Oh, Gracie wants me to tell you that it's the 4th of July and the town will have fireworks tonight. The people in town told Gracie that John Rivers watched from the front porch with friends every year. There is a good view of that part of town across the low fields, but if you want to go to town, I will take you in the big car—it's up to you."

"To watch the fireworks from the porch sounds good, Bill."

The dog barks at me. She is very cute.

Surprisingly, I remember Kathleen and Junior with a similar dog in one of my dreams with them.

I take her from Bill, noticing the dried mud in the hair around her feet. "Just find out if anyone in the village is missing a dog. For now, I'll keep her." Then I carry the dog to the kitchen and put her down on a rug by the counter.

Gracie gives the pup a few crumbs of dry cereal and says, "Sorry about the commotion this morning. Did it wake you?"

"Yes, it did, but it was time to get up anyway. Have you seen Mrs. Forrester?"

"Yes, she's having her breakfast," but then Gracie stops me before I go to the dining room. "Miss, the pup is dirty, use this sink to wash your hands and I'll get your breakfast ready. Amy is having scrambled eggs, bacon, hash browns and biscuits."

"That's fine with me."

When I arrive in the dining room, Amy looks up from sipping coffee and says, "Good morning. I heard the commotion out back with that dog."

"Well, the pup is very cute. If no one claims her, I'll keep her."

Amy's face has a disgusted look. "I can't believe you! Why in the world would you want to keep a dog? She'll just be a lot of trouble and they're dirty. They chew on everything and make messes."

I shouldn't be surprised at her response, but I'm going to be strong about this!

"Bill is going to the village to find out if she belongs to someone, but in the meantime the dog will stay here."

Amy gets a funny look on her face and I wait for the next comment. She says, "I hope you don't keep her in the house. I think that brings problems."

"Oh, I am going to keep her in the house. She'll be no trouble. When I was young we had a small dog that stayed in the house. After I was put in the orphanage I never found out what happened to her."

For some reason I think of the fireworks tonight, maybe from Amy's explosive dog comments. "Oh, Bill reminded me that today is the 4th of July and the town is having fireworks tonight. He says we can see it from the front porch very well, or he will be glad to take us to town. I told him watching from the porch will be fine."

To my surprise, Amy agrees. She must have enjoyed that breakfast.

CHAPTER SEVEN

After breakfast, I go into the kitchen to see the puppy. *Amy follows along but I am sure loving the pup is the last thing she wants to do.*

Gracie says, "I just fed her some of our leftovers."

I reach down to pet the puppy and she jumps up and licks my hand. I scoop her up in my arms and she licks my face. I feel instant love for this little animal. I silently hope that no one will claim her. Then I look at Amy's dissatisfied face, but her attitude just tells me to pet the dog even more because she won't.

I'm hugging on the dog when Gracie says, "Oh, Miss, let me take her and wash that dirt off. She may have fleas too. We have a washtub in the cellar. I'll take her and clean her up so she smells good."

Amy says, "Thank God!"

After Gracie takes the pup from me I see Amy looking at me strangely. She says, "I would never have guessed that you had a love for dogs like that. For me, I love horses. My husband and I used to visit friends who had horses and we would ride all the time when we were first married."

Gracie speaks up, "Mrs. Forrester, we have two horses—I think they are males."

Amy speaks with an official voice, "When Bill comes back he should take us out there and show us around."

Her tone of authority is beginning to annoy me.

Gracie turns, not to Amy but to me, and says, "I'll tell him when he returns. He only has a small list of things to get this morning. It won't take him long."

When we get settled in the small parlor with another cup of coffee, Amy says, "Did you sleep well last night?"

"Yes, I didn't wake up until the pup was barking and Bill was yelling."

I have decided I will not tell her about my dreams. I am convinced that the family members are giving me a glimpse of their lives for some reason, and she doesn't need to know.

Amy puts down her cup. "Well, I went down to the library to get a book and came across a Bible with names written in it. I left the Bible there for you and took a novel to read in bed. I didn't go to sleep until very late—I kept hearing creaks in the walls and floors, I hope that's not a regular thing in this old house."

Amy's comments about noises in this house are not worth talking about, but the fact that Amy found a Bible is very interesting.

"Well, that Bible may tell me more about my family. Let's go get it. You'll have to show me because I'll never find it in there without you."

"I thought you would be interested and told Gracie about it this morning. I left it on the bookshelf. I'll show you," and she gets up.

We walk to the library and she goes right over to the bookshelf in a corner of the room and starts touching the books. "I think I put it back in this section, but I don't see it now."

"What did it look like? How big was it?"

She stops looking and hesitates. "It had a worn, cracked, brown cover with Holy Bible in gold lettering on the side. When I opened it the pages fell to where the family was listed. I only saw some of the Rivers' and Walters' names and shoved it back with the other books."

We search all through the books in that section and also the other areas, but Amy keeps going back to that one corner, insisting that's where she put it.

Amy and I are standing in the corridor outside the library discussing the Bible, when Bill comes to join us from the kitchen.

"Miss Walters, I asked around at the village about the pup. I found out they had seen her a few times but had no idea where she came from. I went to Jamie's Pet Store and asked about it too. From the description I gave, they said it was not one of theirs."

I look at Amy and Bill with satisfaction. "Well then, she's mine, and I even have a name for her. We will call her 'Boots' because she had so much mud on her feet this morning she looked like she had boots on them."

Bill looks around. "Where is she now, Miss?"

"I think Gracie is washing her in the basement tub."

"Thanks, Miss. I'll go and see if I can help with the pup."

As we go back to the small parlor Amy is continuing the story about the Bible not being in the library.

"Well, don't worry about it—maybe, without thinking, you put it back in another place when you left the room last night. It will show up."

Bill comes in with Boots. She is all cleaned up and looks wonderful. Gracie even cut the hair around her face and feet. She is dried off pretty well and I reach for her, "Put her on my lap, Bill."

Bill covers my lap with a dry towel and Boots is all ready to snuggle down.

Bill says, "Miss Walters, I picked up a few things for the pup at Jamie's Pet Store," and he hands me a bag. Inside I discover a collar and leash, cans of dog food, and a dog bone for chewing.

"Thank you, Bill. That was very thoughtful."

"Yes, Miss, I bought them with our allowance money for food. I have the receipt. I hope that's all right."

"Of course. Boots will need them, and now I can take her for walks without worrying about her running off. Give the dog food to Gracie, and when the accountant comes I will give him the receipt."

I put the collar and leash on Boots, finish my coffee and get up. "Come on, Boots, let's take a walk and ask Bill about the horses." Amy gets up excited and follows Boots and me to the kitchen, where Gracie tells us Bill is outside.

The sun is shining through large oaks on the way to the stables and it feels pleasantly warm. The stable is a short distance from the manor house and as we walk I see the horses out in the pasture, and Bill is at the fence.

Amy runs over to the fence and whistles. She climbs up on the fencing as the two horses come running over and she leans over to rub their faces. I occasionally rub their noses as they stick them through the fence. Boots smells around in the grass, apparently less interested.

Amy says, "Bill, tell me their names."

He says, "The white and black one is 'Kota,' he's the gentle one, and the brown one's name is 'Major.' He's more rambunctious and energetic, perhaps because at one time he was a racehorse. The people in town say that his leg was injured, and John Rivers bought him when he was going to be put down. His leg looks fine now."

Once I can get Amy away from the horses we get a tour of the stables. The windows in each stall and doors to the stable are open. Two stalls have the horse's names written above them. There are six other stalls indicating that one time there were more horses here.

Amy says, "Bill, do you know how long these horses have been here?"

Bill scratches his head. "I've heard that John Rivers bought Kota and Major a couple years before he died. When we were hired we found out that he had made arrangements for a few farmers to look after them until an heir was found, but I took over when I was hired. They say he always had horses. He was breeding them in his earlier years, and sold the young ones to the racing crowd in Richmond."

Bill stands up from his cleaning and says, "This is my favorite job—being around the horses."

Amy says, "I see there are saddles for the horses in case I want to ride sometime."

Bill looks over at her. "Yep. Just let me know when and I'll get one of them ready for you."

Amy answers, "And Bill, when you get time, the horses look like they need a good brushing."

There she goes again! I think the horses look fine. I can see Bill's friendly expression changing, and I notice he sighs and goes back to work in the stall. I feel like sighing too.

As we leave to go back, Bill looks up from the stall and says to me, "Miss, if you want, I'll have time tomorrow to take you around in the truck to see the property and meet a few farmers."

I nod in agreement, "That will be great, Bill."

Back in the kitchen I remind Gracie that my meeting with her and Bill had not happened that morning because of the dog. I suggest we meet after lunch, which is only an hour away.

Amy and I go to the library. It is a very quiet, peaceful place. I look around and admire the way the books are kept. It seems they are in order by category. Amy still complains about the musty smell.

The room looks the same and takes me back to that dream again, when Kathleen and I disturbed her father in the library as he tried to hide a bag he had in his hand.

Amy and I sit down in the soft chairs that appear to have not been used very much, and she starts offering suggestions for the meeting with Bill and Gracie about staying on with me at the manor house.

I thank her; however, I know their duties will change. They will not be caretakers, but servants, since I will be responsible for managing the property. I sincerely hope they decide to stay, as it will give me a feeling of support when I take charge.

Shortly after lunch, Amy and I get settled in the small parlor as Gracie and Bill come in. I motion for them to have a seat and tell them it has been very nice having them help me to feel comfortable here.

Gracie says, "We certainly hope all is satisfactory for you, Miss Walters."

I smile in agreement. "You have been a tremendous help," and Amy nods her head.

I clear my throat. "This is why I wanted to speak to you today. I'll need assistance for some time to come, and would like to hire you on a permanent basis as servants—with no salary change. If you will be in agreement, I'll call Mr. Whitaker and let him know."

Gracie and Bill look at each other, and Bill says, "Gracie and I will have to talk this over and let you know."

I am not prepared for that response; maybe they have reasons that take them elsewhere.

I see an uneasiness on their faces, and say, "That's fine, Bill. Let me know what you decide to do as soon as possible."

Then Amy starts a conversation about the horses and Bill talks about Kota being the best one to ride but likes Major for his spunk.

I'm not really listening—thinking mostly about how I will get people to replace Gracie and Bill if they don't stay.

That afternoon I call Mr. Whitaker about hiring Gracie and Bill to stay on with me as servants with no change in salary. Mr. Whitaker agrees and will cancel their contract as soon as he hears from me.

After my call, I go out the kitchen door with Boots. Bill sees me and offers to take Boots for a walk. Bill's cheerful attitude with the dog shows me that he loves animals and doesn't mind taking care of Boots. His initial responses about her I'm sure were made because he didn't know how I would react to a dog on the property.

CHAPTER EIGHT

When I go back in the house, Amy is in the foyer with Gracie at the open door to the small stairway we saw last evening. Amy says, "Jenny, I was coming to get you. I asked Gracie to show us where it goes. I thought you would want to see this."

Gracie finds the light switch and leads the way. A door at the top takes us into a large empty room. Gracie explains, "This is just an extra room and I think the servants used this way to go to the upper rooms. The Rivers' family may also have used this room to accommodate extra servants or guests."

Gracie may be right. I do remember games and toys here in this room and children playing with Kathleen and Junior. It was always odd because the other children only pretended to see me.

The room has shelves and cupboards, a desk, bookcase, and a small table and chairs. There's a bathroom with just a sink and toilet, probably added in recent years. We go through a door at the far end that leads to the hallway upstairs and the bedroom suites.

After our tour of the extra stairway leading to what I think was a children's playroom, Amy and I retire to our bedrooms to freshen up.

That evening when the sun goes down, Bill sets up a place for us on the front porch to watch the fireworks with comfortable lawn chairs and a table for drinks and snacks. The night air is comfortable and there is a full moon. I notice the stars are giving a display of their own.

I am very impressed with the fireworks. Gracie and Bill are there too, and are saying their "oohs" and "ahs" along with us as various shapes and colors appear in the night sky. The noises from the fireworks are keeping Boots close beside me.

That night I have trouble sleeping. I walk around looking out of my windows at a very clear sky. I can't see the moon but it is lighting up the trees in the mountains across from me. Then I notice the sounds in the house. Amy is right—there are creaking noises in the old place. Imagining my ancestors in the house should give me a feeling of foreboding, but the heartfelt dreams I have had make me all the more aware that they did exist, and I feel comfortable.

I'm thinking about the painting of Helen and her children in the big parlor. I really don't know much about the Rivers family even though I had glimpses of them in my childhood dreams. I wish Amy had been able to find that Bible! I'm hoping the old newspapers at the library in Helen will disclose a few more facts about my relatives and what happened in the area when they lived here.

I put on my robe to go down to the kitchen for a glass of milk. Boots stirs and looks at me like I am a stranger. She has been sleeping soundly and puts her head down to go back to sleep. I realize she must be very young requiring more sleep.

Out in the hallway the air is still. There is a foyer light in the downstairs area and large creepy shadows appear on the walls behind me from the staircase handrails. Going down the steps quietly I hear the clock ticking in the library and the door is slightly open. As I approach the library door I see there is no light in there so I close it.

On my way to the kitchen I hear the library door open again. It startles me! I hesitate to turn my head around to look back.

Am I having another dream? Will there be an ancestor coming out of that room?

I falter, but my heart is beating like an oversized drum, and I turn around slowly, anxious about what might be there.

Standing at the library door there's a man, and instead of a person from my dreams I see Bill Waller! I step back surprised with my mouth open wide like I'm trying to bite an apple.

He approaches and says, "Miss Walters, I'm sorry if I've startled you. I had just turned off the light in there when you came over and closed the door. Frankly, you surprised me, that's why I didn't say anything."

I sigh, and my heart gets it's rhythm back. "It's okay, Bill. I couldn't sleep and was just going to get me a glass of milk and saw the library door was opened."

He passes me. "Well, I'm going to bed now, sorry again," and quickly goes into the kitchen.

As I slowly walk to the kitchen I have to laugh. In my frame of mind I almost expected one of my ancestors to appear behind me.

In the kitchen I pour a glass of milk, but I don't feel like going to bed. I want to see Helen and the children again. I walk to the parlor, turn on the lamp, and set my glass of milk down on the table. I ease down into the wing chair that Amy says needs new cushions, and look up at the painting.

This time I'm shocked! I see a small dog in it! It looks similar to Boots with a white face and a little brown on the front of its body. The dog is peeking out behind Helen's long, blue, lacy dress on the right side, which is covering its paws and part of its chest.

In my dreams with Kathleen and Junior I do remember a dog like Boots, named Princess, running after us.

It's late but I don't want to leave the parlor yet. I lean back into the chair and close my eyes wanting to know more about my ancestors…

Standing across from me are two people on a side porch. One man looks like it could be the young man in the painting in the small parlor, but a bit older. The other man is much older.

"Father, why are you always mad at me—I just like going to Richmond."

"That's a lie, John. I know what goes on there with those women. It is shameful and I hear about it."

"Father, I do everything you ask. I try very hard to attend events with you and help take care of those affairs in Richmond that Grandfather left us with."

"Yes, but it is those other 'affairs' I'm talking about."

The younger man raises his hand up as if in desperation. "They don't mean a thing—just being with a lady my age is very enjoyable."

The older man says, "John, marriage to a respectable person is what is necessary. I won't rest and neither will our departed ones with Mother's bloodline until there are legitimate heirs to care for rivers run. I hear from them about this. Don't you?"

"Yes, Father, I do, and often. I will think about what you have said." Then they walk past me to leave and I watch them go as they continue talking about the departed ones...

My dream begins to fade when I laugh out loud from suddenly realizing that Donald Junior must be the older man and a father figure. I hear a commotion behind me.

Boots is hurrying into the room. "Hello, girl. How did you get out of my room? I suppose you are telling me to go back to bed, huh? Well, I'm ready now."

In that dream his father called him John, so I'm sure it was John Matthew Rivers. Donald Junior said he and the departed ones from his mother's family, including John, wouldn't rest without an heir and talked about hearing from them. How interesting! They must have had dreams from the ancestors too! He also mentioned Richmond again. I wonder what that's all about?

While Boots sits there patiently looking at me, I look from Boots to the dog in the picture to compare them, and there is a resemblance. I hug Boots, feeling so much better about having these dreams.

The door to my room is ajar, but I thought I closed the door. I feel more relaxed and get into bed.

As sleep comes I think about the fact that John Rivers never married.

That night I don't have a dream—but a kind of vision. I recognize Helen, with Donald Junior and John Matthew pointing their fingers at me.

It shocks me to have them here beside my bed.

Then Helen speaks with determination and says, *"You must be sure!"* Then all three repeat that to me over and over, *"Be sure!"*

The morning light awakens me as it escapes through the drapes. Boots licks my face and jumps down off the bed.

Then I remember the vision and I shiver from hearing their words in my head over and over again. What does it mean? Do they want me to search for another heir? Didn't the law firm do that?

I get out of the covers and prepare myself for the day.

In the hallway I hear no noise in the house; however, the smell of coffee is strong, and my love of coffee leads me down the steps with Boots. When we enter the kitchen, Gracie is standing there at the stove.

She says, "Hello, Miss. Bill said he saw you downstairs last night. Didn't you sleep well?"

"I did, Gracie, after I got a nice glass of milk."

Bill sees us from the window and comes in the backdoor. "Hello Miss. I can walk Boots this morning, if you want."

"Good morning, Bill. Thanks."

Gracie hands me a cup of coffee. She tells me she is fixing pancakes and sausage for breakfast. That sounds great and I go into the dining room.

Amy is dressed in heavy overalls as if she's planning to ride one of the horses. "Hi Amy, are you going to ride today?"

"I might ride but I'm going to visit with the horses first. Gracie has a few apples for them."

"Well, that's nice. I don't think I'll try riding, but I might go out there with you for another look at them." Amy nods her head sipping her coffee.

While waiting for breakfast, I say, "Well, last night I heard the noises you've talked about and couldn't sleep. I came downstairs to get a glass of milk and went to the parlor to enjoy the painting again. You won't believe it but there's a dog in that painting—and it looks a bit like Boots."

I don't tell her about the encounter with Bill.

Amy looks surprised. "Really? I didn't see it when we were there the first time. I'll have to look again. That's interesting."

"Yeah, I thought so too. The lady's dress is covering most of the dog and that may be why I didn't notice it."

It's a nice warm day, and after breakfast Amy and I take a walk around the outside of the house. Bill comes back with Boots and I take her with us. Amy emphasizes the correct names of the perennials and roses among the weeds scattered in all directions. I do see where Bill has worked and a lot of weeds have been removed, but it only makes a slight difference in the gigantic job.

We sit on an old bench that has splinters coming off the wood and I have to agree with Amy when she says work is needed on just about everything in sight on the outside of the house.

I will need to talk to the accountant about my finances and maybe I can afford a gardener and a few necessary repairs to the house.

About that time, I see that Bill is driving the truck in our direction. He stops and gets out. "Miss Walters, would you like to take a ride around the property this morning?"

"Yes, Bill. I'd like to go."

I look at Amy and she is shaking her head negatively and says, "I'd like to ride one of the horses today if Bill will prepare one of them for me."

While Bill gets a horse saddled for Amy, I finish my coffee, and go over and hop into the truck with Boots. The old green truck needs paint and has a few dents, but the tires don't look too bad.

Bill gets in and we start down the dirt road. He says, "I saddled Kota for Mrs. Forrester. I think he will be gentler than Major."

"Thank You, Bill, that was nice of you to think of that."

CHAPTER NINE

Bill is taking me to see the property in the old farm truck. I'm very glad for this opportunity to meet the farmers. They have been allowed to rent the property and produce vegetables and fruit for themselves, for us, and the local markets.

Bill makes a turn to the right side of the house into the trees on a very narrow lane. He says, "Your farming property is divided into five 50-acre sections and rented to five families. I have a copy of the plan and how to reach each farmer." He hands me the copy and I look it over briefly.

We travel along a fenced area and then we make another turn down a bumpy road. He stops next to a large field where two men are picking vegetables.

Bill gets out of the truck and I follow along. When we get to the fence, the men come over to us, as Boots, on a leash, rummages around in the grass beneath my feet.

Bill says, "Hello Larry, this is Miss Walters, the new owner of Rivers Run. I'm taking her around on the property today."

Larry, leaning on a rake, adjusts his straw hat to see us better. He leans over the fence to shake hands with me. "Great to meet you. We haven't had such young beauty here at Rivers Run in a long while."

I thank him and say, "How are things going today."

"Well, we need rain—sure hope we get it soon."

He looks clean-shaven, and tan from the sun. I can see a lock of his blonde hair, but the sun is too bright and I don't see his face very well. He looks like what I would describe as a typical country farmer and dressed for the part.

Larry introduces his son, Roger. I smile and shake hands. Then Larry looks at Boots and says, "She's been running around here a lot. Looks like you're gonna' keep her."

"Oh, yes, I call her Boots. She's getting use to me and I love having a dog."

His son, Roger, smiles and reaches through the fence to pet Boots.

He's tall and appears to be in his twenties. He has a nice build, gorgeous dark brown eyes, and blonde hair trying to work its way out of his straw hat. He's very nice-looking even with his soiled overalls and the blotch of dirt on one of his suntanned cheeks. I can just imagine him in clean dress clothes.

Roger just smiles and chews on a blade of straw, or something, and I look down at the ground. Both of us seem at a loss for words so for several minutes we follow the conversation going on with his father and Bill.

Mr. Jackson says, "Roger graduated from the University of Virginia, majoring in Agriculture. Marsha and I are real proud of him. He's been a great help here on the farm. He's interested in changing everything, using new gadgets and suggesting ideas that I know nothing about."

That information is very interesting. He's educated even if he doesn't look like it.

Then Bill speaks briefly about Larry's comments as Boots starts walking along the fence. Roger and I follow—Roger on one side, and me with the dog on the other. When I glance back, Mr. Jackson and Bill are smiling, talking, and watching both of us.

Suddenly I feel conspicuous and extremely self-conscious of what I'm wearing, and I pull at my white peasant blouse to straighten it. I'm uncomfortable and he seems to be too.

Bill and Larry Jackson start talking about the crops while Roger and I continue to walk along the fence neither one of us speaking. Then he smiles and his eyes seem to light up as we look at each other, making me oblivious of the humidity, the weeds and bugs that I usually try to avoid.

Roger pets Boots again through the fence, "Miss Walters how do you like living here?"

No sense telling him how the house is deteriorating. He probably already knows.

"Oh, it's nice but I'm still a bit overwhelmed. My friend, Amy Forrester, is staying with me for a time while I settle in. She loves the horses and is riding one right now. I want to meet some of the people farming the property, so Bill is taking me around today." Then I add, "Roger, please call me Jenny."

He smiles, "Okay, Jenny."

We both hesitate to speak and I look over the fence at all the crops they have planted. I'm sure it represents a lot of work. He reaches through the fence and pets Boots again and there are more awkward moments, but I think I like his hesitance.

It shows me he is not arrogant or aggressive, like many I knew at the orphanage. Some of those guys I had to avoid completely.

Roger Jackson looks off in the distance as we continue standing there at the fence, and he says, "I was glad to hear that the place has someone to take care of it again. John Rivers was ill in his last years and we noticed things were neglected." I nod but don't comment.

There is another awkward lull in the conversation and then he says, "If you need to go to town for anything, just call me and I'll show you around."

He writes down a number and hands it over the fence. "Jenny, we don't live far from here. This is our phone number if you need anything."

"Thanks, Roger. I may take you up on that offer. I would like to see some of the shops in town. I would also love to go to the library sometime and Bill has enough to do without chauffeuring us."

He raises his eyebrows and gives me a cute smile, "Just give me a call. Pop unhooks me from the plough now and then," and I laugh.

It's nice to know he has a sense of humor.

Then he tells me about a nice tavern in town for lunch. I thank him again for offering as we walk back to Bill and his father.

When we approach Bill says, "Well, Miss, let's go see the rest of your property, if you're ready."

"Yes, let's do." I shake hands with Larry Jackson and tell him it has been nice meeting him and his son, Roger.

"It's good to meet you too, Miss Walters."

Then I say, "Roger has offered to ride me into town one day, and I might call him. It will be good to have someone to show me around the first time."

He looks at Roger with a grin and back at me with another, "Well, I know he will be glad to help you out any way he can." As we walk to the truck I look back and Roger nods, smiles and waves goodbye.

After that encounter with Roger, I sigh and get my self-control back. I definitely will call him for a ride to town.

Bill drives along the road a bit farther and points out Jim Vanderhoff. Jim sees us, stops a large green farm machine and gets down from it. As we get out to meet him, Bill says, "That machine plows, plants crops, and does other things as well, and is one of those things that the estate provides for the farmers to use along with harvesting equipment."

We walk to the fence and I'm told about his wife, Judy. When introduced to Jim I notice he's very tall and thin. We shake hands and I apologize for stopping his work and, after a few comments about the lack of rain, we leave.

Driving farther on the property I meet Fred Sanders. I am introduced and we only talk with him a short time. Fred says I should meet his wife, Laura. He also mentions his daughter, Mary, of high-school age, and his son, Charles, who goes to college. He says he's been working in his field of vegetables. He takes off his hat showing his light brown hair with a touch of gray that matches his mustache. Before we leave I thank him for taking the time with us.

As we ride along Bill says, "I don't see Tim Bogart out in his field. He's probably at the market. Tim has a wife, Barbara, and two girls, Alice and Lydia, that go to college."

When we make a left turn on the property road we see a lady picking tomatoes from a small fenced in area. Bill stops the truck. "Oh, that's his wife."

Barbara Bogart comes over to the fence from the tomato plants. She is a little taller than me and is probably in her forties, dressed in overalls and a thin shirt with her blonde hair in a ponytail. Bill and I get out of the truck and he introduces me.

I shake hands with her and she says, "It is wonderful to meet you. Call me Barbara. Tim went to the market and he will be sorry he missed you." She invites us to stay for ice tea that she has in a cooler. I thank her but tell her we must get back.

Bill makes a turn to another area of the property to meet Jeff Hoffman who is busy on the edge of a field of corn. Bill says he has several helpers with him today. Mr. Hoffman comes over to us and I am introduced. He is an older man that looks to be in his fifties with graying hair, stout build, and a good smile that makes me feel comfortable. We talk about the weather and the lack of rain. He's very pleasant but seems to be anxious to get back to work, so Bill and I don't linger.

When we are in the truck again, Bill says, "He has a wife, Betsy, who works in one of the shops in town and two sons, Jeff Junior and Joseph, who work in Richmond."

Leaving the Hoffman farm we start back to the house. "Well Bill, thanks for taking me to meet the farmers. You seem to know a lot about them and that is a help."

"Jenny, I've been talking with them almost weekly since I took over as caretaker and I've learned a lot. I thought it was best to get acquainted and let them feel comfortable with Gracie and me."

When Bill and I return to the manor house, Amy is in her room changing clothes for lunch.

"Hi Amy. How was the ride?"

"Oh, Kota is wonderful. He is so gentle and does everything I want him to do. I gave him an apple when I got back. I rode all around the fenced-in property. It's lovely and goes into a nice shade tree area."

I sit down in a lounge chair. "Good for you. I met four of the five farmers, and also a guy that will take us to town when we want to go. His name is Roger Jackson. He is the son of the farmer, Larry Jackson. I'll call him some time and he'll take us."

I don't tell her how good-looking he is.

Amy seems pleased and says, "That's good since you probably won't ask Bill to take us."

I don't comment even though it is an obvious deep dig at me.

After lunch, Gracie starts us off on a nice long journey through the house after I tell her I would like a tour. We have seen most of the first floor so she takes us to the huge garage. It is connected to the house by a covered walkway.

On the way I notice the covering is made from wooden slats, some broken and a few missing entirely—*something else I'll have to get fixed.*

In the huge garage Gracie shows us a ten-year-old black Cadillac for Bill to use to chauffeur us around. Next is a small Buick that she says is available for us when we want to drive ourselves. There is also Gracie and Bill's Ford. Several tractors and trucks are there along with other farming equipment. Gracie tells us that the farmers use them and keep them oiled, gassed, and ready, while Bill takes care of the cars.

We start back to the house and Gracie takes us down a few outside stairs to the basement. The room we enter is a large workroom with tubs and lines to hang clothes. The washing machine and dryer are in operation.

At the other end there is a storage area. The shelving has jellies, jams, and vegetables canned and supplied by the farmers' wives. There is also a bin for potatoes, pumpkins, sweet potatoes, and other vegetables provided by the farmers.

I am very impressed with the basement facilities but think that a few rugs on the cement floor could make things more comfortable down there.

As we follow Gracie up to the first floor, I say, "The first night we were here we saw most of the first floor rooms, but I would like to see the big room again."

"Of course, Miss," and she goes in that direction.

As we go into the big room Gracie says, "I understand from people we know in town that this room was used for all the parties that were held by the late John Rivers—even his funeral was held here." Gracie shows us again exactly how the windows become openings to the outside porch.

Amy says, "Those drapes need a good cleaning. Haven't you and Bill had enough time to get that done?" I give Amy a look and shake my head.

Gracie looks at me as she answers, "They need taken down and sent out for cleaning, Miss. There is a drapery store in Richmond that might be able to help you with that. The drapes in the other rooms probably need cleaning as well."

"I understand Gracie. I'll call them tomorrow." Amy doesn't comment but looks away, closing her eyes in disregard.

CHAPTER TEN

Before we leave the big room on our tour of the house, I am fascinated with the paintings on the walls, and so is Amy. They are mostly all landscapes and scenes of markets with crowds of people. There are many painted by one artist, and his scribbled initials are hard to read. I study it and come up with "MAMahon" but Amy is not sure.

Gracie says, "Most of these appear to be scenes from the village but I don't know."

From the ballroom we go up to the second floor and visit the other six bedrooms. They all have old furnishings and faded colors on the bedding and drapes. Gracie says, "If you want to use any of these other rooms let me know."

I don't think it will matter because all the drapes and bedding need replacing.

Amy says, "I'm very happy with my room; however, my bed needs a softer mattress."

"I will replace it with one of the other mattresses, if you wish," Gracie offers.

Amy answers, "Yes, please, it may be more comfortable."

I tell her mine is fine for now. "Eventually I may be able to replace the mattresses and the drapes in our rooms at least."

Then I see a small wooden stairway leading to what must be the attic, and my suspicious mind especially wants to see that part of the house.

When I start up those stairs Gracie says, "Miss Walters, we haven't been up there to clean anything yet. Since we've been here Bill and I have been more concerned with the living areas. They were in very poor shape."

Amy says, "It should be cleaned properly right away so Jenny can explore what's up there." I look at Amy with an expression of disgust. She looks up at the ceiling as if to cancel out my feelings.

I just sigh about her voice of authority.

Gracie turns to me. "Of course, Miss. I'll see if Bill can start on it today."

I run my fingers through my hair in frustration with Amy. "Gracie, just let him know about it and I'm sure he will get to it when he can."

I turn to see Amy shaking her head at me, and I give her a look that I hope will turn off her cranky engine. I laugh because I often wanted to do that when I worked for her but knew I couldn't.

When the tour is over I thank Gracie and tell her I'm going to my room. Amy comes over but I hope she won't stay long. I think we both need time to relax.

Gracie offers to bring us ice tea and I agree that would be nice. It is late afternoon and I've had a busy time today.

The week goes by with me getting used to the arrangements and the noises at night when everything is quiet. I'm not noticing the creaking as much but it is disturbing when the wind is strong, because the loose shutters rattle and I make crazy words and music out of the sounds.

One day the following week Gracie tells me there is a gentleman at the door who wants to speak with the owner. I tell her I will see him in the parlor.

He comes in with a nice smile and introduces himself as Mr. Johnson. I introduce myself as the new owner and heir of Rivers Run and offer him a seat. He's a short man about Bill's age, dressed in a suit and tie. His hair and mustache are beginning to show gray.

He says, "I am from the Lombardo Real Estate Office in Richmond and represent a gentleman who wants to take this rundown place off your hands as soon as possible."

I am very surprised and say, "Mr. Johnson, I just inherited Rivers Run and I know it needs major repairs but I have no plans to sell."

"What? You're going to stay?" He walks back and forth shaking his head, comes disturbingly close, looks at me and says, "I tell you right now, Mr. DeLuca is ready with a very generous offer. To sell Rivers

Run will save you much anguish. Do you know what it will cost to keep things from falling apart?"

After that remark I take his card and say, "Thank you for your concern but I have no intention of leaving. If I decide to sell, you will be the first to know."

As he continues with his sales pitch, Gracie and I gradually usher him out of the house. From the porch he continues to delay his departure and tells me I should reconsider, and I just smile as Gracie shuts the door.

I love the house no matter its condition, and if I even thought about selling I can just imagine the dreams I would endure. I laugh to myself because I am beginning to relate to my ancestors, enough to know their wishes.

After my visit with Mr. Johnson, I tell Amy what he wanted.

"Oh Jenny, I think that is wonderful. You should sell this place. Just look at what will have to be done if you stay—things look like they can't be repaired! You and I can go to New York and start a gift shop business—and with your money and my business knowledge it would be grand!"

Remembering my dreams with Kathleen and Junior and my love for them, I turn with a look of disbelief that she would suggest such a thing.

"Amy, I'm not going to sell. This is my ancestors' lovely home, and I feel a connection with it already." She just sits there looking displeased and shakes her head.

I also think again about her last comment—"with your money it would be grand."

One day in August I make notes of things to buy when I go shopping again as I will need fall and winter items now. In the middle of the survey of my closet I notice the big box with my family mementos.

I should go through it. There are a few framed pictures of my mother and father that I could set around my room.

Just as I reach for the box, there's a knock on my bedroom door, and it's Gracie.

"Miss, the accountant is in the library and wishes to speak with you." I sigh from the interruption, and go downstairs to meet him.

Bob Humphrey is medium built, about forty years old, casually dressed in brown slacks and a short-sleeved, tan knit shirt. His cheerful round face, dark brown hair and eyes, and a thin mustache give him a polished appearance.

We shake hands, and after the exchange of first names, he sits down at the desk and I sit across from it.

He says, "Jenny, I'm here to close out and finalize your statement from the bank if that is agreeable with you."

"Bob, if you will, I would like you to continue everything the same way you have done before. I want you to take over my account regarding this estate and work for me just as you have in the past for Mr. Whitaker."

"That's great, Jenny. You know, I got a call from him the other day and he told me that you might want me to continue here. It has been a pleasure to serve the law firm, and yes, I would be happy to serve you as you wish. I will continue to come here around the 10th of each month to balance the bank account and take care of any other matters regarding your finances."

He looks up from the papers. "I want you to know that the only funds going into the account monthly is the rent money from the farmers. There is a good balance left in John Matthew Rivers' account from his various investments that is being transferred from his bank in Richmond and that should help with expenses, but you must be careful with what you spend." Then Bob asks if I have any questions or concerns.

"Yes I do, Bob. Everyday I notice things that you probably have noticed also that need replaced or repaired, and general maintenance that may be necessary just to keep things going."

"Jenny, you'll probably have enough money to take care of most repairs and your monthly expenses. Check with me about major maintenance and fix just a few things at a time until you can get a feel for this obligation. I'll advise you whenever I can, just call me." He provides his business card and a checkbook for me, and explains the system he has for handling my finances.

I shake his hand. "Thank you, Bob. That gives me an idea of what I must do. I'll leave you to your work now."

When I start up the stairs to my room, Amy is coming down. She says, "I thought you were doing an inventory of your clothes closet."

"The accountant arrived and I was interrupted. He is going to continue working for me. He knows all the ins and outs of this place by now. He has also made me aware that I need to watch my spending."

Amy's face has one of her familiar disgusted looks. "Oh, I could have helped you with the accounting. I did all mine for the gift shop."

I don't comment but try to smile thinking that will never happen here.

She continues down the steps saying, "Whatever," along with a facial expression of a dig at me so deep that, if we were outside, I think it could uproot trees.

The days go by routinely and one Friday after lunch, Amy goes out to ride Kota. It's a lovely day and I decide to take Boots for a walk around the property.

I walk along behind the back of the house and see the hills that are visible from my back windows upstairs. Most of the property that is farmed at Rivers Run is flat but the landscape near the house takes me down into a nice long, shady path between large oaks, toward a stream. I continue down to a tree that has a limb near the ground, providing a nice seat by the water.

The stream, at this point, is about thirty feet across, not very deep, and the water rippling along over rocks makes a pleasant sound. The sun is out and as I sit there I see what Donald and Helen were talking about in a dream—the brilliant and magical "diamonds" in the water. It appears to be shallow at this point with groupings of rocks, but I see that the river gets deeper and wider, and rapidly goes past me. I know it eventually goes into the larger body of water that I view from my bedroom.

Perhaps Helen and Donald Senior were sitting right here when they saw those lights in the water.

I feel so connected to them as I watch the ripples turn into sparkling lights from the sun as the water moves along. I remember how Donald compared the diamonds to good times and the rough, dark water, to bad times.

My short walk on the property has been very revealing, and that afternoon when I describe the place to Amy, she seems pleased with my new discovery and suggests we have Gracie prepare a picnic lunch one day and enjoy it there.

One day in the library with Amy I discuss the change that will happen when the caretaker contract is ended for Gracie and Bill.

She says, "If they stay as servants you should add a few additional jobs for Gracie, such as putting our clothes away instead of leaving them on the bed after they are washed and ironed."

"Amy, I think what she does right now is sufficient."

I'm again wondering how long Amy is going to stay before I tell her where the door is located.

"I just want to remind them that their salaries will not change when they take on the servant duties, and I want them to call me Jenny."

As she opens a new book she makes a face with tight lips, "Well, I certainly wouldn't put the staff on such friendly terms, but it is up to you."

"I definitely want them to stay. I'll have to meet with them about this."

"I'll be glad to sit in on the meeting so you don't forget anything."

She has convinced me that I don't need her in that meeting, and since she is engrossed in a book, I decide that now is a good time to talk with Bill and Gracie.

CHAPTER ELEVEN

Leaving Amy in the Library, I find Gracie and Bill in the kitchen together. I greet them and ask them to join me in the small parlor.

When Bill and Gracie are seated, I say, "I am now willing to manage the estate, and Mr. Whitaker will cancel your caretaker contract. If you stay here with me as servants, the duties will be similar but without management involved, and I'm keeping your salary the same. I'll need to know today if you will stay."

They seem to be troubled by something, but what could be the matter? Gracie is always cheerful and Bill seems to want to do everything I ask.

I sit and pet Boots for several minutes waiting for Gracie and Bill to respond to my offer—not wanting to rush them.

Seeing the hesitant looks on their faces, I am concerned. I add, "I know there is a need sometimes for extra help, and I will hire people as needed, and perhaps a gardener."

Bill says something to Gracie and she responds but I can't hear what is said. Maybe they have a crisis in their family or something tragic they don't want to talk about. I sit back in the chair waiting, and continue petting Boots.

Their uncertain demeanor reminds me of how I felt when I was told at the orphanage that I was going to a new foster home.

Bill hesitates and then says, "Yes, Miss Walters we have decided to stay."

Then he looks at Gracie. "What the future holds for us is not certain, that's why we are hesitant. You will be the first to know if and when things change."

Both of them look at each other as if they don't have a clue either, and at that time I wish I could read minds.

I smile and say, "Welcome to Rivers Run. I would love it if you would call me 'Jenny.' I think it will add to the friendly atmosphere in the house. Mrs. Forrester is my guest and you will continue as usual for her unless she tells you otherwise."

Bill says, "Thank you....Jenny. Gracie and I will try to remember that."

I shake hands with both of them. "Please let me know if there is anything you need in your quarters to make your stay more comfortable, and I expect you to let me know if the house needs anything to keep it running smoothly."

Bill says, "Miss Jenny, I know you have seen all the things that Gracie and I have *not* done here—but frankly, I cannot do many of the repairs. You may need to hire a contractor."

"Bill, I understand completely and I am going to get help to fix things, and I'll need your recommendations to find adequate help. We'll talk soon about all that."

I know Amy will be happy they are staying, but I'll tell her later. I wonder what she finds so interesting about books.

Reading has never been something I enjoy. In the foster homes the people would give me a book and tell me to go read, and I knew they were trying to get me out of the way. I would sit in a corner somewhere and pretend to enjoy the book that I couldn't understand while they went on with their lives.

Later I see Amy going up the stairs to her room. I say, "Amy, suppose I call Roger and see if he wants to take us to town? We could get some lunch and do some shopping. It might be fun." She agrees.

I go to the phone in the library and make the call. I recognize Roger's voice and I say, "Hi, this is Jenny. I know this is on the spur of the moment, but I'm wondering if you want to go to town this afternoon? If so, Amy and I can be ready shortly."

"Sure, Jenny. Oh—think about having lunch. There's a nice place in town. I'll see you in about thirty minutes."

Roger arrives, and looks like I knew he would in nice casual clothes and stands out in a white polo shirt and khaki pants. His hair is combed back with a small blonde curl escaping over his forehead. We approach and he takes my hand.

I introduce Roger to Amy and he nods and smiles, but Boots jumps up on him, getting his attention. He leans down and pets her as Amy gives me a side look, blinking rapidly, her mouth displaying a silent "Wow." I didn't think I would get that response from her, but Roger does look handsome.

I tell Gracie we probably will have lunch in town and she picks up Boots, giving her a hug.

I'm glad she and Bill are getting attached to the dog.

Amy and I walk out with Roger to his tan Ford Bronco and Amy gets in the back seat. It's nice and comfortable, and he says his mom and dad bought it for him as a graduation present.

On the ride out of the property Roger points out special trees and plants as we pass. He tells us about what his dad was told about the last sharecroppers. They stayed with the Rivers because they were treated well.

Roger says, "I've seen a small plot of ground in the woods on the property where they are buried, and the Rivers family provided the funerals and headstones."

We also learn from Roger that he knew the last servants living in the manor house. Their first names were Martha and George Woodward. Some people in town joked about them, calling them the Washington's. They were old, and when John Rivers died two years ago they retired and left for Florida.

Driving through town Roger tells us that he met the last heir several times. He was told that John Rivers held parties in the manor house almost every weekend until his later years. He says the talk in town is that in his younger years he was quite a gentleman with the ladies.

That reminds me of the dream I had where John Rivers and his father had a talk about his "affairs" with the ladies.

Roger points out the different stores in Helen, and tells us about some of the owners. Amy and I comment on the pots of flowers hanging everywhere and how we admire them.

He parks in a space at a diner called Helen's Café and says, "This has the best food in town."

"That's great—I'm hungry," says Amy.

As we enter the cafe Roger gives a smile to a woman approaching who is dressed in a blue café-style outfit. She is probably in her forties, with a rather heavy-set figure, has a lovely round face, and bright reddish hair piled up on her head. She acknowledges Roger and gives us a pleasant smile.

Roger introduces us to Helen Dupont and then says, "Ladies, this diner is named after her, not the town."

We shake hands and Helen says, "It's great to meet you. Come sit and enjoy." She seats us at a corner table that has a round-shaped booth and a nice vantage point.

The menu has a variety of sandwiches, subs, and hamburgers, along with pizza of every kind, a few side dishes that sound great, and many dessert choices of pie, cake, and ice cream combinations. We are served our drinks and then order.

While waiting for our orders, we discuss the quaint, old-fashioned décor and the colorful pots of flowers in the corners of the diner. Most of the customers are young teenagers. Some are putting money in a Jukebox and playing popular tunes. There are a few families with small children.

One man gets my attention as he walks in. He's tall, dressed casually, and has a young manly face with nicely trimmed, light brown hair. He is seated at a table by the door. Several people smile and greet him with a nod.

When the food is brought to the table we stop talking as our appetites take over. Then Roger says, "You see that gentleman over there"—and he points to the man I had noticed—"That's Ward Wendell. He teaches history at the local college. Say, he might be able to reveal some facts about the Rivers' family. I'll introduce you if he's still here when we leave."

Gracie told me about Mr. Wendell when I asked her about the painting in the parlor. I tell Roger I'd like to meet him.

We enjoy our lunch and on our way out we approach Ward Wendell's table. Roger says, "Mr. Wendell, I'd like to introduce you to Jenny Walters. She's the heir and new owner of Rivers Run."

Mr. Wendell gets up from his seat and turns to me, and we shake hands. "Miss Walters, It is most gratifying to meet you. When the lawyer came here checking with the locals about heirs, I told them Helen Marie Rivers' maiden name and that she had a brother who could have possibly had a Walters' family member still living—apparently, it was you."

I shake hands with him. "I'm very glad to meet you, please call me Jenny." Amy has stood back from the encounter and I turn to introduce her. "This is Mrs. Amy Forrester. She is here to help me settle-in at Rivers Run."

He says, "It is nice to meet you. Just call me Ward. We seldom get such attractive newcomers to town. Is your husband with you on this trip?"

Amy hesitates for a moment then says, "No Ward, I'm a widow. I have come to be with Jenny for a short time. Please call me Amy."

Then Ward hesitates with that news and pats her hand. "I'm very sorry, Amy. I am, however, very pleased to meet you and Jenny."

He hesitates, looks at me, and then Amy, and says, "I hope I can call on both of you at Rivers Run. I have not been there since John's funeral."

He continues to talk pleasantries with Amy as moments go by, and she seems captivated.

As Roger and I stand by the door, he looks at me and says, "I think Amy has found a friend."

I see how Amy looks at Ward and I can only hope.

Ward Wendell stands there in Helen's Café very reluctant to end his meeting with us, gives Amy a wonderful smile, and finally releases her hand. Still looking into her eyes, he says, "I will look forward to our next meeting."

He reaches into his pocket and gives me a business card. "Here, call me when it is convenient for me to visit."

"Ward, you are welcome at Rivers Run anytime we are there, give us a call. It has been a pleasure meeting you today."

He slightly bows his head, "My pleasure, dear, and with you as well, Amy."

Amy smiles and we turn to go—Roger leading the way out.

From Helen's Cafe we go shopping in several stores on Main Avenue. It is great fun just looking at what the shops have to offer, but

I'm still thinking about Ward Wendell, his obvious attraction to Amy and her response, and his comments about finding some facts that led the lawyers to me.

It's late afternoon when we arrive back at the manor house from our shopping. We thank Roger for taking us and he says, "It was fun. Call me again sometime."

When we enter the house Gracie is coming out of the parlor. She says, "Oh, you're back. Did you have a good time?"

Amy says, "Yes, Gracie, we did. We met Ward Wendell at Helen's Cafe."

"That's good. He is a very nice young man. He came here often to visit the late John Rivers. At least that's what he told me when I met him in the town library one day in the History Section."

Then she changes the subject. "Would you like a snack?"

I answer, "No, we had lunch in town."

"All right then. If you change your mind, I'll be in the kitchen."

CHAPTER TWELVE

After we return from our visit in town, Amy and I go to our rooms upstairs with Boots trailing behind. Amy says she will be over to visit after she gets into something comfortable.

When Amy comes in I'm lounging in my chair with Boots by the windows overlooking the hills. She hops into the other lounge chair. We enjoy the scenery as the late afternoon sun goes down behind the mountains and the clouds begin to show edges of bright gold.

Time goes by before either of us talk. Nothing but the view and the quiet are necessary to replenish my mind.

Then I break the silence, "Gracie and Bill are going to stay at Rivers Run as servants, and I have told them to call me Jenny. I told them they should still address you as Mrs. Forrester. It's up to you to make things less formal, if you wish."

Amy runs her hand through her hair. "That's good that they are staying, Jenny. I like them, and Bill really loves those horses too. I've watched him around them—he seems devoted that's for sure."

She sits back to relax. "I do hope you won't be sorry you have put them on an informal level with you." I don't comment.

I noticed how her attitude changed while she talked with Ward Wendell and I ask, "What did you think of Ward Wendell?"

"Oh, he's very nice, and he has beautiful green eyes. I couldn't stop looking at them."

I laugh. "Well, he couldn't stop looking at you, either. We might have a romance going on here sometime—what do you think?"

"It was just nice to be admired again."

I recognized that when the two met.

That evening we have dinner and discuss things that need repairs in the house to make it more livable and there are a great deal of concerns. Amy retires early with a book.

I feel like going outside to sit in the cozy lounge chair on the front porch and Boots follows me. It is a perfect summer evening and there is a good breeze. Boots sits down beside me as I make myself comfortable and sigh, enjoying the moment, closing my eyes to rest them....

Suddenly the sky is dark, and I am standing off the front porch next to a carriage. I look up and recognize a young john Matthew rivers who is standing beside me, and it is very cold. There's a beautiful lady in the carriage.

John carries a quilt over his arm and says, "Here, Margaret, let me put this quilt over your legs, and the ride home will be warmer for you."

The lady smiles down at him. "Thank you, John."

Then John steps up into the carriage and covers her lap with a beautiful quilt and says, "My grandmother made this one and embroidered her initials on the bottom."

"John, it is beautiful. I will cherish it."

"Margaret, tonight was very nice and I am glad you are feeling well. I hope it has been pleasant for you. The family being out to a New Year's event made your visit possible. This was better than meeting at a restaurant in Richmond. Don't worry, if I can make some Richmond connections, you may have a place of your own soon."

She smiles, "Yes, John, I'm looking forward to it."

Then John steps down from the carriage, and tells the driver to take her home. I follow John back to the porch...

Boots stirs, and I awaken, shocked that I was in another dream.

John's visit from a lady named Margaret? I wonder what happened to her and if John Rivers got a place for her in Richmond. Once again he is referring to the Richmond connections. The dreams are very revealing and troublesome, but I don't know what they are trying to tell me. Did John love Margaret? Could there be an heir from that background?

The next morning after breakfast, with the dream still fresh in my mind, I go with Amy to the library. "Hey, Amy, did you finish that book you were reading? If so, I'll take it and try to read it."

She laughs. "Yes, I did, even with your interruptions." I have to laugh too. She hands me the book. It is a mystery and romance novel entitled, "Beyond My Dreams." I doubt I will enjoy it, but it has a pretty cover and I'm thinking the title seems appropriate for me.

I look at the first pages of the book. The first paragraph is interesting.

The girl in the story, Lydia, is a dancer at a club in a town called San Jose. She is walking down an alleyway after dark.

Boots hops up in the chair with me and I pet her, going back to the book and the alleyway with Lydia.

A few minutes later Gracie comes into the library, interrupting my story. "Miss Jenny, Bill has cleaned out the attic and, whenever you wish, I can go up there with you."

"Oh, that's good. We can do that tomorrow after breakfast." Gracie agrees, and Amy says she would like to go with us.

I can't wait to hear the things Amy's going to point out to me that need attention. I had better bring a notebook to make notes. I sit back and sigh.

I continue reading the mystery about Lydia being followed in the alley until my eyes tell me they don't need to find out what happens next.

I leave Amy in the library and walk around the house, inside and out, considering the repairs that need to be done. I jot them down in a notebook and decide to talk with Bill about them, wondering if I will have the finances to cover the costs.

In late afternoon, while I try not to think of my responsibilities, I walk Boots around the yard, remembering my time in dreams with Kathleen, Junior, and Marty. It is so refreshing to think of them and takes my mind off the troubling questions about my ancestors.

One night the following week, I hear the creaking sounds in the walls and listen to them for several minutes, noticing that those sounds don't bother Boots at all as she snoozes next to me. I drift off thinking about the picture in the parlor of Helen and her children....

The atmosphere changes suddenly and I am in the moment with a very old man and a young man in the library. The young man says, "Father, I have been with you several times when you made your visits to Richmond. I think I know what I have to do in case you are no longer here. You told me what Grandfather did to cause this problem and I understand he was under pressure. These people we deal with mean business and I understand that too."

The older man says, "Son, I just want to make sure, for your sake and the sake of Rivers Run, that you know everything you have to do after I'm gone. Your grandfather was under pressure at first but he didn't realize it would take so long and that later the individuals he was dealing with would also have to have a younger generation to continue the operation. We will keep it going here because then there is no way it will be discovered. When you leave this world I hope there is an heir to take over this project if it is necessary. Dad had me do it and now I have you."

"Father, I'll try to make sure there is someone—even if I have to sell Rivers Run to one of those people, then they can take over the project."

"Son, those guys are dying off and as the years go by there may not be anyone left in that organization that knows about this. Then the agreement will just stop, and surely you know you will not benefit at all from this unless there are contacts in Richmond. The investigation is still ongoing apparently, and it could be devastating for Rivers Run if discovered. Bruno DeLuca does have a young son. His name is Romano, and he may take over the project after Bruno dies or possibly one of his relatives."

I feel something move and look down at Boots and rub her head. Then I realize I had another dream.

I was there with them, just like the other dreams I've been experiencing! I believe it was John Matthew Rivers in this dream with his father, and they were discussing a matter I could not understand at all. It was all about a Richmond connection. It seemed that Donald Senior had made a deal with some bad people and it continued right down to John Matthew Rivers—and possibly the one who would come after him—and that's me! Was it money they were talking about? What is it I must do? What will happen unless I find out more about it? I think about that real estate offer from Mr. Johnson to someone in Richmond. Was the buyer's last name DeLuca?

I prepare myself for the day and go down to breakfast still thinking about the dream. Amy is there and I greet her.

Gracie comes in with breakfast for both of us and says, "I think I know what you both like now and I just get cooking." She has French toast with butter and syrup, hash browns, sausage, and coffee.

Amy looks at the French toast. "I would rather have pancakes."

Gracie says, "Sorry, I'll fix pancakes for you, if you wish."

"Yes, Gracie. I'd like that."

I look at Amy and shake my head in disbelief and turn to tell Gracie that's not necessary, but Gracie has already left the room.

"Amy, don't you think that was a bit much. You could have eaten the French toast!"

Her satisfied smile says, "It worked," and she sips coffee.

I have mixed emotions, but smile back, although my mind has an image of her leaving Rivers Run with her suitcases.

After breakfast Gracie comes into the small parlor. "Well, ladies, would you like to see the attic this morning?" We both agree and follow her.

When Gracie opens the door to the attic area she says it looks a great deal better. There is a cleared area to walk into and we follow her in. It appears that the floor of rough wood has been waxed and some of the old boards actually shine. The room is long and wide and there are four nice big windows facing the back of the house, letting in light very well.

Gracie turns on the overhead lights and says, "This room is above the old part of the house. The kitchen, servant's rooms, and the small parlor were apparently added on to the back later."

Boots starts sniffing around boxes.

I remember what was said in a dream where the old John Matthew Rivers talked to Helen and was concerned about not leaving an heir. He said he might write something that would leave the truth with someone. Maybe it will be here in the attic.

There are a great many pieces of furniture along the walls, and I lift rough jute material, placed on top to keep dust off, and discover bundles of curtains, rods, tablecloths, and linens. Amy tells Gracie that those linens could be used and should be cleaned and stored downstairs.

Amy is asserting herself again but it is a good idea.

Gracie looks over at me and I nod in agreement.

There are old lamps, tables, chairs, an old rocking chair, a small children's table, along with broken bedsprings, and old mattresses. Rusty lawn tools, rakes, and shovels sit like they have waited too long for someone to use them.

Amy says, "Gracie these old things should have been discarded."

I knew I'd be sorry Amy came with us.

Gracie again looks at *me* and says, "Miss Jenny, I did not know what you would want to do with those."

I smile. "Thanks, Gracie, if Bill doesn't think they are usable, get rid of them."

CHAPTER THIRTEEN

As I look around in the old attic, I notice Amy is interested in a small, antique desk. It's clean but she wipes it off as if it isn't, and smiles pointing to the name "John" scratched on it. We laugh, thinking that John Matthew Rivers probably engraved it when he was very young.

She looks in the drawer and holds up several notebooks, with pencils, pens, and an ink well with dried ink. Flipping through the ragged and torn notebooks, she says that some pages have been torn out and those left are blank.

I guess that's not where he left the information he said he would write.

Going over to a long wooden chest that Amy uncovers, I ask where the key is that will open it. Gracie says, "When we cleaned yesterday Bill added a few keys to our house keys. Let me try them."

Amy starts sneezing, "Gosh, I thought they cleaned everything up here."

Gracie shakes her head, makes a disgusted noise with her tongue, and I say, "It is probably the dust coming from the papers you disturbed in the opened desk drawers." Amy gives me a look of displeasure that I'm beginning to ignore.

A few keys are tried on the lock of the chest. One connects and Gracie steps back so I can open it.

As the lid slowly opens we hear an agonizingly, prolonged, deep *m o a n* that vibrates throughout the room and sounds like someone suffering. Amy looks behind her, comes closer, and I jump and go closer to Gracie, who stands straight up. We look around but it's just us here.

A few seconds later, my heart starts beating again when I realize it was a noise from the chest lid, and it dawns on Amy and Gracie too because then we laugh about our reactions—but that was a ghastly sound.

The chest is lined with cedar and the inside is full of clothes. On top is a lovely silk blue gown with white lace around the neck and cuffs. Other clothes that appear to be from the same era are stacked one after the other—dresses, petticoats, leggings, along with baby clothes, bibs, and blankets. On the sides are shoes, hats, and gloves.

I hold up a few of the dresses and they look like they will fit us. Amy says, "These are very fragile. They have been here a long time. They won't hold up very well if we try to move them." I agree, and pack them back very carefully.

There is a small box under the shoes and I pull it out. It's covered with white satin material. Opening the latch and raising the lid I see a book and several items that may be souvenirs of some kind, with a key among them. The book has a plain brown cover that is locked and I think maybe the key may open the little book.

I close the box and tuck it under my arm. "I'm taking this with me."

The lid of the chest is closed carefully, and we hear another "m o a n" from it. We look at each other and laugh, as Gracie locks it.

Now that I have seen everything up here, I turn to go with the box in my arms. Gracie and Amy follow with Boots.

It is doubtful John Rivers left any written notes in this box or the attic, but I may come back and look again by myself.

Amy says she's going to read in her room, apparently unimpressed with what we found. I go into my room across the hall, anxious to see what is in the box, and set it down on a table. I am pleased that I have found something of interest. It might answer some questions.

I am just about to open the box when Gracie knocks on my door and calls me. "Yes, Gracie?"

"Jenny, you have a visitor. Mr. Roger Jackson is in the parlor."

"All right. I'll be right down." I put the box in the cedar chest at the end of my bed, wondering what he wants—we went to town only yesterday.

As I go down the stairs I'm not too happy with Roger's interruption keeping me from exploring the box from the attic.

Stepping into the parlor I see him looking out the window. "Hello, Roger. How are you today?"

"I'm fine, Jenny. I was about to go in town near the library and thought you might want to go with me. I remember you said you wanted to go there sometime. I could drop you off, do my errands, and come back for you."

This is a nice surprise. "My goodness, Roger, that would be grand."

I check with Amy, but she is busy reading and doesn't want to go. She says *our* library is giving her enough to read.

Roger and I leave in his Bronco and in no time he is parking in front of the library. He looks over at me, smiles, and his brown eyes sparkle. He says, "Gee, I'm glad you could come with me."

I am thrilled with that remark, and I say, "Thanks for asking. I get tired of staying at the manor house, but don't want to bother Bill to take me to town. I guess I could get Amy to drive the little Buick they have in the garage for us to use."

"Don't you drive too?"

"Actually, being under the county orphanage plan until I was eighteen made it difficult. I walked to Amy's gift shop where I worked, and didn't need a car. I'll get Amy to help me get my license."

He turns the key off to the Bronco but doesn't get out. "You were an orphan?"

I guess he hasn't heard about my childhood experience.

"Well, to give you a short version, I'll just say I became an orphan in 1971 when my parents died in an accident. I was only seven years old and, at the time, they didn't know about my heritage with the Rivers family."

He runs his fingers through his hair. "Oh, I'm sorry—I didn't know. The only thing we heard was that they had found a female heir for the place. Gosh, I was about ten when that happened to you. It had to be terrible. I guess this inheritance took you by surprise for sure." I don't comment as he gets out and comes around to open my door.

Now I know he is three years older.

The town library looks new, made of brick, with a small porch and white pillars on each side of double doors. Once inside I see typical library tables and chairs, catalogue card trays, and shelving filled with books in categories. As I approach the counter, a middle-aged lady asks if she can be of help.

"Yes, I'm Jenny Walters from Rivers Run," and I introduce Roger. He says, "Oh, Julie and I have met."

She nods at him, smiles at me, and says, "Oh, you're the new owner and heir. It is very nice to meet you. I'm Julie Cramer, the Librarian," and she reaches over the counter to shake hands.

I smile. Word about me has gotten around pretty well.

I thank her and explain, "I am interested in knowing the history of Rivers Run and my ancestors that lived there—perhaps from old newspapers."

Coming out of the enclosure she makes a hand motion for us to follow her and we go over to a machine. She says, "We are suppose to get a computer that will make things easier in the future, but for now this is where you may find the information you want." She shows me how to operate what she calls a microfiche that carries many older newspapers and town information, and also a copy machine.

Before I begin, Roger puts his hand on my shoulder and says, "I think I'll leave you with this and do my errands. I shouldn't be very long. Do you need anything from the butcher shop?"

"No thanks. Bill and Gracie take care of what we need for the house. Take your time. This may involve me for a while."

Soon I find that the Opal Register doesn't have the details I want. I remember the lawyer told me that Donald Andrew Rivers and my great-great aunt, Helen Marie Walters, were married in England. I really wanted to know who attended the wedding and items of interest when they were first married. There is only a marriage announcement about the two of them, and a paragraph on the next page indicating that the marriage and reception were held at the Holy Trinity Church in London. There are no details.

I scroll down through several weeks of news in the area and the first thing I see about Rivers Run is a notice about the two of them arriving from England in December 1867 with no pictures. There is no other information about them. It only lists weather problems, describing rain and wind in Virginia at that time.

More scrolling and I find a birth notice concerning Donald Andrew Rivers Senior and Helen. It's about their first-born child, giving the date of their son's birth in 1869, and his name, Donald Andrew Rivers Junior.

I am very excited now and keep operating the machine until I see another Notice about Rivers Run. It is the birth of a little girl, Kathleen Louise, to Donald and Helen Rivers two years later.

Reading on, I find there was an epidemic and several sharecroppers and others from the town had lost a few people. The Opal Register printed an article about Donald Andrew Rivers. He had gone to Richmond and brought a doctor back to Opal to help the families.

I am overwhelmed when I remember that was probably the illness that was told to me in that first dream when Donald talked about the diamonds in the water.

The Opal Register seems to keep up on events that involve Rivers Run and I make copies of several pages concerning the family when Donald Andrew Rivers Junior married Sophia Marshall. They had a son, John Matthew Rivers, born in 1893, and a son, Robert Andrew Rivers one year later who died in childbirth. The Register tells about the sadness of that event that surrounded the family.

There is also another article in 1894 about another loss in the family concerning Kathleen Louise Rivers killed in a conflict in Southern England. She was only twenty-three. Her volunteer work with the Nurses Unit #224 in Richmond, Virginia, is noted.

This saddens me and I sit there surprised at my reaction—but I knew her in my dreams. She talked to me and we had such fun together. I am shocked when I realize that I had been transported in dreams that started with me around 1978, taking me back in time almost one hundred years, to be with her and Junior when they were my age! Maybe it has something to do with the bloodline that has been mentioned in my dreams with the ancestors.

In a small section of the Opal Register I find out about Helen Marie Walters Rivers. She died of Cancer on July 3, 1904 at the age of fifty-five. The death is recorded after reading about the town's celebration of Independence Day that year. Suddenly it occurs to me that Amy and I arrived at Rivers Run on July 3rd this year. I sit back in awe. My arrival on exactly that day is an interesting coincidence.

Then I read where the town of Opal is renamed Helen, to honor Helen Rivers. A ceremony at the town square several months after Helen's death commemorates the occasion with Donald Rivers Senior making a speech. It has a faded picture of him and a young man listed as his son, Donald Junior, who must have been in his thirties. I can't really make out what they look like because the picture is old and dark. I make a copy of that as well as several other stories.

I find a full-page in The Register dated June 1918 about the death of Donald Andrew Rivers Senior at the age of seventy-two. The article has many stories from families in the town of Helen who respected and loved him for all the things he had accomplished and financed in the township over the years. It states that the ownership of Rivers Run passes to his son, Donald Andrew Rivers Junior who is forty-eight years old.

Had Donald Senior financed things with money from his dealings in Richmond? How deeply was he involved? Will it matter to me now?

In an article in 1929 one story catches my eye. It is about John Matthew Rivers. It notes that several young women, without mentioning names, have been known to frequent the manor house without male escorts. One young lady had been seen with John Matthew Rivers in Richmond several times in fancy restaurants and other places of business. The dates of those notices tell me that John Rivers was in his late thirties at the time. I want to know the names of the ladies to which the articles refer, but they are never disclosed. It did mention that John Rivers often met with many prominent people while visiting Richmond.

I know through my dreams that his father was not happy with him concerning his affairs with lovely ladies. Could they have been Lia and Margaret, the ladies John Matthew had mentioned in the dream where he talked to his grandmother in the painting, or were there others?

CHAPTER FOURTEEN

Reading more news articles in the library I learn that when John Matthew Rivers is forty-four years old he becomes the last known heir in the Rivers Family when his mother dies in 1937, two years after his father passed.

John Matthew Rivers never marries but often invites the whole town of Helen for parties and events. He enjoys musical groups and circus people, having picnics on the property where everyone enjoys good food and drinks. There are a few pictures of the events with him dancing with the local people. From the pictures, I am sure now that the painting in the small parlor of the young man with blonde hair and blue eyes is John Matthew Rivers.

The article also tells about his love of dogs, just like his grandfather. One article is about him giving puppies away to people of the town. The article also tells about his love of horses and his business, breeding and selling horses to the racing clan in Richmond.

Reading the next page I find that after his mother is buried he has workers build a large ornate iron fence and gate that surrounds the family graves, adding more land with gardens and bridges in the cemetery.

Scrolling down I find the article about John Matthew River's death just before Christmas two years ago. The large funeral at the manor house was a huge Christmas event for the town with food, music, decorations, and photographs. Some photographs are in the article, and I make copies. After the service he was interred in the family cemetery.

A month later an article is written about the fact that there are no heirs. It has a nice picture of him, and the newsman that wrote the article has included pictures of the cemetery, his gravesite, and the large tombstones of the family members who had passed. Next to it is a note that the property could be up for sale with numerous pictures of the property and the river.

I continue scrolling and find an article dated June 20, 1985, that is all about an heir that has been located. It is interesting to read about me coming from Shadyside, Virginia, to manage the estate.

I make copies of the information I want, sit back in the chair at the library, and think about all I have discovered. It has added a few things of interest, answering many questions that had not been revealed by Mr. Whitaker.

I sigh with content and realize that the dreams I had as a young orphan, putting me with the first family in the manor house, were a blessing. I am so thankful that now dreams with the old family members continue to provide a glimpse of their lives and sometimes their feelings. I have been given an actual connection.

Suddenly the family cemetery comes to mind. I must visit there very soon and put flowers on all the graves. I sit there for a moment with the vivid truth.

If authorities had discovered my connection with the Rivers family when my mother and father died, I would not have been an orphan, and would have known John Matthew Rivers, and perhaps even lived at Rivers Run.

That thought disturbs me greatly!

With my unnecessary abandonment still repeating in my brain, I gather the copies and thank Julie for her help. I start out the door and Roger is there sitting in his Bronco in front of the library.

As I join him he says, "I just arrived. Did you manage to get some information?"

"Yes, I think so and I made copies. It is sketchy but I believe I have what I want to know about the Rivers family. A person would have to be able to read between the lines to know more"—*or be in a dream with them.*

I voice my other thoughts. "I do want to visit the family cemetery one day."

"I can take you there if you want. It's not far from the gardens in the back of the manor house. I went with my father to John Rivers' funeral. I had come back from college for Christmas so I was able to attend."

"Thanks. I read a little about it from a news article and made a copy. I may get Amy to go with me one day." Roger shakes his head and rolls his eyes.

I guess he wants to take me, but I stifle a laugh—a cemetery visit for our first date?

He says, "Okay, let me tell you about John Matthew's funeral. That man was amazing. He had everything planned ahead. There was an orchestra and music. A large crowd of people came from Helen and I think some came from Richmond. The funeral was in a large room and food was served. It was a grand Christmas event and people talked about it for months. Martha and George made sure the celebration had everything. It was the last thing the servants did before closing the house, retiring, and leaving the area."

Roger looks over at me, and speaks with concern, "The problem was no one knew what was going to happen to the property. We were told that the state would take it over and probably sell it unless an heir was found or someone bought it, and that could have been a problem for us for sure. My dad was concerned because he rents the property, but you know that. Now all the farmers are concerned that you might sell after seeing the shape of things at the manor house."

"Oh Roger, I can imagine that those things bothered all the farmers. I don't think they have to worry about me selling the place— I'm totally enamored over my inheritance and want to improve things here. I have had one gentleman from a Richmond Real Estate Office approach me about selling, but it's not going to happen."

Roger nods his head, "My dad will be glad to hear that. He has had several meetings with the other farmers. He had been hoping to convince John Rivers to sell him the rented property so he could build a house on it and move from our little place in town. His death put a stop to our hopes and dreams."

After he says that, he looks at me with a strange hopeful look in his eyes, and I get it—I don't say anything, but I should consider the possibility and ask Mr. Whitaker about it.

Roger says, "How about lunch? We could go to Helen's or there is a barbecue place you might like."

That box of things from the attic is still on my mind.

"No, Roger, not today. I need to get back. Gracie is probably ready to serve lunch."

"Okay, Jenny, maybe another time. I'm real glad you came with me today. I miss being around people my age." Then he gives me a special look and says, "I like you, Jenny."

There's something to think about, and I tell myself to calm down, but I have to smile.

"I like you too, Roger. Thanks for inviting me today."

As we get closer to Rivers Run he says, "There is a theatre a couple miles from here. Maybe I can interest you in a movie sometime."

I hesitate to go on a date with him even though I am tempted.

I sigh, "Perhaps—we'll see."

Back at the manor house I thank Roger again as he leaves. I go upstairs to my bedroom with Boots on my heels and she jumps on my bed.

Amy comes over. "Hi, how did it go with Roger?"

I flop on the bed with Boots, and Amy sits next to me as I show her various articles and notices from the copies I made about the Rivers family. "Some of this information is very interesting."

While Amy reviews several news stories, I still hold the article about the Rivers' wedding in England. When I turn the page over to read the rest about the church, another continued first page story jumps out at me—there was an investigation ongoing about hundreds of uncut diamonds stolen from a large jewelry company in England. According to the news, Britain's Scotland Yard and the United States were working together, and were investigating many Sicilian Italian immigrants whom they suspected in both countries.

I sit with Amy as she reads the other papers and I look them over again, but I am still thinking about those stolen diamonds. I feel faint all of a sudden. Did the authorities ever find them? I feel my heart skipping beats and trying to catch up with my thoughts. Donald Senior did say in that first dream that Rivers Run would always have diamonds. Was he talking about good times—or something more valuable?

I'm still thinking about the robbery when Amy says, "Jenny, I'd say you learned a lot, but it also confirms many things that the lawyer told us."

She turns a few pages. "The article about the funeral of John Matthew Rivers is nice."

"Yes it is. Roger says he attended the funeral. He said it was a grand event for the town that Mr. Rivers had specifically planned. Many people from town attended. Now I want to go to the family cemetery."

I think I have learned a lot! I sit back on the bed trying to get my head around this stuff, and realize I still have the news article in my hand about the stolen diamonds. I fold it and place it back.

We sit for a time just going over the stories about the family and the sharecroppers. Then I tell Amy about the concern of the farmers about their rental property after John Matthew Rivers died, especially if there was no heir and the State of Virginia took ownership.

"Now the farmers are concerned that I might sell. I have to call Mr. Whitaker to let him know that Gracie and Bill are working for me now. While I'm at it, I'll talk to him about the farmers to see if I can sell the rented property to them. After all, that's more land than I need—and what will I do with it if they don't farm it?"

"Well, it wouldn't hurt to see what he thinks, and it would give you more money if you can sell the property to them."

After Gracie fixes us a late lunch, Amy goes to our library and I go back to my room with Boots. I open my cedar chest and remove the box that I took from the attic chest. There are several bracelets, a heart-shaped clasp, a gold locket, handkerchiefs with the initials HMW, and an old brown book that has a locked latch. I hold the hankies to my heart knowing they were my great-great Aunt Helen's. How precious it is to have these things.

The gold locket is beautiful and pops open easily. There is a picture of a young girl on one side and a young boy on the other. They don't resemble Kathleen and Junior from my dreams.

Then I notice a key lying there in the bottom of the box. I try it on the book latch and with just a nudge it opens. The first page has the beautiful hand-written signature of Helen Marie Walters. I rub my finger across the signature, thinking about her. I know she is the woman in the painting and it pleases me to know she was once holding this book and writing her name on the first page. I settle into my lounge chair by the window to see what's in it. Turning to the next page I see she has written something before she was Mrs. Donald Andrew Rivers.

December 10, 1866

Dear Diary,

I don't know what to do about my brother, Patrick. He is so tired of anti-Irish discrimination, the famine, and going to England for work and being sent back when work is done. He still won't come with me even though my aunt will accompany us across to her place and will take care of everything for us, just as she did for Harrison. Patrick has a family and says he doesn't want to try it. It is very hard to leave mother and father but the famine is worse and they want us to go. They cannot do us any good in Ireland and the visions from our ancestors tell them we must go. I told Patrick he should do what Aunt Fiona says to do and it should be all right. Aunt Fiona has all the right connections and I'm ready to go. Patrick's children deserve more in their future than poverty. Poor Kathleen, wife and mother, having to deal with all the abuses and troubles in town and her raising little Meghan and Melvin in those situations. I will keep them in my prayers.

She has written about an Aunt Fiona! My middle name is Fiona—maybe my dad knew about the story of his great-great- grandfather, Harrison Walters, and gave me my middle name in remembrance of his great-great aunt who helped Harrison across to England—seems strange, but logical, and I will think it happened that way.

CHAPTER FIFTEEN

This page of Helen's diary has told me a lot. I close my eyes for a moment. *Living in poverty and fear must have been terrifying but her departure and leaving her mother and father had to be even worse. This also tells me she and Harrison, my great-great-grandfather, were Irish not English. I turn the page...*

January 1, 1867

Dear Diary,

I'm in England finally. I crossed into England with Aunt Fiona in her carriage. The papers were sufficient because the guards let us through. Aunt Fiona is known in the right circles, she says, and reassured me as we traveled. Her house is beautiful. She says everything is taken care of in my credentials as her niece. It was difficult leaving my home but I love Aunt Fiona, and her British husband seems very nice. He seems in agreement about the situation. Now, I must get used to the new things. All I have is the locket Patrick gave me with the pictures of Meghan and Melvin. I will keep it with me forever. *The pictures in the locket are of Patrick's children!* I turn the page to find she has skipped many months before writing again.

August 10, 1867

Dear Diary,

I have been in England for months and have met a man who fascinates me. I met him at an affair at the Cunningham's last week. He is an

American. He is a fine gentleman and I love his eyes. He has asked to accompany me to the park this Sunday and my aunt has given permission. I can't wait to see him again. His name is Donald Rivers.

I find on the next page that once again she skips time before writing again. *What happened in those skipped months?*

October 5, 1867

Dear Diary,

I am so overwhelmed with joy. Donald Rivers has asked me to marry him and I accepted with Aunt Fiona's blessings. He wants me to go with him to his place in America. I am so glad I came across with Aunt Fiona. I would never have met Donald Rivers in Ireland. He wants to marry me next week on the 15th. He is planning on leaving immediately. There seems to be something urgent for him in America. I must get my things in order. He says we will be very happy there. I sent a note to my brother Patrick to tell him about it, and he wrote back and said he will not leave Ireland. They are having a small break in the problems there. God knows it is about time. He says things are looking up. He is upset with me for what I have done. Leaving was a big decision but I'm happy and can't look back now.

Rubbing my hand over the remarks in Helen's Diary, I am amazed. This is wonderful. Here is an account of a few days of her life. I wonder what happened to Patrick, her brother, and his family? She writes nothing about the wedding or part of December, making me frustrated as I read on.

December 18, 1867

Dear Diary,

We arrived at Rivers Run two days ago. The trip over on the U.S.S. Atlantic was long and hard. Then we took a boat down the east coast *from New York, and when we docked at a small coastal town we took a carriage to Opal, Virginia. I was sick for most of the trip. Donald was understanding and patient with me. The house in Opal is very nice and cozy. The winter weather is cold and harsh here but no worse than England. The servants seem adequate and my chambermaid, Bonnie, can't do enough for me. My life in Ireland, and family I left behind, are on my mind often. I love Donald but can never reveal any of that circumstance to him. It is the one sad thing about our relationship because he is so forthright and honest, and I worry that the truth could change everything for us. I am so glad I can keep busy with my quilting. It takes the stresses away and gives me comfort when Donald goes to Richmond.*

I continue turning the pages of the old brown book and wonder what it is that my great-great Aunt Helen is keeping from Donald Rivers.

Why couldn't she tell him about the poverty and upheaval in Ireland that made her leave? Maybe she didn't want him to know she was Irish.

No more is said about her secret, but I discover how she feels when she is expecting her first child. She writes that she does not look forward to the birth but her husband will have the very best doctor from Richmond to be there for her. Donald Junior was born on May 1, 1869 and Donald Senior held a big party a month later, inviting some old friends and neighbors. Helen was able to attend with the baby.

The next page of her notes skips to the birth of her baby girl two years later, born on June 5, 1871. She names her daughter, Kathleen Louise, after the wife of her brother, Patrick, who did not go with her to England because he had a family.

In the next page of the book she only lists special events and dates like a calendar. The dates of the childrens' birthday parties, the first days with their tutor, Mr. Morris; their riding lessons with the horses, times when Junior and Kathleen had teen parties on the veranda, and Kathleen's nursing interests and abilities.

She gives a very nice account on the next page of Junior's wedding to Sophia Marshall, June 2, 1890. From her descriptions I believe it took place in the large room. Her account is very short but so distinct that I can just imagine how it must have looked at the reception with those windows opened and everyone sauntering out to the porch and the grounds.

The very next event in the book is the birth of a grandson, Donald Junior's boy, John Matthew Rivers, on June 18, 1893. A year later, the mood is changed from joy on that page, to sorrow when she briefly records that Robert Andrew Rivers, another son of Donald Junior and his wife Sofia, dies in childbirth. These were all notes with a line or two about her feelings.

Then there's a short note about Kathleen's death in Southern England in 1894 and her service in the nursing unit. She writes that the family is extremely heartbroken and she fears she will never recover from the loss.

I can just imagine dried tears on these pages.

Those are the last notes in the little journal and leaves many questions in my mind as I close the book—specifically the secret she kept from her husband.

What happened to her Irish brother? I know my ancestry is traced through her other brother, Harrison Tomas Walters, my great-great grandfather, and he came from Ireland too. Aunt Fiona's husband must have had powerful connections to get her and my great-great-grandfather Harrison into England.

It is very interesting and puzzling, but for now it is all the information I have. In a way, I am really sorry that I have opened her book. I didn't get much more information than I got from the library except her view of things.

I look over to the bed. Boots is asleep. The soft chair is comfortable and I feel very relaxed. I rest my head back on the cushions....

My eyes suddenly see a young John Rivers in a garden holding a woman around her waist. I hear music in the background and look around. There are people dancing in the big room with the windows opened to the porch. I stand there with john and the woman. She is very lovely wearing a beautiful lavender gown with lace on the edges, cut very low in the front, worn off the shoulders. His hands are busy touching her as they kiss and he says, "Lorraine, you are so lovely. We must get together more often. As you know I am alone here now with just the servants."

He kisses her again and she pulls away, turning toward the house. "John, you are easy to love but I must have a solid foundation with more. I don't think you are ready for that."

John rubs her shoulder. "Just stay tonight and we'll talk about it. I must go to Richmond tomorrow and I'll take you home." He then follows her toward the music, his hand around her waist. They go right past me as they go into the ballroom setting. I reach out to touch the sash on the back of her dress. She just walks on, looking up into John's eyes with desire.

I try to follow but yawn loudly—and the dream fades away.

When I open my eyes I'm back in my room. I shake my head trying to remember the dream.

It is very interesting. John has another woman friend. What happened to Margaret? Now he has Lorraine. As I get ready for bed I laugh. I had thought that he had those parties because he had no family anymore and was lonely. Now I'm thinking he couldn't have been very lonely after all.

Someone is knocking at the door. "Yes."

Amy comes in but leaves the door open. "Well, finally. I've been knocking but I didn't want to just barge in. I thought maybe you were in the bathroom and didn't hear me."

"No. I must have drifted off to sleep."

"I'm sorry if I woke you. I took a nap too. It's time for dinner."

I put Helen's book back in the box with the other things except for the locket. I feel sure Helen wants me to wear it. It is a beautiful, golden, heart-shaped locket with long golden chain-links, and clasp. I put it on and go to the mirror to see it. To wear it makes me feel very close to the family. I return the box on top of the linens in the cedar chest. Boots jumps from the bed, joining me to go to dinner.

Later when we are in the small parlor having ice tea, Amy notices the locket and she has me open it. Then she wants to know about the children. I tell her I don't know who they are but I know they are my ancestors and I want to wear it.

Amy says, "Was there anything else of interest?"

I know I'm not going to try and explain that diary information to her!

"Not really. Just a few trinkets and some handkerchiefs." Then I tell her about Roger's invite to a movie. "When Roger found out I didn't drive, he offered to teach me and help me get my license, but I told him I thought you would do that for me."

Amy smiles and says, "I think he likes you and he wants to get to know you better."

"Well, I'm not in any hurry to start anything serious with him. He's very nice, but I have too many things to think about right now and going out to movies with the first person I meet is not one of them."

"I think you're smart. After all, your obvious good fortune might be attracting him. Give it some time."

That's just what I think too. Then I realize that she doesn't offer to help me get my license.

CHAPTER SIXTEEN

It's September and one evening, while the sun is still out, Amy and I decide to take a walk in the gardens. I put a leash on Boots and take her along. Amy loves the flowers that Bill has planted and we walk around the new blooms while she admires each of them and discusses the fact that they won't be blooming much longer.

We sit on a bench and I notice the rough splintered edges and wait for Amy's derogatory remarks, but surprisingly she doesn't comment. I enjoy the fading sun and the vivid colors in the distant sky while Boots sniffs around in the soil.

Amy says, "When I see this beautiful sky, I think of Eddy. He and I loved to sit and admire nature and sunsets. I guess that's why we started the gift store—it was fun filling it with beautiful things and showing them off to customers."

I know she misses her husband. Maybe this place is not good for her, reminding her of what she is missing in life.

"Amy, are you happy—you know you are welcome here, but perhaps you need more in your life."

She turns away and wipes tears. "Jenny, I am fine for now. I'll always miss my husband no matter where I am. It's just that he would have loved this place. I do miss my gift store but life will go on."

We walk back to the house in silence.

Amy says, "Let's have a glass of wine in your room." Gracie pours wine for us and we take it upstairs. We enjoy the wine and the end of another perfect day.

After Amy leaves, I remain by the windows, and close my eyes thinking about the diamonds in the water…

Suddenly I am in the library, and I'm with Donald Junior. He pulls out a small pouch from an inner pocket of his suit.

I follow him to the outside of the room where he nods to a short, rather stocky built man standing there, and says, "I hope this is all you'll need right now, Marco, until next time."

Marco says, "Very good, Donald. Bruno has been waiting for you. That's why I decided to come to you myself, and bring it to him this time. He has been very upset, and he says it is very time-consuming to deal with this problem." Marco shakes his head and says, "I have cleared it in the bank accounts so now he can do his job."

Donald says, "Marco, I'm tired of this and should turn you guys over to the authorities, but I'm afraid it will cause trouble for Rivers Run and my grandfather's name. He should never have gotten mixed up with your organization!"

"He had no choice after he lost to the boss. After that, the agreement they made was for keeps, and you, your son, and those after him, are in this as much as I am now, until it's over in our business and it may take years to use them in small amounts. I guarantee they are still investigating, and several times we have been the ones that have had to cover our tracks. In all cases, we have kept Rivers Run out of it."

I cough and it wakes me from the dream.

This time I saw Marco, talking about Bruno and the agreement. Would they still be alive? In that other dream they said Bruno had a son, Romano—and did he have a family? I still wonder about going to Richmond. What they need must be here. If so, where is it? What did Marco mean when he said he had cleared it in the accounts?

I say my prayers and get between the covers, but I know I won't sleep. These dreams are upsetting!

The next few days are uneventful, and I use the time to walk around the old house and make notes of what needs changing or fixing. Several rooms need painting. Bill recommends a contractor named Michael O'Malley, who lives in Helen, and a meeting has been arranged.

This also gives me an opportunity to search for someplace that may have been used to hide something—I laugh to myself because I don't even know what I'm looking for—all because of dreams.

Mr. O'Malley arrives around 2:00 p.m. the next day. He comes in a large green truck that has ladders and equipment hanging off the sides. He's about forty years old, tall, tan, very muscular, dressed in overalls, and a work shirt. When Bill introduces us he removes his straw hat and I can see his smiling brown eyes and thin mustache. He wastes no time giving Boots a nice pat on the head, and from that gesture I think he and I will get along fine.

He says to call him Mike, and I walk him through the house. I show him many places that need serious attention—either by fixing the plaster, the broken wooden trim, or faded paint. He is congenial and helpful with suggestions, Bill agreeing with him, adding several places that I had not noticed that need repair.

When we walk to his truck, I ask about the outside repair and paint for the entire manor house. Mike looks at Bill with a questioning look, kicking loose gravel with his boot, and Bill looks at me with the same look—neither one saying anything.

The cost is probably what they are considering.

I shrug my shoulders. "Doesn't it need a new paint job? It's the first thing I noticed when I arrived."

Sighing, Mike says, "Yes, all of it needs attention, Miss Walters, but it will take a lot of time and money to complete the outside with paint and repairs. I should also recommend someone to inspect the roofing. We have had several bad storms and it may need attention as well."

I stop to consider that. "Thanks, Mike. You are right. I should have that checked. Please prepare the contract with a separate cost of the outside work and roofing inspection. Bill and I will look it over and then I will discuss the costs with the accountant."

"Yes, Ma'am. I know a well-qualified roofer, but it will take a few days for the estimate. How about next Monday, same time?"

"That's great. Thanks, Mike." I watch as he walks around making notes before he leaves, and I thank Bill for coming along with me. Bill has been a great help and I am beginning to feel more confident about taking control of these challenges.

After the contractor leaves I go looking for Amy to tell her about the plans I have made for repairs. When I walk into the library Amy gets up from her chair with a big book in her hands.

"Oh, there you are." She approaches me, very excited, holding up a brown book. "I was bending down tying my shoe and saw this on a lower shelf—I sure don't remember putting it there!"

I sit down in one of the chairs with the Bible, quickly turning the pages to see the place Amy said had names in it.

The pages are brown from age and I turn them carefully. In the middle of the book is a section with names. I recognize the handwriting of Helen from the book I found in the attic. I haven't told Amy about those writings yet and probably won't bother now.

Amy watches over my shoulder and I look through what has been recorded. The page of the Bible recording the family history has the last name "Walters" in the center of the page and begins with her parents.

Her mother's name was Cornelia Elle. Her father's name was Riordan Brogan. She notes only their deaths in the late 1800's, when she was at Rivers Run.

Under those names she has listed two brothers: Harrison Tomas and George Patrick – and adds her name: Helen Marie. She does not mention the families of her brothers. From Helen's diary, I know that Patrick had several children and Harrison had a son that was my great grandfather.

From there she has centered the name "Rivers" and lists the dates of birth of her husband, Donald Andrew; her children, Donald Andrew Junior, and Kathleen Louise; and her grandson, John Matthew; and Robert Andrew, the grandson who died in childbirth.

There are no other names listed. I feel satisfied that she recorded George Patrick. It doesn't answer what happened to him however. I only know that Harrison Tomas Walters was my great-great grandfather, according to records found by Mr. Whitaker.

Looking over my shoulder at the Bible, Amy says, "That is very interesting. It looks like she had another brother besides your great-great grandfather. I wonder what happened to him? Maybe he died when he was young, but she doesn't list his death."

I say, "Yes, that may be possible."

I close the Bible and Amy puts it back on a shelf. Then Gracie announces that dinner is served.

After dinner when we retire into the small parlor with a piece of carrot cake and coffee, I'm still thinking about George Patrick Walters.

His wife's name was Kathleen and they had two children that Helen had mentioned in her diary. Their names are Meghan and Melvin and they are the two children in the locket. What happened to them? The Bible only gave me more questions. I settle down in the soft seat—fall is fast approaching.

I finish my coffee and look down at the locket around my neck thinking about Helen's diary and the dreams. Maybe the cemetery will give up a few answers to my questions.

"Amy, I think I'll go to the Rivers' cemetery tomorrow if it is a nice day. I am not sure exactly how to get there, but I'll ask Bill. I feel terrible that I have neglected to go until now."

"You should go, Jenny, and I'll go with you. I'd like to see it."

That night before I turn the lights off in my bedroom I think of Helen's diary. *It disturbs me to think that Helen felt she couldn't tell her husband she was Irish. I imagine it was the animosity against Ireland at the time.*

I am so glad that I am acquiring renewed confidence in handling the affairs of the estate. When I finally close my eyes I hope for another dream to tell me more. The house is very quiet tonight and I awaken several times, but sleep finally comes with thoughts of my ancestors coming to my mind…

Suddenly, I am awake and walking in the dining room with a young John Rivers and a man who is older. Their breakfast is on the table. John Rivers is marching back and forth in front of him and stammers, "Father, it will be all right. Lia was a servant with no family. We will bury her in our cemetery. I have found a family who will adopt the baby girl. Please believe me, if she had not died I would have kept her and the baby in Richmond. She would have been comfortable until I could provide a place."

"Yes, I know John, but this could be very embarrassing for us unless your story is believed. How can I approach our friends? There will be so many questions and they will think the worst. I just wish you were not so loose with your affections." He then wipes his brow and sits down near the fireplace. "Your mother is very upset." He sighs and looks into the fire.

"Father, stop! I have seen people in the village and told them how devastated we are. You won't have a problem, I promise." He goes over and sits beside his father and together they look into the flames of the fireplace....

CHAPTER SEVENTEEN

When I awaken in the morning the sky is overcast with clouds but there is a warm breeze coming through the windows. I stumble around getting dressed, realizing that I had an unusual dream last night.

The fact that Lia had a baby and died here is astounding. Now I really want to go to the cemetery, not just for the Rivers family but to see Lia's grave. If it's there, it will help me believe in the dreams.

After breakfast Amy and I get directions to the cemetery from Bill who is filling the horse troughs. He tells us he keeps the gravesites cut and cleaned every week and warns us of a forecast of rain late today. Again I think I need to get help for Bill because I can see there is just too much outside work in the gardens for him, especially since fall is bringing leaves to remove and other preparations for winter.

We cross the yard in the back of the house and for the graves we cut red and white roses from the bushes that still have blooms. From there we go down a small hill and walk on a path leading into a woodsy area next to the stream. Coming out of the tunnel of trees and bushes I see the gated area. The fencing around it is iron with intricate designs of flowers and ornate circles. Over the gate are the words, "Rivers Repose." I stand there a few moments admiring the artwork, while Amy walks ahead.

We open the gate, enter the cemetery, and walk on gravel paths that go through green grass to the gravesites. Donald Senior and Helen Marie are buried on a slight hill under an elm tree. I place several roses and sit under the shade tree on a bench. Looking up at the sky I feel at peace with whatever happens in my life here at Rivers Run.

The graves of Donald Junior and his wife, along with the baby, Robert Andrew Rivers, who died in childbirth, are across a bridge and small stream. Further along I see a memorial stone with Kathleen Rivers' engraved name and date of birth. Engraved also on the stone is: Nurse Unit #224, and the date, May 15, 1894, when she was killed in Southern England.

She was twenty-three. How sad for her mother. I remember the fun we had as children in my dreams and it gives me a moment of sadness.

Then I look for the gravesite of John Matthew Rivers, the last heir, still thinking about my dream concerning Lia. Where is her grave?

Amy finds John's grave across another walkway and I spend time there on a bench under a shade tree.

I am so sorry that he was ill and couldn't keep up with everything the house needed. I'm also sad that he didn't know about me when I lost my parents.

I continue to look for Lia's grave. Bill has done a good job keeping the cemetery looking its best. The grass is trimmed and there are no weeds. The stream down below the manor house is meandering through the cemetery very slowly as if it doesn't belong. Perhaps part of the stream was redirected to the cemetery when John Rivers added the fencing and the gate.

Amy and I have placed flowers at every Rivers' gravesite and she is sitting on a bench relaxing, but I know from my dream last night that there is another grave here somewhere and I have kept several roses for that purpose.

Standing at John Matthew Rivers' grave and examining the way the stream makes its way out, I think I see a headstone that could be a gravesite under a tree. I walk down a hill and cross a small bridge.

The grave's inscription reads, "Lia Moretti, a household servant from 1922-1933." It shows she was born in 1900, and came to work for the Rivers family when she was twenty-two and died when she was thirty-three.

I feel elated—I have her full name. From that recent dream I know she died having a baby—but was John Matthew the father? He was forty when she died. Could there be another heir someplace? He said in the dream that the baby was adopted.

At Lia's grave I look over at Amy who is still relaxing on a bench. I call to her to come and see this gravesite. She gets up reluctantly and comes over. After reading the gravestone, she seems just as surprised as I knew she would be.

Amy says, "Why is she buried here?" I just shake my head, show surprise, and don't say anything.

I'm afraid that if I speak I'll blurt out what I know from the dream.

She stands there in thought for several moments. Then she says, "John Matthew Rivers was a young man and she was in her twenties when she came to work for them and she died eleven years later." I can see Amy's brain has been working overtime.

She looks at me with her eyes blinking wildly and says, "Ah ha! Maybe he loved her and that's why she is in their cemetery. I wonder how she died?"

"Oh, Amy, you are too suspicious. He was a nice man, that's all. It says she was a servant, and they all probably loved her. Perhaps she had no family, died of some ailment, and they buried her here." The subject is dropped after that comment, but Amy still has a suspicious grin, as I place on the gravesite the roses I have been holding, and we walk away.

I really don't know the truth either—only the things I learned from my dream last night.

Amy says, "These old families have secrets we will never discover." I shake my head and walk away.

If Amy only knew what the dreams have disclosed and the questions that are still unanswered.

Leaving the cemetery I close the gate and we follow the stream that flows into the huge body of water that I see from my bedroom window. I want to show Amy the area below the house where the stream is shallower.

When we get there I notice there is no sun, just clouds and no "diamonds" in the water. Amy says she is impressed with the peacefulness, and we both think it is a good day to enjoy a picnic.

We're looking at the water but hear thunder behind the hills, and look up to see dark clouds approaching our area.

Amy looks at me and raises her eyebrows. "Maybe another day?" I laugh as we head for the house.

The rumbling in the sky becomes more pronounced as we enter the kitchen out-of-breath after running uphill. Gracie has fixed a stew that has a wonderful aroma, and after the tour of the cemetery and the uphill run, both of us are ready to indulge.

The afternoon rain falls pretty steadily, keeping us indoors. After another cup of tea, Amy goes to the library to start reading another novel. I go along and try to read the novel I had started about the dancer, Lydia.

I sit comfortably and start Chapter Four. *I find Lydia, the dancer, discovering that she is being stalked. Lydia falls asleep and has a vision of him appear in her dream. He is talking to someone about her.*

Suddenly, this story with dreams is becoming too much like my own life.

I close the book, deciding that mystery novels are not my thing and pick up a romance novel that Amy has suggested.

For me, there are enough mysteries in the Rivers family.

We are settled in the library when Gracie comes in and tells us that Mr. Ward Wendell has come to welcome us to Rivers Run and she has taken him to the parlor.

Amy quickly gets up and closes her book, and I say, "Well Amy, this might be a good way to spend the afternoon."

Amy wants to freshen up first, so I tell Gracie that we will be down to see Mr. Wendell shortly, and we go to our rooms.

After I wash my face and hands, I knock on Amy's door and she comes out looking fantastic in a dressy beige pantsuit with brown embroidery on the collar and sleeves.

Wow! She's trying to impress him!

When we walk into the parlor Ward stands up to greet us, and Boots reaches him before I do. He pets her gently, looks at us, and I tell him the dog's name.

He says, "Jenny, I thought with the rain today, visiting would be a good way to pass the time, and I did not want to wait much longer to welcome you here. I hope it is not inconvenient."

"No Ward. It is very nice of you to come, and you're right, the rain makes it a perfect day for your visit. Gracie has served refreshments. Please help yourself."

Amy offers to pour him coffee. He thanks her as she pours coffee for the two of them.

They are still standing, busy smiling at each other and making small talk about the weather, as I pour myself coffee and sit there with Boots.

There's a package in Ward's chair and he is so engrossed with Amy that he almost sits on it but catches himself.

He straightens up, "Oh, Jenny, I almost forgot. This is a copy of my book that has just been published." As I open the package, Ward sits with Amy on the faded blue loveseat.

He continues, "It is all about the history of the area during the civil war and after the war, with photographs. At the time, Opal was the name of the town and was involved when the north marched through here. The name of the first farmer who owned the property was Lucius Dovell."

He sips coffee and continues. "Donald Senior bought the property from him with money from his father, Martin Stephen Rivers, a banker in Richmond. That information I received when I had discussions with John Rivers."

Very interesting! His father was a banker in Richmond. What about the Richmond connection? Did his father somehow get his son mixed up in a strange deal?

My mind comes back to the present when he says, "There is a picture in the book of Mr. Dovell's small house that stood here then. Some old notes implied that Donald Rivers repaired the old house and used it until the manor house was built behind it. I'm sorry to say that all the photographs are not the best quality."

I'm impressed. "Oh, thank you, Ward. It is wonderful to have this history. Your title, 'Virginia Before and After The Civil War' is fascinating. You must be very proud of this, and I am so pleased that you thought of me."

Ward's face lights up and he smiles. He says, "You are most welcome. John Rivers was very concerned about not having heirs, and it's good that they found you. He told me once that he was considering selling the place because he couldn't really take care of it any longer."

Ward gets up, sets his cup down, walks around, and says, "I had many visits with John and when he died we lost a man with many memories of things he had been told by his parents. He once told me that the property was named Rivers Run, not so much because of the family name, but because of the river running through the property. He told me his grandfather and grandmother loved the river."

Amy says, "That is a wonderful fact to know."

He says, "Yes, it is, and I wrote about Rivers Run because of the things that happened on the property and in the town of Opal.

I put the book next to me on the chair. "I will treasure it."

As we enjoy our treats and coffee, it is obvious that Ward and Amy do not need me around. It is nice to see Amy open up to another person like she is doing. The two of them are laughing and chatting about the little town of Helen.

I sit and listen as Ward talks about his encounters with the different people he has met in the area who had known a few of the Rivers family.

While Ward talks, I look up at the painting of my ancestor and her children and ask a question, changing the subject rather abruptly, "Ward, I think I know that this painting is Helen Marie Rivers and her children, but can you tell us any more?"

He looks up at the painting, "Oh yes, my dear, you are correct. I talked with John Rivers about it the first time I visited. We were here in this very room. He told me that Donald Senior had that painted. Kathleen was three years old and Donald Junior was five. He said that Kathleen and Junior wanted the little dog to be in the painting but it was very hard to keep the dog there very long. Finally, the artist had to paint the dog in that spot from memory." We laugh.

Then Ward gets up and walks around. He says, "Actually, there's another story about dogs. Donald Senior loved them and had a brown male beagle and a white female Poodle that had several litters. He always gave them to people in town that wanted them and called the breed Beagle-Poos. The dog in the painting was from one of those litters. Some of the mixes actually turned out brown and white, just like your dog, Boots, here."

Ward looks up at the painting, scratches his head and says, "I think John Rivers said the dog's name was 'Princess.' He told me that for years the people in town had litters from those dogs. You could see them around everywhere you went."

I am very happy with that information. I say, "Thank you, Ward, for that story. Maybe my little Boots could be a part of that background— just as I am."

Ward agrees, "Yes, she could be."

CHAPTER EIGHTEEN

I sit back and relax with Ward and Amy and think about those things Ward has told us, while Amy starts talking about her shop in Shadyside.

The conversation stops for a minute, and I ask Ward if he knows anything about the artist that painted most of the paintings in the ballroom, especially his name.

Ward says, "Yes, John Rivers took me in there one day and I was admiring the paintings. He explained that the artist, a young friend of his, brought several of those paintings for him to see. John Rivers bought all the ones he had that day and asked him to paint several others that were favorite places in town that he visited. They were of the town hall, the park next to it, the old library, which has been replaced since then, and the old courthouse area."

Then Ward stops, rubs his chin. "I usually never forget a name." Then he looks deep in thought. "I believe the name of the artist was Marvin Allen Mahon, but John called him Allen."

"Oh, thank you, Ward. They are beautiful and look so real, almost like photographs. I wonder whatever happened to the artist?"

"I don't know. John Rivers always seemed enamored with his work though, and told me once that he paid for him to go to Paris to study and often gave him support at exhibits. I thought that was unusual, but he was old and very generous."

Ward turns back to Amy, "Sorry, what were you saying about your shop?"

Then Amy tells him about herself, her husband, Eddy, her gift shop, and the inventory that she left at Shadyside.

I am surprised that she is discussing those things so easily; however, I've noticed Amy loves to talk about her circumstances and how she took on that obligation.

Often I find myself turning her off when she goes on about it.

I look over at Ward who seems to be engrossed in what Amy is saying. When she stops talking he gets up and goes to the window as if suddenly his thoughts are somewhere else. Moments go by as Amy and I sip our coffee.

Ward paces and then walks slowly back, sits, rubbing his chin before finally speaking, "Amy, wouldn't it be nice to set up your gift shop right here on the property—I mean if Jenny would be receptive to it? It would give both of you something to do, and I think many people would love to come and shop here."

I am stunned as the idea bounces around in my brain.

Amy looks over at me and around the parlor as if trying to find words. She sighs. "Yes, Ward, that would be very nice; however, that's out of the question, Jenny has enough to consider here on the property. Besides, next year I may travel to New York City and start a new life there."

Initially I agree. It will be time for her to go.

He looks surprised and rubs his chin at Amy's response and for a moment is without words. Then he shrugs his shoulders. "Well, it was just a thought."

Ward looks at me and sighs. He says, "You know, I wanted to buy this place from John Matthew. He was getting very old and unable to do very much any more. I offered to buy it and let him live in it until he died."

Then Ward shakes his head and says, "He said he would consider it but there were things he needed to do first. Then time went by and he passed away. He never said what those things were or whether he did them or not. I sure wish I had followed-up on that idea and pressured him more about it."

Ward's offer to John Matthew Rivers to buy Rivers Run is interesting, but my mind is continuing to think about his idea for a gift shop here.

I say, "Ward, the gift shop may be a good idea but it is quite a lot to think about right now. Amy is right, I've been too busy getting this place to look like a real home, and there has been more than enough to do."

He walks back and forth and says, "I know, Jenny, but this place has a lot of history and everyone in town is concerned about what happens here. When John was alive many people from Richmond visited and loved the place. I'm sure you will get the Richmond crowd to shop for gifts. There are not many of these old homes left and with a few improvements, the manor house would show well too. I think it will be a mistake not to discuss the possibility."

The subject is gently dropped after that, and it is late afternoon before Ward Wendell leaves Rivers Run. Walking out of the parlor he takes Amy's arm and she smiles. I'm not surprised when she accepts his invitation to accompany him to dinner in Richmond Friday evening.

After he leaves we go into the library. I have Ward's suggestion and Amy's comments hopping between other thoughts in my head.

Is it something I should consider? Like he said—it would give us something to do and I'm thinking it would bring in much-needed money for the estate.

On Friday night, I watch Amy prepare herself for the date with Ward. The weather is getting cooler and Amy dresses appropriately in a tan linen dress and brown pumps with a matching cape over her shoulders. Her blonde hair has grown and she wears it pulled back slightly from her face with curls in the back.

I tell Amy how nice she looks and she smiles and steps lively down the stairs, greeting Ward who has arrived, and I watch them leave.

Before I return to my room I tell Gracie I would like dinner in my room tonight.

Boots settles down with me on my bed as I think about the dream with John Matthew Rivers' father, Donald Junior, and the Italian jeweler.

Then I think about the man in Richmond who wants to buy Rivers Run, and Ward Wendell making that offer to John Matthew Rivers to buy Rivers Run and take care of it, allowing him to live here until he dies. I feel exhausted from these scenarios and what they mean, and close my eyes…

Suddenly, there is a fire going in a fireplace and I see Helen near a bed with a young lady. She is very pretty. She is wearing a white uniform with a heavy black cape over her shoulders and is bending over the bed closing a suitcase.

Helen dabs her eyes with a handkerchief and says, "Kathleen, you can't be serious—you, joining the nurses unit, and leaving for England? We just had your 'coming out' party and there were several young men who wanted to come back and take you out. It is your obligation to get married and have children. I have told you how important it is to have heirs for this great estate. What will we tell everyone?"

"Oh, Mother, I'm sorry. We have discussed this before. I just can't stay and be married. I want to see the world and help out where I can. The people I am going with are wonderful and I want to go. The conflict is minor. It is what they call an Anglo-Ashanti War with a King who rules a small Colony and is refusing to surrender his sovereignty to England."

She leans over to pack another item. "Father knows about it and doesn't seem to mind if I go. He likes traveling. After all, he went over there and found you didn't he—and then he came back!"

She locks the suitcase and turns to her mother, "Don't cry. I won't be gone very long. My service won't last forever and it will be a great experience. Then I'll come back and do whatever you want. Besides, you have your quilting that keeps you busy."

Helen holds Kathleen's hands and seems to look at something on her wrist. "Kathleen, What is that on your wrist?"

"It's a bracelet that has my identification and my Nurse Unit Number. By showing this bracelet I am allowed into the medical camps to serve."

I realize that I am witnessing the last moments of Helen's time with her daughter, Kathleen—and I feel tears come down my face because I love her too.

I step closer to reach out to them. I yell, "Kathleen don't go!" --but somehow, maybe because I'm older, I can't connect—what would it change anyway...

Kathleen gives her mother a kiss on the cheek and they hug before she leaves. Helen sits down on the bed crying, and says out loud, "This is definitely not the 'diamonds in the water' time of my life." *I want to console her and step nearer...*

I hear a noise—the dream fades, and Boots jumps up startling me. Gracie is at my door, and wiping tears from my face I tell her to come in.

She rolls the cart of food over to my chair. I get up, still thinking about my dream, but awake now. "Thanks, Gracie, it looks wonderful."

When Gracie leaves I walk around. I am stunned that another part of Helen's life has been revealed to me.

Poor woman, watching her only daughter go to God-knows-where. It must have been horrible for her!

I recall that Kathleen mentioned Helen's quilting in the dream. I go to the cedar chest and open it. I've seen a few quilts in it but had never examined them. I spread one out on the bed. It has beautiful designs with colors of yellow, purple, and pink, just like the sky colors seen from my windows. I look for Helen's initials that John Rivers mentioned in a dream with Margaret when he gave her a quilt. I find them on the very edge and rub my fingers across beautifully embroidered initials, *HMR*.

Then I take another quilt out of the cedar chest. The colors remind me of the gardens. I see the colors and shapes of red roses, yellow daffodils, and green leaves with her beautiful initials on the edge. There are other blankets, but they are not her quilts.

Putting the quilts back, I try to enjoy my dinner. When I retire for the night Amy has not returned. It's very quiet in the house and I sleep soundly.

At breakfast Amy looks relaxed and is all smiles. "Well, I hope you had a good time last night," I say, sipping my coffee.

"Oh yes, Ward and I went to a very nice Italian restaurant called Romano's on the outskirts of Richmond. They had a band that played music and we danced. I got back after Midnight."

I remember in a dream that Bruno's son was named Romano, and I laugh to myself because these Italians are into more than banking and jewelry.

Then I remember my plans with Gracie today and say, "Well, I'm going to spend the day in the kitchen helping Gracie bake cookies for a benefit in town. Gracie says they raise money for the disadvantaged people of Helen."

Amy says, "That's not for me, but I'll come and watch."

After a couple of hours mixing, baking, and listening to Amy's comments with her directions, we end up with ten dozen assorted cookies. Gracie will take them in the morning.

Since Gracie and Bill have worked for me as servants, they enjoy Sundays off, and every Sunday I have been making breakfast. I don't mind at all but of course Amy has not been agreeable, complains slightly, and after breakfast goes directly to the library while I clean up.

CHAPTER NINETEEN

It's Monday and Mike O'Malley has brought his estimates, and I am reviewing the costs of the various repairs to be done on the house. It will be costly but the review shows that everything is necessary.

In the afternoon I call the accountant, Bob Humphrey, and discuss it with him. I also tell him about the plan to sell the rented land to the farmers.

He thinks the work on the manor house will take time and with money coming in every month there will be sufficient amounts to cover everything on credit. He will watch my finances closely, however. He also tells me that selling the land will help the financial problems. He totally approves of both plans.

After my conversation with him, I go to check on Amy. She is back in her soft chair with a book in her lap. She appears to be deep into her reading. I sit in the chair across from her and stare in her direction wondering about the gift shop that Ward had suggested.

She looks over at me while I'm watching her. "What?"

"Amy, maybe Ward is right. We should think about opening a gift shop here at Rivers Run. We could both be involved. You might love working and living here."

She looks surprised and shakes her head, "And where would we put the shop?"

"I have considered that. I think there is plenty of room in the garage, and if we put it there the cost will be minimal. It would be far enough away from the house for privacy, but still be close."

Amy stares at me and I see a change on her face—like a glow when a person gets a surprise birthday gift.

With the possibility of a gift shop still hanging there in the room like the heavy drapes, Amy then shakes her head back and forth, rubbing her chin and staring at me.

She scrunches up her mouth, "Where would the parking area be for people that might come?"

"Bill can help us with that small problem. I'm sure when John Rivers had parties they had a place for the cars."

Through dinner Amy and I talk more about the gift shop possibilities.Before we retire for the night Amy stands at my bedroom door, "Jenny, I think it is wonderful that you want the gift shop here. I really appreciate it."

I smile, thinking about the possibility, "I am glad it pleases you. Have a good night."

After saying a prayer for guidance and direction on the gift shop idea, I close my eyes but memories of my foster care as a young girl ignite, and all the problems I had then come back like a ghostly vision, but I know that I was strong through it all, and I'm convinced that my strength will help me through anything that happens now as well. I am so thankful for my peaceful life here as I finally drift off...

I am standing in the foyer with John Rivers and a woman I recognize as Margaret. She appears distraught. "John, I must talk with you."

"Come in Margaret. We can go into the parlor." Then I follow them and he serves wine.

Margaret says, "John, I had to get my cousin to drive me here. I have not seen you for weeks, and Angela had her fifth birthday and you did not come. I wrote you that nothing is happening to my other Worthington plans."

"Margaret, I've known you for a long time. You know I have obligations with this place and there was never a promise of more than a home for you and Angela. It took some business dealings but now you have a home. If you thought there would be more, I'm sorry. I never meant for you to believe that. Because of Angela and your needs, I have continued the support." He hands her an envelope. "You must leave me alone after this." Then he arranges for his driver to take her home.

Without another word, Margaret wipes her eyes, gets up and John escorts her out to the car. I walk along and hear him try to console her on the way.

As the car leaves, I stand there amazed as John turns to go back into the house. Here he is turning away a possible heir, or is Margaret just someone he tried to help out of a difficult situation and she is coming back trying to get more?...

The dream fades and I awaken troubled, just as John must have felt back then and it is difficult for me to sleep.

I wonder what Margaret meant by "other Worthington plans" that did not happen for her?

At breakfast Amy says, "Well, I slept very well last night and hope you did too."

"Yes, I did."

It would be too late now to reveal my dreams.

With a second cup of coffee, Amy and I take a walk out to the garage to check out the location for the gift shop. Looking it over I can envision it. The garage is big enough for a portion to be used for it, even with the farmers' equipment there.

We walk back and forth, taking measurements and getting excited about the idea. When I look at Amy I can see she is beginning to be inspired.

Looking up at the trees nearby, Amy says, "Jenny, I don't think any trees will have to be removed to make a parking area, and that's good."

My voice comes out with a spirit of determination. "Amy, let's do it!"

We come together and hug and I start a two-step dance in front of the garage. Gracie and Bill are tending to flowers around the porch. They run over and Bill says, "What's happening, Jenny?"

I say, "Not a thing. Everything is fine. I want to put a gift shop right here in the garage!"

Gracie and Bill come closer. Gracie says, "I had overheard Mr. Wendell talking about a gift shop but thought nothing would come of it."

The look on Amy's face shows irritation and I have a feeling it's about them hearing our conversations. She returns their smiles with a cold look of distaste but I'm glad she doesn't say anything.

Amy and I watch Bill and Gracie as they look at the area in the garage from our view, but I notice they hang back for a moment.

Their smiles seem half-hearted, and resemble how I felt as an orphan, getting in on things that make other people happy but have nothing to do with me.

I feel a need to make them more involved as we stand there, envisioning the gift shop. I say to them, "Do you think it is a good idea to remodel a small area of the garage for the shop?"

Bill looks it over again. "It should do all right."

"What about a parking area, Bill," I ask. "Can we put that in the back of the garage, or where would you suggest?"

Now I see interest in their eyes and he answers. "You could make a good size parking area on the side of the garage with an entrance there, to allow for public traffic on the property. I don't think you will want it out front in the privacy area or outback where we pull our cars and equipment into the garage. I suggest a separate road off the driveway with signs to the gift shop."

I feel relieved that Bill has voiced some ideas.

Gracie is smiling now also with more enthusiasm. She says, "You know, Jenny, I could do some extra baking and have cookies and cakes for sale in the shop too, if you want."

I think that's a great idea, and say, "Yes, and it will bring customers into the shop and additional money—and perhaps a portion of the money from the bakery goods could be yours, Gracie."

Amy looks at us, and from the frown on her face I can see that didn't go over well with her. She says, "I'll have to think about that. Let's wait and see how the shop brings customers first."

I sigh and say, "We have to give this some thought. We must remember that Amy will be the deciding member of this project."

It quickly comes to mind how this might adversely affect all our lives with Amy having control. I look around at the four of us and notice a slight change in the momentum.

Changing my course, I say, "Bill, perhaps we should talk with our contractor friend, Mike O'Malley, about this project before we get too excited about it."

Amy walks back looking over the area of the garage again, and with another frown she says, "We have to talk, Jenny—in private."

I have no idea what she wants to discuss, maybe it's about the money for the project, and I say, "Okay, Amy, let's go into the library."

I turn to go back into the house, but Amy has not totally changed my enthusiasm. I have been inspired.

I ask Gracie to bring us ice tea as Amy and I go to the library. Amy sits at the desk in the corner and takes out a pad of paper.

"Okay, Jenny, we have to figure out what this means if we go ahead with this."

Sitting behind the desk in the library, Amy reminds me of a strict counselor I once knew. I recognize her negative attitude all too well and wait for her to speak.

"The shop will be in your garage and already there are plans that may not be what I want—that just won't work!"

Amy shakes her head back and forth. For several moments I wait while she looks around and down at the floor.

She says, "There is only one way it will work—I'll just have to rent an area from you since it will be part of your garage—just like I rented my shop before, and how the farmers rent land from you."

That scenario is interesting but stops me cold.

I naturally thought it would be our shop together but still a part of the estate. It is disappointing, and I feel my rising balloon of joy losing altitude. However, I have learned a lot about Amy since living around her. I somehow thought she and I were closer, but now I understand—she wants the gift shop to be her own!

I sigh and look back at Amy who is waiting for a response from me.

Renting out a portion of the garage, which is really a part of the manor house, doesn't seem right, and I remember the warning from Miss Brewster about people taking advantage.

Determined, I walk back to the desk, "Amy, I'm sorry. The rental to you would not be right. I feel obligated to the estate and feel that if the garage is used for this, it should be a Rivers Run responsibility. After all, the garage is definitely a part of the manor house."

Amy gets up from the desk, walks to the window with her back to me.

As I wait for a response from Amy I think about how she loved being the owner when she had her gift shop in Shadyside, Virginia, and it's obvious she wants to do the same here.

I walk closer to her, "If I make it a part of Rivers Run, how do you feel about being the manager and continuing to live here as my guest?" She continues to look out the window for several minutes, but soon turns around to face me and I see a decision in her eyes.

Will she decide to leave Rivers Run?

CHAPTER TWENTY

I stand there with Amy in the library waiting for her response to my offer to make her manager of the gift shop that I want to build in the garage, wondering how I will manage this without her.

Amy turns around and walks back to the desk and says, "Jenny, I wanted to be the owner, but I do understand your side of this. I am not happy; however, it will be fun to work in a gift shop again and this offer seems all I have now. I will take the manager position once the gift shop is built. For a price, I'll turn over my inventory I have in storage to give the shop a good start, if you will agree," then she writes an amount for the inventory on a piece of paper and hands it to me.

With relief I look at the price. "Amy, it looks good and your inventory will be helpful. I think a gift shop for Rivers Run is an excellent idea and I'm glad you want to manage it. Now all I need is an estimate on the building of it, and I will include your price for the inventory when I talk with the accountant."

I will still have to speak to Mr. Whitaker to make sure this is done legally concerning the use of the garage for a gift shop.

Amy gets up from the desk and comes around to stand beside me and offers her hand to shake on it. We shake hands and hug—but there are no words to describe how I feel having to exert my authority over her for Rivers Run, but it is for the best.

Amy immediately leaves the library and I don't see her again until dinnertime. I can see her attitude is one of disregard as she goes about her own needs for the rest of the evening.

The next day I call Mike, with Bill standing by, and tell him about our plan for a shop in the garage. Bill gives him the approximate measurements that Amy and I have decided will be necessary.

Mike arrives on Friday with a group of workers to begin the work on the manor house. After he gets them started on repairs, he shows Amy and me a few pictures of his completed remodeling jobs. We walk around with him in the garage to discuss everything we need and I'm happy Amy is there to add her ideas.

That afternoon Mike provides a rough estimate and Bill seems to think it will be a good contract and I'm glad to have his views about it.

The next week I realize that many weeks have passed since Bill and Gracie started their new service with me, and I have been very pleased with their work. It is a beautiful warm day in the change of seasons and when it's time for lunch I suggest that we have a picnic, with Gracie and Bill, down by the stream to celebrate the new beginnings.

Gracie packs a great lunch with sandwiches, fruit, ice tea and dessert. Bill sets up chairs and a table. Amy seems to have put aside her feelings over Rivers Run ownership of the gift shop, and we have a wonderful lunch.

I watch the stream cascading along, and feel a special peace. The water is sparkling with "diamonds" as it rises and falls over rocks with various shades of color and trickling sounds. It is simply mesmerizing, indicating to me that the gift shop will be a good thing.

In that first dream with Donald and Helen about diamonds, was Donald Senior talking about real diamonds somewhere—and what about Rivers Run never running out of heirs?

When Amy discusses her plans for the gift shop I still have visions meddling with my thoughts. I take a deep breath and try to focus.

Bill and Gracie seem as eager as I am about getting started. Bill says, "Mrs. Forrester, I am good at carpentry, and can help Mike make the counters and shelves for the shop. That should save money."

Amy seems happy, smiles and says, "That's wonderful Bill, and please call me Amy."

Finally, she has put Bill and Gracie on a first-name basis with her. That pleases me.

The lunch is very enjoyable and productive. Amy talks about how she thinks the shop will add to our lives.

Bill doesn't say much during our conversations but when there is an awkward silence he quotes what he says is an Irish Blessing. "May the road rise to meet you, May the wind be always at your back, May the sunshine be warm upon your face, May the rains fall soft upon your fields, and until we meet again, May God hold you in the palm of his hand."

We all seem overjoyed and I look around at the smiling faces. I think the Rivers family would be pleased with me, taking charge and using their property in this way.

After lunch everyone helps to get the picnic things back into the house. We are laughing and Gracie and Bill start singing a song. It sounds like an old song that I think I've heard and I try to sing along. This day has accomplished the desired relationship I want between all of us.

The next day, Ward visits and Amy goes to lunch with him in town. He is very pleased about our sudden plans to have a gift shop. I'm sure Amy will tell him all the details during lunch.

I make a call to check with the accountant. After I give Bob a brief about everything involved for the gift shop and the amount on the contract with Mike, he thinks it is a good thing for the estate and the town, and advises me to sign the contract.

After his approval on the gift shop contract, I feel like wandering outside to do some thinking. I walk around the grounds, the new gardens, the benches, the fountains, and the house.

Maybe my ancestors are happy that I am heir to this place and want me to be aware of my obligations. It is astounding to me that they share certain happenings with me. The dreams still seem to indicate that I need to find heirs. Is it really the ancestors—or is it this old house that's trying to tell me something?

It was George Patrick Walters' name written in the Bible. What was it that Helen would not tell her husband Donald? Was Patrick a criminal? I wish a dream would reveal this secret! And what about Donald's secret. Did he ever tell Helen about his dealings and the business connection in Richmond?

When Amy and Ward arrive from lunch, Amy goes upstairs to freshen up and Gracie brings Ward into the small parlor to be with me.

When he sits down I have a request, "Ward, there are two names in the history of Rivers Run that I would like you to check for me. One is George Patrick Walters. I believe he was a brother to Helen Marie Walters. The other is the artist, Marvin Allen Mahon, who painted the landscapes in the ballroom. He may live in this area."

He gives me a questioning look. "Of course, Jenny. I will be happy to do so; however, back when I was checking the family tree I don't recall a record of another brother to Helen Marie Walters."

He writes down the names in a small notebook and tells me the artist of those paintings could be in the area but would probably be very old if he is still alive.

"Yes, Ward, I know the artist might be very old, but he may be living. George Patrick Walters is listed in the family Bible and may have come to America after Helen married Donald Rivers. Those are just names I am interested in."

Ward sighs. "Well, there are many ways to investigate names. I will let you know what I find out."

When Amy arrives, Gracie serves refreshments. I can see that Amy and Ward are getting very close. Amy says, "Jenny, the weather is so nice. I'm going to show Ward the place by the river," and they leave.

While alone I relax in the small parlor. I look up at the painting of young John Rivers who was very good looking, and all at once I think of the problem the farmers faced with their rental property after he died. The repairs to the house have kept me occupied and I have not called Mr. Whitaker about selling the property to the farmers.

I go into the library and make the call and he answers on the first ring. When he finds out it's me, he says, "Miss Walters, is everything all right?"

"Oh yes, Mr. Whitaker, but I would like to have your advice on something that has come up."

"Of course. If I can be of help I'd be delighted."

"I have met most of the farmers on the property and would like to know if I can offer them a way to buy the property they rent from Rivers Run. As you know I have no idea about these things—that's why I'm calling."

"I don't see why you can't sell anything you want that is yours. The courthouse probably has it already divided. The farmers have separate roads into their areas, and it seems quite possible. The first thing you need to do is talk to a Real Estate Broker—and of course the farmers, to see what they wish to do as they may not be financially able."

"Thanks, I'll arrange a meeting with the farmers first."

Then I think of the gift shop. "Oh, there's one other thing." I describe the shop we want in the garage and tell him that Amy will manage it once the shop is ready to open. I also bring up my concerns about the garage being used.

He stutters and seems very surprised. "Well, Miss Walters, it will be a good source of income for you and I know the people in Helen will be thrilled, and don't worry, the property was listed commercial when we thought it would have to be sold. That will not be a problem. I'm glad you called about these things."

Later I sit with Amy and tell her about my conversation with the lawyer.

She says, "Jenny, I'm glad you keep me informed but it really isn't necessary."

I sense she feels differently about her part in all of this and I feel relieved. Right from the start I felt she overcompensated when she thought I was unable to take charge.

The next day Michael O'Malley comes over and Amy and I go through the plans for the gift shop. The parking and entrance on the side of the garage sounds good to him. Amy is very happy with his drawings, and the cost is what I had discussed with the accountant. The contract is signed and Michael tells me he should be able to have the plans approved by the county in four weeks.

In the evening after dinner I meet with Gracie and Bill to let them know about the final plans for the gift shop, and also my plans to sell the rental properties to the farmers.

Bill looks down and says, "Miss Jenny, are you sure that is a good idea to turn over ownership of all that property? I heard that for some reason John Rivers never wanted to sell to them." Gracie looks thoughtful about it too.

I smile, "This will be good for the farmers, Bill. They have been renting for so long and I suspect they would like to build a house on part of it in order to live where they farm the land. If all of the farmers buy their rented land, Rivers Run will still have 50 acres. At any rate I need to find out if they want to do it before making plans. Nothing will be done for a while."

With no response from them, I say, "Bill would you arrange a meeting with the farmers? I thought it would be nice to ask them to dinner Friday evening around 7:00 p.m. That will give Gracie a few days to plan for it."

Bill says, "Yes, of course."

I turn to Gracie, "Will that be all right, Gracie?"

"Yes, that's fine. I'll bake a nice salmon dinner."

CHAPTER TWENTY-ONE

The next day I see Bill in the library. "Hi Bill, I know Amy likes reading books—do you like reading too?"

Bill looks startled. Then I notice he's holding the old Bible in his hand. He sighs, "I like to explore old Bibles. This one is very old and has the names of your ancestors in here. There's one in particular—George Patrick Walters. Did your family ever mention him?"

Now I'm stunned! "Why do you ask, Bill?"

"I'm just curious and heard you talking to Mr. Wendell about him."

Once again Bill had heard a private conversation of mine.

"Yes, I did ask him to check on George Patrick Walters because there is no mention in the Bible as to what happened to him, and Mr. Whitaker, my lawyer, never mentioned him as part of the family."

Then Bill puts the Bible back in the bookcase and passes by me, leaving the library, but not leaving my mind; however, I have come to the library to write a few checks and the subject is delayed by other problems.

I am very anxious when Friday evening comes.

How will the farmers react to my offer? I have asked Amy to take part in this dinner with the farmers and we wait patiently for their arrival. If the farmers are agreeable and want to buy the property, I'll check with a real estate broker.

While we wait, Amy says, "Jenny, if the farmers buy their rented land, it will bring you money that you can use to remodel and buy new furniture."

"Yes, that's right."

From the window in the library I see several cars arriving and Amy and I go to the foyer to greet the guests.

With each step my mind is going over what needs to be presented tonight. I'm very hopeful it will be received well.

Amy and I stand there waiting for the farmers as Gracie opens the door. Larry Jackson and his wife, Marsha, come into the foyer first. She is very petite with brown eyes and short blonde hair. He is about five inches taller than Marsha and has coloring of eyes and hair like Roger.

I greet them and they thank me for inviting them before standing aside for the Vanderhoffs.

Jim and Judy Vanderhoff come in the foyer all smiles. She's on the heavy side. Her black hair is cut very short with wisps of highlights on the ends that frame her lovely oval face. He is tall and lanky and reminds me of the actor, Jimmy Stewart. I shake hands with them and Judy says, "We are very pleased to be here."

I recognize Barbara Bogart as she enters with her husband, Tim. She is busy looking up the stairs and taking in the new beauty of the house as he comes over for the greeting. The obvious scrutiny makes me proud of the refinishing of the entrance floors, new rugs, and wall paint.

Tim Bogart is medium built, slightly overweight. He is taller than Barbara. She has her blonde hair twisted in a French bun. I greet them with a handshake. Barbara says, "It is lovely here. Thank you for the invitation."

Next are the Sanders. Fred and Laura enter and smile. I shake hands and Laura says, "It is so nice of you to invite us." She has brown curly hair that is cut short, and Fred has trimmed his light brown mustache and hair since I saw him in the field, and looks very distinguished.

Behind the Sanders are the Hoffman's. Jeff and his wife Betsy are looking around at the tall ceilings. Jeff Hoffman is clean-shaven, his mixed gray hair combed back away from his face. He and Betsy are holding hands. She is almost as tall as her husband and very thin. Her light brown hair is long and wavy. As they come forward she gives me a nice smile and I see that her eyes are hazel. All are casually dressed just as I instructed Bill to advise them.

We stand in the foyer area until I introduce Amy to the group and thank them for coming. I tell them that I wanted to do this earlier but had to wait until I got comfortable here.

Gracie leads the way and takes us into the dining room. The table is set beautifully with the old china and silverware, and lit candles down the center of the table in silver holders.

The farmers' seating choices place me at the head of the table with Amy to my right. They stand behind their chairs around the table with us, and before we sit I bow my head and we all say grace.

Gracie serves a baked salmon dinner that is simply delicious. There is little talk among the farmers while everyone enjoys the meal.

As the dinner progresses the farmers talk about the weather, their plantings, and the harvest of certain crops. It's all very new to me, but very interesting, as I sit and listen.

There is a lull in the conversations with the farmers, so I bring up the plans for the gift shop with Amy as manager. They are all very surprised.

Amy sorrowfully tells about her and her husband's past experiences at the gift shop in Shadyside, as I tolerate the story again.

There is sympathy for Amy, but they seem very happy for her and excited for me to have this new project at Rivers Run. From the positive comments, I'm encouraged.

Barbara Bogart mentions that the wives on the farm are very good at making beautiful homemade items that perhaps could be sold in the gift shop on consignment.

Marsha Jackson says, "Ceramics are my thing and I would be happy to have a place to put them on consignment." Others talk about their crocheted pillowcases and embroidery. Amy seems very pleased with those ideas.

When dinner is over I relax with Amy and the guests in the main parlor with wine, liqueur, and coffee served.

Then I begin with my proposal, "This has been delightful; however, I have something else to discuss with you that has to do with my property."

I see them look at one another with concern and I quickly explain. "How would you like to buy your rented property?"

They look around at each other with favorable changes on their faces.

I continue, "I know this is sudden and it is fine if you do not want to pursue this option. Suppose I give you time and you can get back to me about it."

Larry Jackson looks at his wife and stands up. "Miss…Jenny, I don't need time. I have wanted this for so long, never thinking it possible. If I could buy it, I would build a home for us on it. I am very interested. John Rivers never wanted to sell the property."

The others are nodding their heads in agreement, and I add, "I will work on the best deal for each of you on your payments through a broker."

The room seems to come alive with talk back and forth between the farmers and their wives. It seems they are very interested and I am happy that I can offer this to them. They each thank me and we shake hands.

I say, "I will let you know what happens after I talk with a real estate person in town," then I raise my glass. "Let's make a toast to our new beginnings," and everyone raises the glasses in the air for the toast.

When everyone is seated again I share my knowledge about the painting over the fireplace of Helen Marie Rivers and her children. I tell them the children are Donald Andrew Junior and Kathleen. I talk about the history of Rivers Run that I researched at the town library and about the little dog "Princess" that looks like my dog, Boots.

I'd love to tell them about my dreams with Kathleen and Junior, but I'm sure it would give them doubts about me and my sanity, along with all the things I've proposed today.

The farmers share stories of their dealings with the family in their time. They agree that John Matthew Rivers was wonderful to them and they attended a few of his parties. Mr. Vanderhoff said their children had also been invited to several parties. Barbara Bogart added that at one of the dances for adults, their children, who were quite young, had a party of their own in a separate area and a woman was hired to entertain them.

I love hearing about these things and get a sense of being a part of the family as I remember children's parties and being with Kathleen and Junior.

It's late when the group leaves, and Amy and I go back to the parlor. There are cookies left in a tray and I see Amy looking at them. She says, "How about a treat before we call it a night?"

This is good because I didn't eat very well, having been uneasy about how my proposal to the farmers would be accepted.

Gracie comes in and starts to clean up the glasses and cups left behind. She sees us grab the cookies and provides milk to go with them. It has been a nice evening, and I understand why John Matthew had all those parties.

It's October and the weather is changing. I am thrilled with the repairs that have been made on the inside of the manor house. Things are looking new and grand in all the areas that needed attention. The painters have started on the outside and I can just imagine how it will look when it is finished as I walk around the house with a feeling of joy and happiness.

Michael has had the plans for the gift shop approved and has a crew getting ready for the work in the garage. A few boxes of materials have been delivered and Amy is getting very excited.

When Amy goes to her room one night, I decide to go to the big ballroom and admire my favorite paintings again. I walk around and look at the signature MAMahon on them. There is so much depth and color that I can put myself right into those scenes. There is one particular one that has the Town Hall and the park in it that is so lovely and real. The Cypress trees and Cedars are painted with several colors of light green to a vibrant blue green in the shade and I can envision myself walking through them. The leaves also give me a feeling of a breeze the way they are painted with slight bends in them. I move the chair to sit closer to it. It has been a tiring day, but as I admire the painting for the colors and people, I imagine myself there…

Suddenly there are two people standing in front of me. It's the old white-haired John Matthew Rivers and a young man with brown hair and blue eyes carrying a large item in his arms wrapped in brown paper.

125

The young man says, "Mr. Rivers, this is the painting you wanted of the recently rebuilt Town Hall and the park."

"Thank you, Allen. I believe this one will complete your other work nicely. Your great-grandmother, Lia Moretti, would be very proud."

"Thank you. I went to put flowers on her grave before I came in today. My mother and father never told me about her, and until you mentioned it, I never knew. I truly thank you for taking me to her grave when I was here before."

Allen looks at John Rivers intensely. "Of course I knew my grandmother had been adopted but I didn't know that my great-grandmother died right here at Rivers Run giving birth to her. No one ever told me the name of my great-grandfather. My family told me he died before my great-grandmother had the baby. The Turners, who adopted my grandmother, never told me anything, and died several years apart when I was in school."

John Rivers says, "Some things are better left unknown. It really will not matter anyway. It was such a long time ago. We can be thankful for your grandmother, who lived, and the Turners who adopted her. They were a good Christian family in the village who could not have children. They should be congratulated, along with your mother and father, for your strong character."

"Thank you, Sir." Then he unwraps the painting that turns out to be the one I have been admiring. I notice that the artist looks around to see where his other paintings are placed as John Rivers reaches into his pocket and brings out an envelope. Then with Allen's help he places the painting on the wall...

CHAPTER TWENTY-TWO

There's a rap on the door of the ballroom and my body shakes and my eyes open. Boots jumps off my lap and I hear another noise as Gracie opens the door and says, "Jenny, may I come in?"

"Yes, Gracie."

"Sorry to bother you but I saw you come here and thought you might want Bill to take Boots out before we retire for the night."

"Thanks, that will be nice." She calls Boots and they leave.

Wow! I was having another dream. This time I have seen John Matthew Rivers and the artist who painted those beautiful scenes on the walls. I have learned so much. John Rivers called the painter Allen, just as Ward said. What was it John Rivers took out of his pocket? Perhaps he was paying Allen for his work.

I stare up at my favorite painting again and realize that it is exactly on the wall where I watched John Rivers put it.

The dream gave me a good look at the artist who painted the landscapes and revealed a few things about Marvin Allen Mahon, the artist, and his great-grandmother, Lia Moretti.

In the dream John Rivers told Allen he did not know who the father of Allen's grandmother was, but it seems to put John Matthew Rivers in question. Ward had said that John had supported Allen even sending him to Paris for his painting studies and buying his work. Could Allen be John's great-grandson? Where is the artist now? He could be more in line for an inheritance if he is a direct descendent of the Rivers family, but how would it be proven even if I found him?

My mind is spinning some ridiculously strange scenarios when Bill brings Boots to me. I finally go to bed but I toss and turn with all the information I have been digesting, and I find myself falling asleep for a while and then waking up with those same thoughts until morning, hardly sleeping at all.

When I go down for breakfast the next morning, Amy looks up and says, "Good morning. I couldn't sleep last night because my mind is very busy going over the details for the gift shop."

I just go along with that and say, "I know. I'm excited too."

When we are in the little parlor with our second cup of coffee, I sigh. I feel very tired, sit back with Boots curled up on my lap, and close my eyes. Amy is sipping her drink, resting her eyes, and doesn't alter the quiet.

I look up and see the portrait of young John Matthew Rivers with questions.

Everyone loved the man for his generosity but what had happened with Lia Moretti? She worked for them from 1922-1933. John Matthew's mother and father, Sophia and Donald Junior, were still alive when Lia died.

Gracie comes in to announce that Ward is here to see Amy.

Amy explains, "I asked him to take me shopping in Richmond today. It might take my mind off the gift shop for a bit." I agree.

While Amy is in her room getting ready to go with Ward, he comes in to the little parlor with me and we make small talk.

He says, "Jenny, I haven't found out anything yet about George Patrick Walters. His name doesn't seem to show up anywhere. The artist, Marvin Allen Mahon, is alive, and has been in the area with several exhibits of his work, but he doesn't have a local address."

"Thank you, Ward."

I go up to my room after they go and decide to look for Allen in the pictures taken at the funeral of John Rivers. Looking through them carefully, I finally spot a familiar face. It's Larry Jackson and his son, Roger. In one picture off in the distance are people bowing their heads in prayer and one man in that group looks like Allen. It is very hard to tell though, and I come away with nothing certain.

It's the first Monday of November and carpenters are arriving to begin the work on the gift shop. Amy and I stay out of the way but occasionally look in on them. I suggest that we take a walk on the property in the back of the house to get away from the noise and commotion. Amy agrees and we get our coats and I put Boots on the leash.

The leaves on the trees have turned from their bright colors, and already the ground is being covered with them. Walking down by the water is very relaxing and as I sit there on the bare limb of the tree near the stream to watch the water, Amy sits next to me.

I know she must be very anxious now that work has started on the shop. Her inventory from Shadyside will be arriving by truck next week and we will store it in another part of the garage.

Trying to relax from all those thoughts, I say, "Amy, look at the way the sun shines on the water. Don't you think the little shiny lights in the water look like diamonds?"

"A little bit. It's pretty."

Without revealing my dream, I say, "Well, it reminds me of a comparison that has been made about the shimmering lights—that they represent the good times that happen, and the dark water, without sun, represent the bad times. I think we have had some good times here at Rivers Run, don't you?"

"Well, yes. I guess so. It is nice that I have met Ward, then your success with the farmers, and the repairs made to the house, not to mention the gift shop plans."

I explain that all five farmers are interested in buying the property and I have a broker, Mr. James Rawlings, who will be handling the paperwork. As the diamonds flicker in the water I am inspired. I feel blessed.

I look up to see Gracie coming down the hill with a tray and I see she has a container with cups.

When she gets closer she says, "Thought you might want some hot cocoa. It's a bit chilly today with that wind, even though the sun is shining."

"Thank you, Gracie, that is very thoughtful."

We sit and enjoy hot cocoa and Amy discusses the ideas that are coming from the farmers' wives about homemade items they can provide for the gift shop.

As Thanksgiving approaches I discuss with Gracie and Bill my desire to have the farmers come to celebrate with us. Gracie says she will need some help in the kitchen because their children will be here also.

I volunteer and look over at Amy. I can see from the look on her face that she wants to disappear; however, I tell her we will invite Ward, and then she offers to help.

Gracie says her son, George, works in Richmond, and will be visiting with them for Thanksgiving.

"Oh Gracie, that is wonderful. You, Bill, and your son must be included in our Thanksgiving celebration too."

"Oh, Miss Jenny, I certainly didn't expect you to invite us, but I know Bill would love it."

"Well, I will not have it any other way."

Gracie says Bill will make the calls to invite the farmers for me, and I think that's great.

On Thanksgiving we are up early and very busy preparing the side dishes. Gracie is cooking ham and turkeys, and preparing the desserts. Bill is hauling tables and chairs, candles and decorations into the dining room. Of course we get in each other's way all day and several times I wonder why I wanted this.

In late afternoon the company begins to arrive. After all the last minute things to do, I think it's a miracle that the tasty-looking, buffet style arrangements of food are ready.

To meet all the farmers again is a joy, and for the first time I meet their children who range in ages from high school, to college, and a few are employed. We learn that Mary Sanders and Jimmy Vanderhoff, Jr. go to high school; Roger Jackson, Alice and Lydia Bogart, and Charles Sanders graduated from college; and Jeff Hoffman's two sons, Jeff, Jr. and Joseph, have jobs in the Bower's Real Estate Company in Richmond.

The families go into the dining room and everyone begins to get acquainted around the appetizers. I am so pleased to meet the younger guests because they are my age and we talk about things to which I can relate. Roger Jackson makes it a point to help me with all the names and faces of the younger guests.

When I look toward the dining room door there is a young man I realize must be Gracie and Bill's son coming into the room with them.

My first look gives me a jolt and reminds me of how I felt when I rode the roller coaster at the Shadyside County Fair for the first time.

George is tall and suntanned with an athletic build. He has dark brown hair combed back from an oval face, a dimple in his chin, and is very handsome. He is probably several years older than Amy. He has his mother's sparkly brown eyes that always give me a good feeling when she looks my way, and when he smiles he looks like his father.

Suddenly, I notice he is coming over to meet me. I cough to get the feelings of the roller coaster to stop, and I try to focus as he approaches.

He says, "Miss Walters, I am George Scott Waller. It is so nice of you to invite me and my family," and we shake hands.

His eyes focus on me in a way that stops my concentration, but after a moment the roller coaster feelings subside, and I manage to say, "It is very nice to meet you, George. You may call me Jenny. I'm happy you could join us."

He gives me a nice smile and I say, "Come and meet some of our friends who farm the property here at Rivers Run, and help yourself to the appetizers while you get acquainted."

I take him over and introduce him to all the others while Gracie and Bill begin to mingle with them as well. Bill has music playing from a nice old record player, which can accommodate several records at a time. I imagine he has been busy trying to get it to work and choosing the right music. That is a nice, surprising addition to the meal.

When it is time to eat, Gracie, Bill, and George bring several carts of food into the dining room and place the platters of turkey, ham, casseroles, vegetables, and desserts on the buffet table. I say a prayer of thanks and we begin.

I sit at one of the tables with Amy and Ward. Gracie, Bill, and George sit with us. The tables are very close together so conversations go on across the tables as we eat. Roger sits with his family at a table behind me and leans over to talk to me several times in the course of the evening. I am disappointed when he tells me he must leave early to do an errand for his father. I'm sorry about that because I will miss him, but the slow ballads that are playing are from the old bands and they put a nice, relaxing mood on the affair.

CHAPTER TWENTY-THREE

When the Thanksgiving dinner is over and the guests are gone, Amy and I help with dishes and cleaning the dining room. Before I retire, I sit in the parlor with Amy, Ward, Gracie, Bill, and George, enjoying another slice of pumpkin pie.

I say, "Well, I know this Thanksgiving has been the very best one I have ever had, and I think it would be nice to have a New Year's Eve party to start 1986." The very tired Gracie and Bill, and even Amy and Ward, look at me as if I'm someone they don't recognize, but slowly they agree.

George smiles and says, "I enjoyed this so much and would love to come to a New Year's Eve party—if I am invited that is—and you might even need an extra helper to get it going." With a look from Amy, Ward agrees to be a helper as well.

It looks as if we will have a New Year's Eve party.

Friday and Saturday go by slowly. The pounding in the garage goes on relentlessly and that's a good thing, but it disturbs everyone's concentration to say the least. Gracie and Bill go out with George on Saturday to shop. Amy goes to investigate the new interior of the garage.

I don't want to see it until it looks like a gift shop. Sitting in the small parlor with a quilt over my legs, I'm thinking of Christmas and how to decorate.

When Amy returns I get a full report on what else they have completed for the gift shop, and she says it is going well.

On Sunday, I'm sitting alone in the small parlor having another cup of coffee when George comes in. He's carrying a suitcase and looks very handsome in a tan overcoat and brown pants.

His eyes are sparkling as he approaches, making me slightly unhinged. He says, "Jenny, it has been a real pleasure to see my mom and dad again and spend time with them. I really appreciate all you did to make us feel welcome during Thanksgiving. You will never know how much it has meant to me. Mom and dad have always told me how gracious you have been to them and I didn't believe it—but I do now. I won't forget your hospitality and I look forward to our next meeting."

"George, your mom and dad have helped me through a difficult time getting settled in this place, and your dad has been a real help suggesting the repairs to the house and the work on the gift shop. I hope you will be able to come for Christmas and stay for New Year's Eve."

He comes over to me and I get up to say goodbye. He gives me a kiss on the cheek and a lingering hug. I look up into his eyes and he lets go slowly and, stepping back, gives me a smile and a wink. He picks up his suitcase and steps back toward the door.

I raise my hand up limply giving a wave. He leaves the room saying, "Until we meet again." I give him a smile, secretly thinking, "Wow."

There is a feeling of excitement in the manor house. Christmas is now a week away and the place is beginning to look very festive.

A beautiful fir tree from the property, positioned in the main hallway, adds to the excitement, and last night Amy and I, along with help from Gracie and Bill, decorated it with lights, painted pinecones, and strings of popcorn. Fir tree cuttings decorate the front door and the stairway bannister, and several places in the parlors, the bedrooms, and dining room, adding special smells that seem to say, "Christmas is here." I had Bill buy several new strings of lights and he has hung them around the porch and in the foyer.

The gift shop is nearly finished, and a few of the farmers are already making arrangements to buy the farm property, with the broker, Mr. Rawlings, assisting them.

Amy and I have been busy with the gift shop supplies that have come from her storage in Shadyside. We've had to find a place for them in the garage. She believes she will be ready to open for business on February 15th.

Two days before Christmas, after breakfast, Gracie, Bill and George come into the small parlor. Bill says, "Miss Jenny, George is here and will help with Christmas and New Year preparations."

I say, "Good to see you again, George. We love having extra help, don't we Amy?" Amy sips her coffee and smiles.

Bill says, "I'm putting him to work immediately."

George smiles down at me. This time his eyes and a certain smile have a look of mischief that makes me uncomfortable and I wonder about him.

I say, "Gracie, give him a cup of coffee and some breakfast so he will have the energy he needs," and Gracie and George go to the kitchen while I take another sip of coffee and think about how I will deal with him. I will definitely watch him closely.

On Christmas Eve I am in the parlor with Amy, Gracie, Bill, and George, enjoying the time around the tree when we get a surprise visit from Ward, and Amy is thrilled. He has been very excited for Amy about the gift shop.

I ask Ward to stay for our Christmas Eve celebration tonight and to perhaps stay overnight and enjoy a Christmas breakfast with us.

He looks at Amy and says, "I appreciate the offer but I came to ask Amy to come with me to Richmond to celebrate Christmas with my family."

Amy says, "Oh Ward, I would love that so much." She looks around at us and says, "I'm sure I'm not needed here. I'll just pack a few things, then we can go."

I look at them and shake my head disappointedly. "I would love to have both of you here with us, but I understand completely. How about a Christmas Eve drink before you go?" They agree, and I pour everyone a glass of rum punch that Gracie and I had mixed with special fruit.

Many gifts had been placed around our tree and I reach for Amy's. "Here Amy, this is for you to take with you and there's one here for Ward as well." I hand them their gifts and say, "Merry Christmas—but don't open until tomorrow."

I had bought her a shop apron to wear when the gift shop opens for business. We had agreed to call it "Rivers Run Gift Shop," so I had it made special with her name on it as Manager. I bought Ward a set of handkerchiefs with his initials.

Then Amy says, "Ward and I have one for you under there too—you have a Merry Christmas." They leave after she packs an overnight bag.

That night I sit on my bed with Boots and think about a dream I had long ago in a foster home when I was about eight years old.

I remember I was not treated well on Christmas Eve at the foster home and wondered what I would get as my present. The mother and father were drinking and arguing into the night. Their children, Sara and Ben, were sent to bed with me without ceremony or any talks about the next day being Christmas.

On my little cot that night I had one of those dreams where I was in the beautiful manor house. In my dream it was Christmas day, and I was with Kathleen and Junior in a room beautifully decorated. There were many toys and gifts with candy and cookies put in socks that hung on the fireplace. I danced, laughed, and played with them for a long time.

In the foster home the next morning, I awoke and thought of my dream at the beautiful house. I described everything in my dream to Sara and Ben and it seemed to cheer them up. The day went by, and we were given a few new coloring books and candy canes. Between the arguments that we heard in the other room, the mother brought us spaghetti to eat and came in later with cake and ice cream.

I awaken at Rivers Run very rested and go down to the kitchen with Boots just in time for breakfast with Bill, Gracie, and George. It makes us laugh when we say our greeting, "Merry Christmas" all together, harmoniously.

We all sit at the long dining room table that is decorated beautifully, and Gracie has fixed a breakfast with all the extras. I say a prayer of thanks for the birth of our Savior.

After breakfast we settle in the big parlor and open our gifts. The gift from Amy and Ward is a beautiful Nativity snow globe that plays "Silent Night." I adore it and will keep it on my desk in my bedroom.

Scarves, lotions, perfume, and gloves are in the other packages, and we enjoy our gifts together. George bought me a very expensive perfume and I had wrapped a pair of work gloves for him. George gives me a look I'm not sure how to interpret, just like other looks he's given me since he has been here. Gracie and Bill laugh, and Bill says, "He is going to need those gloves."

Later in the day Roger comes over and we exchange gifts. When we open the boxes, we both have scarves and gloves, and we laugh about our similar gifts. I invite him to dinner but he says he is obligated to join his family for dinner because several aunts and uncles have been invited.

George, Gracie, Bill and I have various tasks preparing our Christmas dinner. While things are cooking we sit by the fireplace and I find out about the Waller's and the meager Christmases they shared during the years. Bill adds a touch of joy by saying, "But we survived with love." I don't tell them anything about my hard times as an orphan, but express the joy that I had with my father and mother before they were gone.

Our dinner is delightful, and after dinner we gather in the large parlor for dessert and Christmas treats around the fireplace. George has stacked it with a special wood that he had bought. As the wood burns, it fills the room with pleasant smells and a charming crackling sound. I enjoy my apple pie, as Gracie and Bill discuss how nice it is at the manor house.

It is getting late and Gracie and Bill excuse themselves. Bill says, "We are going to clean up things from dinner. You two stay and talk."

Not wanting to be alone with George I tell them I am getting tired and will be in my room. George comes over next to me but still has a smile that troubles me. "Oh Jenny, stay a few minutes and enjoy the time here. This has been a wonderful day and I hate to see it end—but we know all good things have to end."

I strangely feel he is implying something sinister by his tone of voice, and abruptly get up to leave. He quickly takes my arm, gives me another filled cup of punch, and escorts me over to sit with him on the sofa.

"Now isn't this better than being alone in a creepy room upstairs?"

I give him a smile, sit down with him, and ask my usual question that starts a conversation, "What kind of work are you doing in Richmond, George?"

"I'm working for a newspaper right now. I do all kinds of stories. They send me out when there is a fire or something strange has happened. Sometimes my stories make the news—most of the time they don't. I'm not too happy with it, but it's a job."

"Do you want to be a writer?"

"I'm really not sure. I think I would like to be a person in charge of something of importance, just like you."

What does he mean by that?

He gives me another look I can't figure out, and continues. "I went to college but I majored in business because everyone was doing that and I didn't know what I wanted to do."

I tell him that I went to a pre-college night school for a while and want to go to college sometime in the future because I found that I am very interested in biology.

He doesn't say much about that but wants to know the things I'm doing at the manor house and I tell him about several improvements.

When I finish my drink I excuse myself and get up to leave. He takes my hand and puts it on his arm while we walk to the stairs.

"Jenny, it has been a lovely Christmas and you have made this one my best." He comes close as I try to turn and take the first step. He pulls me close and starts to give me a kiss. I turn my head and he kisses my cheek.

I know I should be thrilled, but the odd feelings I get from him have made me question his intentions, and I take the first step up the stairs.

"I'll see you in the morning, George," so glad he's not going to see me to my room.

CHAPTER TWENTY-FOUR

Late the next day Amy comes back with Ward after celebrating Christmas with his family. Ward leaves her at the door and we go into the library together, have coffee, and thank each other for our gifts.

She says her visit with the Wendell's for Christmas was glorious and their house is beautiful. She is wearing a pair of lovely diamond earrings and when I look at them she looks thrilled.

She says, "When he gave them to me he said he wanted it to be something else with diamonds, but he knew it was too soon."

I smile, "Well, we might have a wedding to look forward to one day." Amy doesn't comment but makes a face that tells another story. Inwardly I have to laugh at her independent thinking.

This week has all of us excited and busy getting ready for the New Year's Eve celebration. Invitations have been sent out. In addition to all the farmers, I invite Mr. Anthony Albright, the Mayor of Helen; Julie Cramer, The Librarian; Helen Dupont, the owner of Helen's Café; and Michael O'Malley, our contractor. The invitations include their older children as well.

So that Gracie, Bill, and George may enjoy New Year's Eve with us, I call a catering service in town, recommended by several farmers, and hire a caterer and his wife, Bessie and Jessie Gray, to do the cooking and serving.

The couple comes to Rivers Run one evening. I want them to meet us and discuss everything with Gracie and Bill, so that things will go perfectly on New Year's Eve.

They are middle-aged like Gracie and Bill. Jessie's tall and has a round, rather pale face, as if he doesn't like the sun. He seems very pleasant and does most of the talking. He has brown eyes and mixed gray-brown hair.

Bessie is shorter, heavier, and has a sweet face. She has light brown hair, blue eyes, and dimples in her cheeks.

They seem happy together, holding hands, and I am pleased with them right away. Gracie and Bill will give them a tour and show them around the kitchen facilities, the dining room and the ballroom.

It's the last day of 1985 and there is a wonderful spirit in this old house. It has been a long time since there was a big party here and I can feel the difference in the air. The preparations have been overwhelming for everyone, but as I stand at the door of the big ballroom, I sense that even the room has been waiting for this kind of celebration. Tables and chairs have been set along the sides of the room, and the floor has been prepared for dancing.

A set of China is being used and I am so pleased. The food will be set out on serving platters that Gracie found in a bottom drawer of an old cabinet in the attic. They have a manor house scene on them with gold trim around the edges. By late afternoon all is ready and as I look around at the lights and beautiful decorations, I sense an electrifying atmosphere waiting to take charge.

In the early evening, Amy and I dress for the New Year's Eve party. On our last shopping trip before Christmas we bought comfortable, but somewhat fancy outfits.

She is wearing black pumps and a lovely wide-leg, dark-blue pantsuit with a formfitting jacket adorned with gold sequins in the shape of small roses around the neck and sleeves.

I'm wearing black wide-leg slacks that look like a skirt with a formfitting, long-sleeve, white and black cashmere sweater and my comfortable black pumps.

As the guests arrive, Jessie escorts them to the ballroom, and Amy and I are there to greet them. A four-member band that Bill recommended called "The Pop-Tops," begin to play an old song from the sixties, and I notice the beautiful soft lights flickering on the walls from the lovely chandelier. Gracie and Bill are there to get things started and to meet and greet the guests as well.

When Roger comes in with his parents he comes over to me, gives me a hug and a kiss on the cheek. "Hi, Jenny, you look lovely. I'll be looking forward to a dance or two."

"Thanks, Roger. That will be nice." He looks very impressive in a black suit and shiny black and white tie. Once again I am intrigued by his smile and the sparkle in those dark brown eyes. His hair is combed back but a small rogue curl of blonde hair is escaping to the right of his forehead.

When the stately, middle-aged Mayor of our town and his wife arrive he stops to talk with me as I shake hands. His wife, Amelia, is dressed in a lovely blue gown and has her brown hair fixed with curls in an attractive upsweep fashion.

He says, "Miss Walters, my wife and I are very pleased to meet you and to have this opportunity to enjoy this time with you. I knew John Rivers and I'm so glad the place has an heir. He was very ill the last time I saw him, and I noticed then that the place needed someone to care for it."

I smile and thank him. Before they go into the ballroom, Amelia and I talk for a moment. She is very interested in the plans for the gift shop.

As guests continue to arrive, I welcome Julie Cramer, the Librarian, and Helen Dupont, from Helen's Café. Michael O'Malley, our carpenter, is right behind them. They greet me with "Happy New Year" and thank me for the invitation.

George has been busy helping Bessie and Jessie with the last-minute preparations and he comes out when there is a lull in the guests' arrivals. He says, "Jenny, you and Amy look marvelous."

He doesn't look bad either in his dark-blue suit and light-blue silk tie.

"Thank you, George. I think most of the guests are here now."

Everyone seems to be getting their places at the tables, enjoying the appetizers and drinks.

After a time of getting acquainted again with everyone, I get their attention and give thanks for the meal and say a prayer for the New Year. Bessie and Jessie are very accomplished caterers, and have fixed a lovely buffet dinner of sliced filet mignon and fried shrimp, along with every side dish you can imagine. It is served on a long table that is decorated with flowers and balloons in one corner of the big room.

After dinner, Roger comes over and asks me to dance. He has a nice dance step and the music is playing a soft romantic melody. We dance together nicely and he holds me close. As we continue to dance through several songs, I notice George is watching us.

When we return to the refreshment table for something to drink, George is now in the middle of the dance floor with Alice Bogart who graduated from college last year. Lydia, her sister, is dancing with Fred Sanders' son, Charles. I'm glad that people my age are here. Everyone seems to be having a lovely time as the night progresses.

Later, Roger and I are standing to the side discussing the plans for the farmers to buy the property. George saunters up to me and by his walk I sense he has an attitude, and it shows when he says, "Jenny, I haven't formally met your friend here.

"Oh George, this is Roger Jackson. He helps his father with the farming on the Rivers Run property. They are planning to buy the land they rent and will put a house on it. Roger, this is George, the son of Gracie and Bill Waller."

They shake hands and Roger says, "I am really thrilled about the property. My mom and dad are going to put the house and land in my name and the burden will be lifted off them as they retire."

George speaks with a voice of doubt, "That sounds good for *you*. I hope they know what they are doing."

Roger looks at him awkwardly, and says, "George, My dad and mom are wonderful people and I would never take advantage of them—ever, if that is what you are suggesting."

I can see Roger is upset.

I look at Roger with a new respect. His sincere response has affected the atmosphere around the three of us for the moment.

I say, "Well, good for you, Roger. I know you are proud of them and they are proud of you."

George looks disgruntled and says, "I'll see you later, Jenny."

I'm disgusted with his suggestion that Roger would do something to hurt his parents, and just nod as he walks over to Alice and asks her to dance.

For a time, Roger and I sit and enjoy the music together, but he doesn't discuss what took place with George. When a new song begins, George asks me to dance. I look back and smile at Roger as George takes me out on the dance floor.

He holds me a little too close, and I want to tell him how he embarrassed me with Roger but I don't talk as he glides around the room.

I notice Roger is dancing with his mother and smiling. I have a new respect for him with the way he feels about his family, and a different feeling about George now that I have a chance for comparison.

After the dance with George he leaves me and I go over to the champagne fountain where Roger is talking with his mother. We toast to the New Year and the plans for the properties.

Roger says, "It's almost midnight, Jenny, let's dance." We put down our drinks and I walk with him hand in hand. We dance through several love songs while the clock continues towards Midnight.

As the clock gets closer to Midnight, Roger holds me very close and we glide softly and steadily to a song Perry Como sang years ago called "True Love," that is played very well by "The Pop-Tops."

When the clock strikes the hour there are shouts of joy in the room. Roger stops, looks into my eyes, and I'm ready when we kiss. It is my first real, sincere kiss.

As my heart beats with the music, Roger holds me tightly and we kiss again as the band plays "Auld Lang Syne." The guests are kissing and hugging in celebration, but my eyes are fixed on Roger, and it seems strange but I don't care about anyone else or how they are celebrating at this moment. We walk off the dance floor, hand in hand, completely occupied in the moment.

He says, "Jenny, this night has been wonderful." I smile and agree.

The New Year's Eve party continues, but guests begin to leave for the next hour. When Roger's parents start to go, I walk out to the foyer with them, Roger holding my hand. At the door we kiss again.

He says, "Jenny, I'll call you tomorrow." With feelings totally new, I smile and nod my head in agreement, not sure how to handle being so close and personal.

Ward is staying over for the night, and he and Amy go to their separate rooms upstairs. As others leave I stand at the door with Gracie,

Bill, and George, saying "goodnight." When everyone has left, George walks me to my room. Gracie and Bill go back into the kitchen to help Bessie and Jessie who are staying over to fix breakfast tomorrow.

At my bedroom door George stops and gets close. He says, "Jenny, I'm sorry that I didn't have a chance to be with you more. Roger made me feel out of place with you. I hope it has not changed our relationship." Then he comes closer.

What relationship? I think I should set George straight somehow.

I back up toward the door. "George, You must understand. I have no definite connections to anyone. You are welcome here because of Gracie and Bill. Other than that I can't worry about relationships. I really like Roger very much."

He gives me an awkward smile that suggests he's upset. "Okay, Jenny. Have a good night." Then he turns and walks away from me in a casual, lighthearted way, as if it doesn't matter to him.

I'd love to know what he is thinking at this point, but I know I cleared up how I feel.

CHAPTER TWENTY-FIVE

When I go to my room, Boots is already on my bed sleeping. After prayers I rest on my pillows and go over everything that happened during our New Year's Eve celebration, especially my feelings for Roger. It's not easy getting to sleep but I'm very tired and finally I close my eyes and begin to relax....

I look around and I think I am in a church. I finally see John Matthew Rivers sitting near me in the same row a few seats away. He has gray showing in his hair around his face but looks very elegant. We seem to be upfront in a church setting. There are people all around us but I don't recognize any of them except the lady in the row in front of us. She looks like Margaret from another dream I had.

The organist plays "Here Comes The Bride" and I look to see a beautiful girl coming down the aisle with a gentleman holding onto her arm. The bride gives Margaret a kiss on the cheek and says, "I love you, mother" and walks to the front and stands by the groom. The man who walked down the aisle with her takes a seat next to Margaret. I listen carefully to the names being pronounced by the clergyman. When he says, "Angela Sarah Worthington," I suddenly get it. This is Angela—Margaret's daughter.

The wedding of Angela and the groom, Daniel Stephen Morris, is soon over. The organist plays a final song, and Angela and the groom go to the back of the church to greet the people. I walk behind John Rivers, and stand there close as he congratulates the groom and hugs the bride. She says, "Thank you for everything, Uncle John." I follow him as people go from the church and throw rice at the couple running toward a decorated bridal carriage.

The dream fades as I cough loudly. I open my eyes and it's early morning. I lay there dumbfounded.

This dream was all about Angela, Margaret's daughter. Her name was Worthington. Margaret didn't wait for John Rivers and must have finally gotten married. Why was I given this dream? Could Angela, or maybe her children, be possible heirs? Her name would be "Morris." However, there would be no way to prove that scenario. I should look further for the proof that John Rivers said he would write. Perhaps he only supported them with money until Margaret married. Angela called him "Uncle John." Was he more than Uncle John?

Still thinking about some heirs that need to be found, I get ready for the day. When Boots and I finally go to the dining room, I see there is plenty of hot food on the serving table in covered servers and Amy and Ward are having breakfast. I greet them and serve myself while Jessie, the caterer, takes Boots outside for me.

Amy says, "That was a great party last night." Ward agrees.

I say, "Good! I'm glad. I enjoyed the party and hope everyone did. I think we should have more of them from now on—just like they say John Rivers did."

The three of us go into the small parlor for our after-breakfast cup of coffee. Bessie and Jessie are going out of their way to help with things this morning they were not hired to do.

I'll need to give them a nice tip when they leave and keep them in mind for other parties.

Gracie and Bill come for breakfast just as we are finishing our coffee. They look in to see us and say "good morning" before going into the dining room.

I guess George is sleeping late this morning, and I am glad I don't have to deal with him.

George bought Gracie and Bill a television set for Christmas that arrived a few days after Christmas to their surprise, and it has just been installed in the large parlor and I want to see how it works. I invite Amy and Ward to the parlor, and Ward turns the television on for us. We watch a local morning show that talks all about New Year's Eve parties in Richmond and the celebrities that were there last night. After a while, Gracie and Bill join us. The morning hours are delightfully spent watching the new television programs and discussing our party.

It is about 11:00 a.m. when George makes an appearance in the parlor with his coffee. Right away he turns on a football game to watch. The rest of us continue a conversation we had started about the house and how nice it looks after all the repairs and paint. As the football game loudly continues, I decide to go to my room, noticing Ward and Amy are leaving too.

I'm sitting next to the windows in my room, rethinking the dream of Angela's wedding, and Gracie knocks on my door and tells me I have a telephone call. It's Roger and he wants to take me to lunch, and he will come for me at Noon.

I am back in my room getting dressed to go to lunch with Roger when someone knocks on my door. George says, "Jenny, can we talk?"

"Yes, George. Just a minute." I finish dressing, put on my coat and open the door to go out. George doesn't stand there but comes in, walks by me, looking at everything. I am perturbed at his abrupt entrance.

He says, "Gee, this room is nice." He goes over to the windows. "It has a lovely view, doesn't it?"

"Yes, George." I stand there at the door and wait to see what he wants to talk about.

He comes over close. "I'd like to take you to lunch in town today."

That's nuts because he just ate his breakfast.

"George, I have been invited to lunch and I'm getting ready to go now."

His eyes go up to the ceiling with a look of impatience, but he quickly recovers and says, "Well, how about dinner then—somewhere quiet, maybe in Richmond?"

"Okay, but not tonight—that will just be too much for me for one day. Why don't we go for a walk tomorrow? There is a nice area you need to see down the hill on the property."

He again looks up as if there is something bad on the ceiling, and slowly says, "Okay, Jenny." He turns and leaves my room, looking back at me as if he is trying to figure out something.

I put on my coat and walk downstairs with Boots following. When I get to the foyer, Roger is coming to the front door and Gracie is in the hallway. "Gracie, I'm going with Roger for lunch."

I give her an envelope with a check and a note of thanks for Bessie and Jessie. "Gracie, pass this along for me, please."

"Certainly, Jenny." She turns with Boots and walks to the kitchen.

I don't see George anywhere as I open the door and greet Roger. He takes my hand and we go to his Bronco.

It's a beautiful afternoon. The temperature is not too cold and the sun is shining in a clear blue sky. I feel different—I know things have changed between Roger and me. It's like I have stepped into another body and another life, and somehow things seem clearer.

Roger seems different too as he opens the car door and I settle into the seat. We don't say very much on the way, but I notice we are not going into town.

"Roger, are we going into Richmond for lunch?"

Roger smiles and reaches over to squeeze my hand. "I'm going to take you to a favorite restaurant of mine. We don't have to go into Richmond."

He makes several turns and drives for a few more miles, then crosses a small bridge over water. He parks next to a rustic restaurant near the water called "Riverside Landing."

It has several piers with boats parked alongside. He helps me out of the car and we walk down to the water. He says, "Jenny, look carefully across this large body of water called Beaver Bay."

When I focus on the land across from us, I see the manor house barely showing through the leafless branches of the trees. "Oh Roger, this is a surprise, thank you!"

He comes close and kisses me while we stand on the edge of the water, and I feel so ready for this moment.

He says, "Jenny, I knew you would love this view of the property. I always enjoy it too." He smiles, "Let's go see if they have anything you'll like to eat in this place."

Before Roger and I go into the restaurant I turn to look at the water and see the "diamonds" shimmering on the surface. How lovely to think of them as good times in life, especially when I feel so good about what is happening with Roger and me.

"Roger, look at the lights in the water—don't they look like diamonds?"

He says, "Diamonds in the water." "Yes, Jenny, they are everywhere out there today. My father mentions them all the time when we go fishing. He said that John Rivers told him about them once. According to his grandfather they represented good times in life compared to the rough, muddy water that has no lights that he thought depicts the bad times. This is definitely an amazing day for me," and he squeezes my hand as we enter the restaurant.

How wonderful. Roger knows about the story of the diamonds in the water, and recognizes them, too.

Inside the restaurant it is rustic but delightful. It is cozy with booths set against several walls, and fishnets draped in corners still adorned with Christmas decorations. Various scenes of boats and ocean paintings hang on several walls. The tables have green tablecloths on them with a red candle in shell-like containers.

We sit at a small table next to a large window where I can see directly across the bay to Rivers Run. We order seafood platters, and everything seems more than perfect.

Roger is very quiet through the meal but during a second ice tea he says, "Jenny, I don't know how you feel about me, but I hope you will let me be a part of your life. I am feeling positive about things since dad will buy the property and build on it."

I look out at the "diamonds" and back at him. "Roger, the New Year has changed so much in my life, and at this point I feel that more heirs will show up."

Gosh, why did I say that?

Moments go by and I say, "I think I must step back for a bit right now and weigh what everything means. As much as I would like to, I can't commit to a relationship just yet."

Roger looks away for a moment and then nods in agreement to my statement, then he says, "Jenny, why do you think there are other heirs?"

Oh, he did hear me. I think seriously about telling him about my dreams and my possible need to search for heirs in the future. I really trust him more than I trust George.

I look out at the water for support, "I think I need to tell you about something. At least I need to tell someone."

I sigh, "I have had strange dreams since I first became an orphan, and more since I came to the manor house. They are all with the Rivers' family who lived in it long ago."

He gets a puzzled look. "Really, Jenny?"

"Yes, Roger, in my dreams different family members appear in various rooms talking to one another, and once or twice they have said that all the heirs must be found or those who have the same bloodline, that have gone before, will not rest in peace. Doesn't that sound strange to you?" I can see Roger is thinking seriously about it as he nods his head in a slow, thoughtful manner.

I sip my lemonade and wait for his response.

Roger smiles, reaches across the table and squeezes my hand. "Jenny, I'm sure the dreams mean nothing and I think eventually you will find that out. There are many things that happen that we can't explain—especially dreams. I believe being at Rivers Run has made you think of your ancestors and it has caused the dreams."

I feel better letting Roger know what I have been confused about, and I am impressed that he doesn't think I'm crazy. As we get up to leave, I ask him to sit with me by the water before we go back.

We walk out and sit on a bench next to the water's edge. The view of Rivers Run looks different from here but very pretty and I notice the high embankment next to the water over on that side, and several green pine trees above that wall of rocks and sand. Looking at the property from the other side of the river is very nice to experience.

CHAPTER TWENTY-SIX

When we get back to the manor house Roger doesn't get out of the Bronco right away but leans over and we kiss. It just seems like a normal thing to do.

When he helps me out of the car I look up into his eyes. "Thanks Roger for listening to me. It means so much to be able to talk to you about the dreams, but please keep this between us."

He squeezes my shoulders. "Of course, Jenny, I'm glad you confided in me. Remember, I'm here for you anytime. No matter what happens or how long it takes, I plan on you in my future."

Roger helps me out of the Bronco and says he'll call me tomorrow. As I take the stairs and go in the house, my attitude changes when I see George there in the foyer. As Boots jumps up to greet me, George has a sly look in his eyes and says, "It's a nice day isn't it?" I agree and go to my room.

He must have been watching us.

George follows me up the stairs with Boots passing both of us. I enter my room and George walks in with me as if this is his room. He says, "I hope you have time for me now. I've been waiting for you to get back because my plans have changed."

I sit in my lounge chair and he walks back and forth in front of my bed. "Jenny, something has been bothering me for a long time and I need to tell you that it concerns your legitimate heritage in this place. I am going back to Richmond today to sort some things out and dig into this more." I don't respond.

He walks to the windows. "In my job at the newspaper, I have had certain ways to look into historical facts and items written years ago. When I go back to the job tomorrow I will continue searching in other places for what might uncover the truth. I just wanted you to know you might be affected in some way—and of course, I have come to say goodbye."

George sits in the other chair. "What do you think about that, Jenny?"

He is trying to hurt me—perhaps because of Roger. I'm not surprised. I hope his meddling will bring to light the truth that I am the only heir. It will be a favor to me. I really don't want to tell him about my dreams—I am beginning to believe Roger—there is nothing to them.

I look over at George, and he's waiting for a response, tapping his fingers on the edge of the chair...

"Thanks, George, for telling me about your concerns. If my heritage is questioned, so be it. You'll need to meet with my lawyer, Mr. Jerry Whitaker. He is with the law office of Whitaker, Johnson, and Associates in Richmond."

Before George leaves he gets up, comes over to my chair, leans down, kisses my forehead and says, "I'll be going before dinner, so I'll say goodbye now."

"Have a good trip, George. You know you are welcome to visit your mom and dad anytime." He waves goodbye.

As George closes my door, I'm actually happy that he is leaving. Then I think about John Rivers. If he wrote something that will answer my questions, George has made me want to find that letter now more than ever.

It's the first day of February and snow is falling heavily. The wind is blowing it into drifts everywhere. It's really a good day to be inside and Amy and I are busy getting the shop ready to open on the fifteenth. Most of the cabinets are installed, and the place has been designed with several types of display counters and shelving. We have bought a cash register for sales, and items we will need for the customers, such as tissue and store bags, gift cards, envelopes, and wrapping paper for sale. All of Amy's storage items from Shadyside have been dusted and set up on the new shelves, along with new and interesting items that Amy has been buying for the last month.

The farmers' wives have been visiting occasionally to see us about what they can do to make the "Grand Opening" a success. Amy has been very appreciative of their suggestions. Laura Sanders, Betsy Hoffman, and Marsha Jackson have brought their homemade items for her to see. The crocheted doilies, embroidered pillowcases, and ceramic figures are beautiful.

To my surprise, Amy has said she will accept them on consignment. Barbara Bogart says she will bake cookies for the big day, and Gracie will bake blueberry muffins and have containers of punch, tea, and coffee.

The parking area on the side of the garage has been made ready with gravel and parking markers. Bill had a sign printed by the local print shop directing gift shop traffic and several signs in the town to advertise the opening.

One day when Amy is out in the gift shop with Gracie and Bill, I think about John Matthew Rivers and his statement about heirs and where he would have put it.

I take a walk around the house, even going into the attic to search his old desk, but find nothing. Searching the cabinets in the kitchen area, I am interrupted by a stampede of people coming into the house from the gift shop. They are talking excitedly about how things are going and discussing further plans that will make it a success. I notice Amy is getting better acquainted with the ladies that are bringing their artistic homemade items.

Amy says, "Jenny, this is going to work out very well I think, but we all got thirsty and Gracie wants to feed us snacks and drinks."

I join them in the small parlor for refreshments, thinking that this searching will have to be put off for another time.

That night when I go up to my room I sit in my lounge chair by the windows, wondering again where John would have put the information about his ladies, and about his grandfather's deal.

Thinking perhaps he placed it in one of the books, I go over to examine the books in my bookcase and see that there are only a few of them on the shelves, but flip through the pages, finding nothing. Small ceramic animals and a few small vases, probably collected over the years, are on the other shelves. I look in the vases but there is no paper stuck in them. There is a box of matches to light the candles that are there.

I am disappointed when I sit back down and look out over the lonely hills as the sky turns dark and depressing with a storm approaching.

Where could that letter be? Should I search in the other bedrooms? I wonder which bedroom was John's. Tomorrow, if I get a chance to be alone I will look in all of those bookcases.

The next few days are frustrating for me working in the gift shop because I have to give up my search for the missing information.

On Wednesday morning, February 5th, I get a call from Mr. Whitaker. "Hello, Miss Walters. I need to come and see you about something that has developed. I'm here in Helen, staying at the Dream Inn on Main Street. The desk clerk tells me that it is one of the places in which John Matthew Rivers invested, and he came up with the name. Anyway, are you available today?"

The Dream Inn! I should tell Mr. Whitaker why John Rivers came up with that name for the inn.

Inwardly laughing, I say, "Certainly, Mr. Whitaker. Can you come now?" He agrees.

When Mr. Whitaker arrives I tell Gracie to bring us refreshments as we go into the parlor. The weather is fine and Amy is riding Kota this afternoon, and I'm glad she is not around. I have no idea about this meeting and what he will tell me.

Mr. Whitaker sits at the desk and opens his briefcase. I sit in front of the desk and wait patiently. He looks at me and shakes his head. "I can't believe this is happening." Then he coughs.

He sits back in the chair and rubs his forehead. I look out the window and wonder what this means.

Is something wrong with the property or the farmers' rental contracts? Then I remember what George Waller said to me before he left about questioning my inheritance, and I wonder…

The drinks are brought in and Mr. Whitaker pours a glass of water, and I have lemonade. He watches Gracie leave before speaking.

"Miss Walters, I have been visited by someone who claims that there are more heirs that should be inheriting Rivers Run."

For a moment I have no words but many thoughts swirl in my brain.

Then I hear myself say, "Oh no, I can't believe it. How can this be? After all the years your law firm investigated the Rivers' and Walters' families!"

He sighs and says, "I must tell you it sounds preposterous and my law office is investigating the story."

He coughs and drinks another sip of water. "The story is strange and more proof will have to be brought forward to completely satisfy all my questions—which has not been done as yet."

After that explanation from Mr. Whitaker about other possible heirs, I get up and walk back and forth.

Well, I bet George is behind this! I wonder what proof there will be? What will happen to all my plans for the farmers…and even the gift shop? My dreams mentioned more heirs—maybe there are more. This makes my dreams all the more real.

"Mr. Whitaker, I have a gift shop ready to open in ten days, and the farmers are ready to sign papers to buy the rented property. What will happen to those plans?"

He stands up. "Miss Walters, the firm is not satisfied yet with the accounts of proof. I will continue to investigate this narrative and get back to you. For now, however, the property for farmers and plans for your gift shop must be postponed until further notice. I don't think it will take long—be patient."

I follow the lawyer to the front door. He says, "Nothing is going to change until my law office is completely sure." He shakes my hand, turns, and goes out the door.

I go to my room and sit down in my lounge chair, looking out over the hills, thinking that there probably aren't any "diamonds" in the water today.

Then Amy comes barreling into my room, "Hey, what's this I hear from Gracie downstairs? I go horseback riding and everything goes crazy? Are you the only heir to this place or not?"

Somehow Gracie must have heard my conversation with Mr. Whitaker.

"Oh Amy, sit down. Mr. Whitaker says there have been some facts that the law office has to substantiate concerning possibly other heirs in line for Rivers Run besides me. The bad news is that until they iron this out, the gift shop won't be able to open, and the farmers will not be able to buy the property they rent. It will all have to wait for final determination."

"Well dang! I can't believe it! Other heirs? What if it's proven? That will be a bummer. I guess that will put me in a bad spot, won't it, and the shop too!"

Once again Amy is only thinking of herself.

"Don't worry, Amy. If it's proven, I will get together with the new heirs and we will discuss everything, I promise."

The days that follow are so strange now. I wander around the place totally empty of thoughts or things to do. Amy is still doing things in the gift shop and hanging out in there, and I don't stop her, even though I don't know what the future will be for the shop. I have also lost interest in looking for John Rivers' written confession until I hear from the law firm.

Mr. Whitaker notified the broker that the various farmers' plans to buy their rented property have to be temporarily postponed.

I write notes to the farmers with my sincere apologies, stating that I will keep them informed of the consequences. I ask Bill to deliver the notes for me. He also notifies the newspaper and puts up signs to indicate that the opening of the gift shop has been postponed until further notice.

Gracie and Bill walk around me very quietly now. I guess they have heard some of the conversations and are wondering where that leaves them. They seem to be treating me differently which almost touches on avoidance. It reminds me how I was treated after my mother and father were killed. No one wanted to comfort me because it would bring the awful truth to light again.

I take walks down to the water but the weather is harsh and cold. The sky is gray with clouds, and the water looks rough and dark. We have had several snow showers and often there are patches of ice everywhere I walk. It is an uncertain and gloomy time, and I compare it to a sudden flooding of mud from the river into my life just as I start to enjoy the diamonds in the water from the sun.

CHAPTER TWENTY-SEVEN

Weeks go by with no word from Mr. Whitaker until March 20th. He calls to tell me that the investigation is still ongoing. He says, "We have decided, however, that you should go on with your plans for a gift shop and the property sales to the farmers. It is taking longer than expected, and our office believes that no matter what, you are still an heir. Whatever you have planned should be continued." I am elated and thank him for the call.

After discussions with Amy, the household, and the farmers, Bill notifies the local newspaper that the gift shop will open on Saturday, April 1st.

I've been listening to Amy's depressing comments about it being "April Fool's Day."

Everything starts up again as everyone involved begins to breathe a sigh of relief, and busy is not the word for it. Life seems to take on a new meaning after dealing with the long period of no action.

Opening day for the gift shop is unnerving for Amy. She's afraid that very few people will come because there is a light sprinkling of ice and the wind is making it colder. At 9:00 a.m. everything is ready. We stand there along with the hot chocolate, coffee, and treats, anxiously waiting as if a baby is about to be born.

The first ones to arrive are the farmer's wives who come together in one car. They have many of their consignment things on the shelves but look around for something to buy, which is very nice, and Amy makes a few sales.

About 10:00 a.m. a car parks in the lot and three women come into the shop. They are older ladies, bundled up with coats and boots, laughing and happy. Amy has on the smock I gave her for Christmas and cheerfully greets them. They enjoy our refreshments and then begin shopping for gifts. By Noon the weather turns warmer and more people are arriving.

I walk around but really don't interact very much. Once again, I'm interested in finding the information from John Rivers and look for time to take on that job.

At the end of the day, I get a report on the sales from the gift shop. It has been a good day for us, and Amy is delighted.

At dinner one evening Amy has a few stories to tell about the customers. She says, "One lady in particular got my attention. She came in later in the day from Richmond. She was very pretty with nice clothes and asked questions about Rivers Run. I told her what I knew about the place, which isn't much. The lady mentioned John Matthew Rivers and said her mother had known him."

This information has me excited. I ask, "Amy do you remember her name, or did she buy anything?"

"I don't remember her name, but if I heard it again, I would remember. I do recall she wanted to know if there were any quilts for sale. Of course, I told her no. Then she said that her grandmother had given her mother a beautiful one from Rivers Run that had initials crocheted on it."

That gets my undivided attention and leaves me breathless! *I remember the dream with Margaret when John Rivers tucked the quilt around her before she left in the carriage. I also remember the wedding dream where Margaret's daughter was married. Her name was Angela Worthington and she married Daniel Morris. This lady that came to the shop might be Angela's daughter. Here I go again thinking the dreams could be real.*

One day in April, I'm about to go and have lunch at the house. I usually bring back something for Amy and work at the counter while she eats. Before I leave, a man steps into the shop looking around, and I recognize him!

It stops me in my tracks! He is the artist! It shocks me and I feel goose bumps on my arms to see him outside of a dream!

He is older than he was in my dream and is dressed in a tan suit and stands straight and tall. His brown hair is combed back away from his face and I notice his blue eyes that are busy looking around at the bare walls of the shop. He is very handsome and looks older than Amy, maybe in his thirties.

I approach him, swallow, try to get my vocal chords working, and the goose bumps from showing. I say, "Hello, may I help you find something?"

He gives me a beautiful smile and says, "Oh, I was just curious. I wanted to see the shop and perhaps meet the owner and heir I had heard about."

"Well, I'm Jennette Walters the one you are referring to, I think."

He says, "Very nice to meet you. I'm Marvin Allen Mahon, but call me Allen."

I stammer because I almost say, "I know." Then I want to laugh out loud, but try to smile instead.

He says, "I just returned to Helen and was curious about the shop. I painted a few scenes for Mr. John Rivers and he liked my work and hung some of them in the house."

"Well, it's wonderful to meet you! Let me introduce you to Mrs. Forrester, the manager. We both have seen your paintings in the house, and I'm sure she would like to meet you."

I introduce him to Amy as the artist of the paintings in the ballroom, and I say, "He would like us to call him Allen."

Amy looks at me with surprise, looks at him and excitedly asks, "You are the artist of those paintings?"

Allen grins and says, "Yes, John Rivers liked my work."

He looks around at the spaces on the shop walls, "Mrs. Forrester, I was wondering if you would display my paintings on consignment? To have a place where they could be sold would be nice."

Amy looks around at the walls that have many empty spaces and says, "Allen, perhaps we can hang a few of them. You'll be charged twenty percent when the items are sold—and please call me Amy."

He smiles and says, "A beautiful name for a beautiful lady," and Amy responds by poking at her hair and thanking him.

This meeting with Allen has gone better than I had expected, and I can see Amy is enjoying every minute of it.

Then he says, "Amy, I brought a few paintings with me today."

At that point I take charge at the counter and Amy walks with him to the door of the shop. They are looking up at the various spaces on the walls and I turn to serve customers waiting in line.

Soon I notice that Bill has a ladder, and Allen's paintings are being placed in various spots on the wall for sale.

Allen says, "They are paintings of two Richmond street scenes and two scenes with barns and hills in the area."

After the paintings are hung precisely how she wants them, Amy and Allen laugh and talk at a table in a corner of the shop before he leaves.

I'm sure she advised him she is widowed because she tells me later that they have a dinner date on Friday night.

I retire for the night completely baffled and intrigued about the quick work Allen made with Amy—or did Amy do her work on Allen?

A few weeks go by and the gift shop is doing well. I am needed more and more to help out. Today I am dusting a few items on the shelves. A woman comes into the shop dressed in a dark blue pantsuit. She goes over to the knitted items and the crocheted things on consignment from the farmers' wives, examining various ones.

Amy comes over to me and says, "That's the woman who was asking about the quilts." I nod and walk over to her.

"Hello, I'm Jenny Walters, the owner. May I help you?"

"Oh, thank you. I came in one day looking for a quilt and really didn't look at the other things that are here. You see my mother has a quilt that I love and she says it was a gift to my grandmother from one of the owners of Rivers Run years ago. I just thought perhaps the new gift shop would have other quilts to sell. I was told there were none, so I decided to come back and shop this time."

This woman is probably in her late twenties. She has short, light brown hair and lovely hazel eyes. "Well, take your time. We have coffee, tea, and treats to enjoy while you're here. Are you from Richmond or here in town?"

"I'm from Richmond." *I am very interested now.*

"May I ask the name of your mother?"

160

"Her name is Angela Morris and I am Pamela Burch, just call me Pam." *Then I remember the dream with John and Margaret. Angela is the name of Margaret's daughter.*

I say, "Pam," it is very nice to meet you. People who have connections to our ancestors of long ago are of interest to me. I understand that my great-great Aunt, Helen Marie Rivers, did quilting and put her initials, HMR, on them."

Pam says, "Oh, that explains those same initials in the corner on my mother's quilt."

Now I am very happy!

I smile, "That is wonderful to know."

Pam smiles and shakes her head in awe. "My grandmother is gone now, but my mother says that John Rivers was like an uncle to her when she was very young. The quilt means a lot to her and I was hoping to buy another one."

I think it would be nice to meet her mother, Angela.

"I wish we had more of the quilts also. I have several but they are not for sale, as you would imagine," I answer.

Pam continues to shop for a while and then she buys a lovely crocheted doily.

As she turns to go I say, "Thank you for coming in. You know, if you would like to come back, I could show you the other quilts. Perhaps you could bring your mother as well."

She smiles, "That would be lovely. My mother will be thrilled I think."

I am very happy about the encounter and she seems agreeable to come back with her mother.

As she leaves I'm thinking that having the gift shop has brought in Marvin Allen Mahon and Margaret's granddaughter—two people who could be heirs. To have them walk into my life is astounding! Maybe these are the people Mr. Whitaker is investigating to find out their heritage.

On Friday, after the gift shop closes, Amy gets ready to go out with Allen. It is nice to see them together. As they leave the house I am pleased. They seem to match somehow, and then I think of Ward. He is a very precise, proper person you might say, and Allen is more good-natured and spontaneous.

I think of Roger, whom I haven't seen for days. He is good-natured like Allen, too. I'm sure he knows I have been busy.

In the days after Amy's date with Allen I hear nothing but nice things from her about their time together. She tells me Allen is more like her husband with his ways of handling adversities.

Amy says, "Allen laughs about the bad weather and treats it as something to be glad about. He says it will make you enjoy the good weather better when it comes along."

CHAPTER TWENTY-EIGHT

The shop continues to attract people from not only our town and Richmond but other places as well. Today when I go to work in the shop I find out that Allen has sold two paintings and Amy is definitely looking forward to seeing him again. She bounces around with a glorious attitude I have never seen from her.

Today, when Ward steps into the shop I can see Amy is not expecting him, but greets him well. He looks around and picks a few greeting cards as Amy makes herself busy helping customers. When he comes to the counter I am there to wait on him. He says, Jenny, how are things going with the shop?"

"Very well, Ward. We have been very busy. Thanks for asking." I wrap his items and he turns to leave the counter, looking for Amy who is straightening several items on a shelf.

About that time the door opens and there stands Allen. Amy goes over immediately and they discuss the paintings he brings with him. They are both laughing about something as they gradually walk over.

Amy introduces Allen to Ward, and Allen says, "Oh yeah, Mr. Wendell. I've heard you're a great history professor; however, history is something I would rather not think about as I try to build on today and tomorrow," and he laughs. This brings chuckles from all the customers standing there at the counter.

Ward gives a slight smile, and says, "Amy, could I see you before I leave?"

They go to the table, sit down and talk. A little later I look up and see Ward leaving. Then Amy gets involved hanging Allen's paintings in places on the shop walls.

Later when Amy and I are at the dinner table I ask about Ward.

Amy says, "He wanted to take me out tonight but I told him I am very tired and would have to refuse. I guess I am not really happy to see him while Allen is here. Ward is very different than Allen. He is a very serious-minded person. I suppose I will have to handle him differently. What do you think, Jenny?"

"You are right about them being different. I wouldn't know how to handle the situation. I guess you may have to chose between the two of them."

"Oh no, why do that when I can enjoy both?"

I scratch my head and realize this is Amy I am dealing with.

I laugh, "Well, good luck with that."

As time goes by it is very interesting to watch Amy handle two men in her life. Surprisingly, both men seem contented with her. Allen is selling his paintings, and Amy has agreed to put copies of Ward's history book on our shelves for sale.

One day while Allen is in the shop and Amy has left for lunch, he comes over to me when no one is around, and says, "Jenny, can I talk with you about something?"

"Sure, Allen," and we walk over to the table.

He gets a faraway look on his face. "I was told by John Rivers that my great-grandmother, Lia Moretti, died in childbirth here at Rivers Run and is buried in the Rivers' cemetery. One day John Rivers took me to see her gravesite. Do you mind if I go and visit her grave occasionally?"

I try to act surprised but I know all about it from the dream I was in with him and John Rivers.

I hesitate to lie, but say, "I saw her grave, but other than a servant for Rivers Run, I didn't know this about her. Did John Rivers really tell you all that?"

"Yes, and my grandmother told me she was adopted by the Turner family. They named her Clara. I was never told who my great-grandfather was. Whenever John Rivers talked about her, I could see he was upset. She was a servant here and I think he loved her and it made me wonder about their relationship."

"Well, Allen, I guess that's something we will never know."

I think about the letter I have been looking for—will it reveal something about Lia, his great-grandmother?

Allen looks downhearted. "Yes, but, he gave me so much support and paid for me to study. I wonder if he could have been my great-grandfather. Wouldn't that make me an heir? My grandmother would never speak about it."

His remarks make me uncomfortable because I have felt the same way about the possibility of his inheritance. I cough several times, thinking of what to say.

Then I say, "Allen, wouldn't John Rivers have wanted you to know if you were part of his family?"

He shakes his head in thought. "I'm sure you're right. I'll just forget about it."

"I am glad your paintings are selling well. It's marvelous to be acquainted with you since we have admired your work here."

At that moment I am glad to see Amy come back from lunch.

One day the following week Pamela Burch comes to the gift shop with her mother.

Angela is middle-aged, dresses smartly, but she looks tired and appears to have a small limp.

I hardly recognize her from the dream I had of her wedding when she called John Matthew Rivers "Uncle John."

I go over to meet them. "Good morning, Pam."

"Good morning, Jenny. I told my mother about the gift shop and she wanted to come with me."

Angela comes over and I greet her. "I am so glad you came with your daughter."

Angela says, "It is wonderful to visit the place again. John Rivers was so very generous to my mother over the years when we really needed the help. Pam says you might have other quilts that Helen Marie Rivers made. I have one that was given to my mother and I would love to see the others."

"Oh yes, please come with me." I introduce them to Amy and tell her that Angela was a friend of John Rivers, and explain about the quilts that I am going to show them. Amy greets them and smiles, continuing the sales with her customers.

Going to the house I notice Angela's obvious examination of the house and the grounds that are looking very beautiful and new.

Angela looks surprised and says, "Oh my, everything looks just as it did when I was a young girl."

I say, "Well, I'm glad you didn't see it when I first came here last year. Over many months we have accomplished the impossible I think."

I take them into the parlor and ask Gracie to serve refreshments while I leave them to get the quilts.

When I return and spread the two quilts out, Angela and Pam examine them thoroughly and discover the initials placed in the corners.

Angela's apparent joy is obvious and I am very glad that this moment has happened.

As we talk over tea, Angela says, "My father, Stewart Worthington, died before my mom did, but I really never knew him very well. He had a job that sent him to other countries and we never went with him. He did come to my wedding, but I always looked to Uncle John for everything. He was more like a father to me all my life and I often wondered about my mother's relationship with him."

Immediately I get a feeling that she is grasping at the possibility of an inheritance for ownership of Rivers Run, just like Allen did.

I say, "I have heard many great stories about my relative, John Rivers, and how generous he was to everyone. I would have loved to have known him."

Then I change the subject and while having tea I talk about the renovations that have been made to the house and grounds, and the gift shop.

When they are ready to leave I walk them back to the gift shop and they buy a few homemade doilies. Before they go I thank them for coming to see us.

I watch them drive away and sit down at the table in the corner of the shop and think about what Angela said about her mother's relationship with John Rivers.

First Allen and now Angela! It makes me wonder if Angela and Pamela really came back to see the quilts or to question the inheritance? How many more possible heirs will come out of the past? I have mixed emotions because, according to my ancestors in the dreams, it will be a good thing to discover them and I should be happy these people are showing up. I hope Mr. Whitaker's ongoing investigation will prove something soon.

On May 12th I say nothing about it being my twenty-second birthday. I don't need to make a big thing of it and the day goes by in the shop. There's a cool breeze but the sun is warm, and the bulbs that Bill planted in the fall appear perfectly placed and the garden is beautiful.

In late afternoon, business is slow and Amy tells me she can handle it, so I leave and go to my bedroom. I start looking through my family things that I'm keeping in my closet. Since the gift shop opened, I really haven't had much time to look through them. Some of the items take me back to those days when my mom and dad were alive. I always felt loved and it makes me want to sit here for hours and think about those times.

I rummage through several items of clothing and there is an old brown piece of newspaper folded inside a shirt pocket. I carefully handle it and I'm just about to open it when there's a knock on my door.

Amy says, "Come on, Jenny, it's time for dinner."

"Okay, Amy. I'm coming." I put the piece of newspaper back. I will look at it later.

When we enter the dining room I see Ward and Roger. They yell, "Happy Birthday." Roger comes over and hugs me and kisses me on the cheek.

Gracie and Bill join us, and we enjoy a delicious meal. There is a birthday cake brought out after the meal. It is decorated beautifully with twenty-two candles all fired up.

My wish is for everything to settle down and be normal again, and if new heirs are to be found, that it happen soon.

Cards and toiletries from Amy, Gracie and Bill are very nice. Gold earrings from Roger are a perfect gift, and I put them on right away. Before leaving, Roger asks me to dinner the following night, and I accept. I have been so busy with the gift shop that we haven't seen each other.

One day while Allen is helping Amy in the gift shop, it dawns on me that I have completely forgotten that paper I found in my parents' things.

With Allen talking about being a possible heir, and Angela saying John Rivers was like a "father" to her, my mind has been on those scenarios.

I go to my room and while sitting in my lounge chair by the window I dig through my parent's things and find the crumpled, brown paper in my dad's shirt.

It is a copy of a Richmond news article dated May 20, 1894. The report tells about a Women's Nursing Auxiliary working in England and states that there was an encounter with an enemy at which time the Nursing Unit #224 was evacuated from the camp. While leaving in a truck, a bomb blasted near them and the truck exploded. They found the remains of the nurses and the article lists the names. I look for Kathleen's name and when I see it, I experience the loss once more.

The article also shows a picture of the nurses when they joined the Unit and even though the article is brown from age, I can recognize Kathleen among the others because she looks like me! I sit back in astonishment.

Her face favors me so much that it is almost like looking into a mirror! Then I realize she was my age at the time.

After the initial shock I wonder how my father had gotten that copy. Did he know of our heritage enough to look for this old news about family members of the Rivers, or did he find it in his father's things?

If I had not experienced those dreams I wouldn't know what this piece of newspaper was telling me. Now I know what happened to Kathleen. I tuck the paper back into the shirt and close the box. It has only given me questions about what my father knew about his heritage, and has given me an eerie feeling about my unmistakable likeness to Kathleen. I suddenly remember that Junior, in those early dreams, told his mother that I looked like Kathleen. She would ignore him and just smile and play with us as if I were there. When she put cookies out for them she put one out for me too, but I never could pick it up.

CHAPTER TWENTY-NINE

Weeks go by with no word from Mr. Whitaker and I am beginning to think their investigation is not proving successful in finding an heir. Then on Monday, June 15, I get a call. Mr. Whitaker says he is in Helen and the investigation is over. He wants to bring the results, and another person with him. The meeting is set for 3:00 p.m.

I tell Gracie, Bill, and Amy to be prepared. Amy says she is going to be working in the shop with Allen if I need her, and I'm glad that she will not be present for this.

Gracie and Bill look disoriented. Bill says, "We'll be available if you need us."

What does that mean—in case there is trouble—or I faint?

Again I wander around.

I probably should look for that paper that John Rivers hid, but I'm too upset to worry about that now—besides what will it matter anyway when the conclusion about another heir is imminent.

I'm in the large parlor when Mr. Whitaker and his associate arrive. Gracie has brought in refreshments. Behind the lawyer I see someone I recognize—*Somehow I'm not surprised but disappointed that George Waller has anything to do with these disturbing consequences; however, here he is, and if he found heirs that saves me the trouble—then Allen, Angela, and Pamela come to mind.*

George comes over and says, "Hello, Jenny, I told you this might happen."

"Yes, you did, George."

George brings me lemonade and gives me a look that I can't quite interpret. It is almost sympathetic and sad. He turns to Mr. Whitaker and says, "Sir, I think we should have my mother and father here with us for this."

What? Does he think I'll need the support too?

Mr. Whitaker tells him to ask them to join us and George leaves. Moments later all three of them come into the parlor and take a seat.

I'm confused, maybe I'll need help after all!

My lawyer stands and says, "Miss Walters, I know this will be awkward for you but, under the circumstances, it is necessary for me to reveal your background and how I found you."

I have nothing to be ashamed of, so I sit through it.

He describes the investigation and how he discovered me, and explains my eleven years in a county orphanage.

I can see that Bill, Gracie and George have been unaware of my heartbreaking background—the loss of parents at the age of seven. Their slight gasps are noticeable as they look over at me with changed expressions.

Then Mr. Whitaker clears his throat. "Miss Walters, this investigation has turned up several people who are definitely ancestors, and I have papers for you to sign. I will try to explain. You see," he looks down at the papers and clears his throat again, "your great-great aunt, Helen Marie Walters, had another brother, and also had another name before she changed it illegally to a British name and became a citizen of England. Harrison Tomas, your great-great-grandfather, also changed his name to Walters, and crossed the border illegally. They both crossed with a woman who was their 'Aunt Fiona.' Her husband had official British connections, apparently, that helped the process, but still they had to change their name."

I remember "Aunt Fiona" from Helen's diary.

Mr. Whitaker stops to take a drink and then continues. "Helen's other brother, George Patrick, was the brother who stayed in Ireland for a time, went to England when things got more civil over there, and never had to change his name. He came to America with his family—his wife, Kathleen, and two children, Meghan and Melvin—five years after your great-great aunt Helen Marie."

He shakes his head back and forth. "I was told a story by George Scott Waller, who found a letter from his grandfather. It revealed that

Aunt Fiona, in order to get them across the border, made a few changes in the name 'Waller' – crossing the second 'l,' making it a 't' and adding an 's.' Those changes made them the English Walters, not the Irish Waller's. It sounds plausible for the year 1867. With security in place today, I don't think it could ever happen again."

I put my head in my hands, trying to comprehend the facts coming together with the information from my dreams—and now it makes perfect sense.

Remembering her writings in the book from the attic and my dreams, I can see why Helen was disturbed about the lie she had to live with. Now I know! This gives new meaning to her story about leaving Ireland and marrying Donald Andrew Rivers—she had to change her name! It also explains why I have the name of Walters, since my great-great-grandfather, Harrison Tomas Walters, also changed his name from Waller to get across the border into England.

Nothing is said for several minutes and the silence is noticeable. There seems to be nothing to say that will change the outcome.

It's official and all at once, I realize I'm not the only heir. Then the name "Waller" takes effect. Gracie and Bill?—and George?

Mr. Whitaker stops turning pages, gets up, comes over to me, and shakes his head. He puts his hand on my shoulder that makes me aware of a big moment coming, like the time I was told my parents were killed.

I wait for his words.

He says, "Miss Walters, I'm sorry this has happened. We thought sure you were the sole legal heir to this place. It seems you are an heir, but the Waller family are also heirs and they will be the main ones because of their ages."

The room gets quiet and George comes over to stand by me. "Are you all right? I'm sorry about this but I had to see it through for the sake of my parents."

I get up and walk to the window and tears come without help.

I think of Gracie and Bill and I'm devastated. They were my servants! I'm without words and suddenly feel faint.

I blurt out, "Excuse me. I have to leave you for a moment. Make yourselves comfortable. I'll return to sign whatever is necessary—just give me some time."

I walk right past the Waller's into the hall without speaking.

Maybe the Waller's suspected something right from the start—why didn't Bill say something? That's why they were hesitant about staying on with me at Rivers Run! It explains a lot, especially Bill looking through the family Bible.

I'm halfway up the stairs when I realize someone is behind me.

George says, "Jenny, please don't be upset. I know my family needs to make amends to what you've endured. There is no earthly reason why things can't work out for you."

I turn toward him on the stairs with tears about to spill over, "George, your father and mother have been my servants, for heaven's sakes! They both have been working for me and following my orders. There are no words to explain how dreadful I feel about that. Perhaps I should leave and not get in the way of your father's rightful ownership."

"Jenny, I don't understand how this happened to you at all, but you are still a member of this family and also an heir to Rivers Run. Come back and discuss things with my dad."

Then he smiles at me in a very sincere manner with his eyebrows raised questioningly and says, "You don't want me to be sad, do you?"

He's being too nice. "I'll be down in a minute, George."

Boots follows and jumps on my bed with me. I sit and try to understand what has happened.

I'm surprised that the heirs were the Waller's, that's for sure. Personally, I'm definitely all right, except I want the gift shop and I want the farmers to be able to buy the rented property. I'm not sure how those ideas will be handled now.

I wash my face and repair my make-up, take a big breath of air, recheck everything in the mirror including my lacey top, and finally reach over and pet Boots, who has been following me since I left the bed. Now I feel more relaxed and capable again and reluctantly take steps to return to the parlor.

When I start down the stairway I notice George is standing at the bottom.

He must have waited there for me.

"Jenny, I'm glad you came back—I didn't want to have to come get you." He takes my hand and we go into the parlor together, hand-in-hand. He has kept a strong hold as if I'll disappear if he lets go. Bill and Gracie are seated and George takes me to a seat and sits beside me.

Mr. Whitaker says, "You must sign official papers to make all this legal in accordance with your ages. These documents give William

Tomas Waller and his wife, Grace Myrtle Waller, complete control of the estate in accordance with the facts now known about the family of George Patrick Waller. George Scott Waller will be next in line, and Jennette Fiona Walters' inheritance will be recognized after the estate has no other heir alive."

The lawyer takes a drink of water then continues, "There is another requested requirement for each of you. Each must live on the property. If an heir decides to leave, they will have to sign a document that will state they want to leave but will be responsible for the estate when there is no other heir."

The documents are there for us to sign and it only takes a few minutes for each of us to make it official.

As I walk Jerry Whitaker to the door, Bill, Gracie, and George stay in the parlor. He shakes my hand, smiles and says, "Now, Miss Walters, go and talk with Mr. & Mrs. Waller and their son, and work out your next arrangements. They seem to be very nice people and will do what is right."

"Thank you, Mr. Whitaker. This has been very unsettling, but I will try."

Then Mr. Whitaker says, "Well, opening this case again has been costly but my company is in your debt." When he leaves, I think about that.

I go back to the parlor and sit with Bill, Gracie and George. Bill says, "Jenny, we want to discuss a few things with you before you lose heart about this and all the things you have planned for Rivers Run."

I say, "Bill, you and Gracie have been so good to me since I came here. I am so ashamed that I treated you as servants! I really felt so unable to take control and I wouldn't have been capable of doing anything without you helping me. I do love this place and all the things I have found out about my ancestors—I mean our ancestors. Now that you have the place, I will bow out of all decisions gracefully, and let things happen for you and your son."

Bill smiles, "Jenny, we understand that our ancestors want all the heirs to live together. We have come to love you as our own daughter. You can help us with the farmers' properties so they can own their places."

That shocks me. "You want to do that for them?"

Bill says, "Yes, we do. You have helped us understand that it is long overdue."

"Well, Bill, what will you do about the gift shop? I hope you will continue with that project also. It is making a substantial profit for the estate."

Bill says, "My dear, we have been very happy about the gift shop. We like Amy and if she will continue with us, we will pay her just as you have been doing."

That is another surprise and I say, "That makes me very happy. Thank you!"

Bill, Gracie and George seem very happy indeed and I am very glad about this outcome, but now it brings to mind a question, and I ask. "Bill, tell me how you and Gracie got your job here. Did you suspect you might be heirs then?"

He says, "We lived in Richmond and heard about the manor house inheritance being looked into. It was in all the papers. We came here when we heard that a lawyer was going to hire caretakers. George had been looking into the Waller name, suspected the Walters name change even then, and insisted that we try to be hired. He thought the proof we needed to prove our inheritance would possibly be somewhere in the house, but we have found nothing."

Bill takes a drink of lemonade and continues. "I eventually saw George Patrick's name written in that Bible in the library with the other Walters, which was interesting. I heard Amy talking about the names in it and had to see for myself. I borrowed that Bible for a few days and returned it the night you caught me in the library when you closed the door on me."

Laughing I say, "I remember!"

Bill says, "Then George found a few old letters in my father's belonging that hinted about the name change and the connection to those ancestors. He continued to search through old things and finally found the proof stuck down in photos of my grandmother. I thought all my grandfather's stuff had been thrown away when my dad died."

That explains many things. I am very relieved. I feel the bridge between us evaporate. "Thank you, Bill."

CHAPTER THIRTY

George and I stay in the library as Gracie and Bill leave with the refreshment cart.

"Jenny, you will have to show me around this place. I feel totally lost all of a sudden."

"I'll be glad to but I'm sure your father will be able to do that for you better than I can."

"Yes, Jenny, but not quite as nicely. I need to get to know you a lot better."

He must have a lot of John Matthew Rivers' womanizing in his blood. I'll have to remember we are cousins or something, even though far-removed.

"George, you will love the estate and when you find out more about our dear ancestors, I'm sure you will appreciate being a member of this family."

Gracie and Bill come into the parlor, and Gracie tells me Amy has come in from the gift shop.

Amy comes into the parlor and says that Allen is watching the shop. She saunters over and gives George a smile. "Well, hello again. What are you doing here?" and George nods his head.

I say, "Amy, things have changed."

She says, "Yeah, I heard a little of it, but tell me more."

I believe not much gets past Amy in this house. She probably talked with Mr. Whitaker on his way out.

I say, "The Waller family are the owners of Rivers Run now. I am an heir but not the oldest. Perhaps Bill can explain."

Bill looks over at her. "Well, it seems Gracie and I have been found to be rightful heirs due to a complex situation involving a name change years ago, and we are now the new owners of Rivers Run. Because of our ages we will take over the responsibilities. Jenny is listed in the inheritance after our son, George."

Amy sits down in one of the chairs and leans back as if to rest with exhaustion. I can see she is frustrated and annoyed as she puts her hand on her chin, looks around at us with a look of dismay and intolerance as only she can do. It seems to take all the air out of the room.

I sense that Amy is not happy, and Bill suddenly gets the picture too and quickly says, "I assure you that not much will happen different for the moment. Gracie and I are going to take one of the bedroom suites upstairs in the other wing of the house along with George, our son, who will also have a suite. We plan to hire new servants. Perhaps Bessie and Jessie Gray will want the job."

Bill looks over at Amy and says, "The gift shop will continue with you as manager, if you want to stay, with Jenny taking part as she wishes."

Amy sits up and seems relieved. "Well, that's good. I will continue doing a good job for Rivers Run. Oh, am I also going to keep my room or should I get Ward to find me a place in town?"

Bill says, "Amy, you are still a guest of Jenny's—you had better ask her that question."

Amy looks at me and I laugh. "Amy, of course I want you to stay on as long as you want. You'll need to be in the shop early in the morning and often late at night as you have been doing."

After that is settled, I think about dinner. "Gracie, how do you feel about cooking dinner tonight?"

She "tsks" with her tongue against her teeth, and says, "Of course I'll fix dinner! How about a buffet style meal, and you and Amy can join in tonight and celebrate our first night as heirs." I think that's a great idea.

During dinner everyone seems happy about the circumstances. Amy is happy about her concerns being met, and George sits back and seems to be relieved about how the situation has developed.

Nobody realizes the relief I have to relinquish my duties to Bill and Gracie. I had been dreading someone strange being an heir that may have upset everything.

That night in my room I ponder the situation, hoping the ancestors are resting in peace since the rightful heirs have been fully validated. I am so glad it's over.

Maybe the dreams are over too. Exhausted, I close my eyes with peace in my heart....

Suddenly, I'm in a different bedroom because I see a beautiful garden scene from the open window and feel a breeze. The colors are purple and pink on the bedding. I see a middle-aged couple. I recognize Helen, who looks very thin, and Donald Senior, tall and still very handsome. They are sitting on the bed. He says, "Helen, I can't believe you didn't tell me about this when I first met you. Did you think it would matter?"

"Oh, Donald, how did I know at that time that it wouldn't have made a difference. I have walked the floor so many nights since I have been here at Rivers Run, thinking I could never reveal this about my family to you. I am so ashamed, but I thought you would not forgive me if the secret came out. That's another reason Harrison, Patrick, and I never kept in touch. We never wanted how we crossed to England to be known."

Donald embraces his wife and wipes her tears away. She coughs and tries to get her breath when he says, "My sweet, it does not matter at all. Here it is May 1904 and so much time has passed. Your story need never be told outside this room, but you should invite your brothers here and make them welcome."

"Thank you, Donald. Once I feel better, I will invite them."

Then Donald hugs Helen and says, "There are also things I have never revealed to you that you need to know as well." Then he says, "but I'll tell you after dinner tonight."

Helen says, "That's fine, Donald. Right now I am so relieved since you know the story and are so forgiving. The doctor says this illness of mine is just a setback. The bad cough seems to be better." I watch the two of them embrace...

I am shocked that Helen told Donald about the family secret and once again I feel the urge to touch her.....

I cough and it wakes me. I wipe tears from my face and realize that I cried while I watched the scene unfold between Donald and Helen.

A dream has allowed me to see her reveal the truth to Donald about her secret of the name change from Waller to Walters, and it was before she died in July 1904. All I can imagine is that she wants me to know that she told him about her brother, Patrick, and also why Harrison, my great-great-grandfather, and Patrick, never kept up with the Rivers. I am growing so close to my people because of these dreams and feel so loved and protected. Now I know exactly how it happened and I feel sure everything is in accordance with their wishes that the other heirs be found.

I wonder what Donald was going to tell her after dinner? Perhaps it is the connections he has in Richmond. Maybe it will be revealed in another dream. These dreams have brought me closer to everyone in the family and I am so glad.

The next day after breakfast I get a call from Roger. Since the weather is good, he wants to come over and take me horseback riding with him this afternoon, and drive back to his home after our ride, to join his family for dinner. I think it will be a good time to tell him what changes are being made at Rivers Run, so I agree, and have Bill prepare Kota and Major.

I tell Amy when I join her in the gift shop. She laughs and wonders how I am going to ride a horse, being totally unprepared, and tells me what to wear. Allen is coming to help her in the gift shop today, so she doesn't mind not having my help. George also wants to help her in the gift shop.

I am amazed and amused.

Roger parks his Bronco and I meet him outside. The horses have the saddles on and I just look at them dumbfounded. I tell him I don't know how to ride a horse. Then Roger picks me up and puts me in front of the saddle on Kota and then hops on the saddle. As I lien on him for support, he takes the reins and directs the horse to gallop around until we get to his rented property.

When he opens a gate to their property, I see exactly how much property they have and the place where his parents will build their house. Roger says they have chosen about ten acres for a house and barn. That will leave the other acres for farming.

Roger helps me down from Kota and we walk through the woods. I tell him about the recent changes at Rivers Run—the fact that I no longer have the responsibility and that the Waller's are owners now, and explain about how it happened with the name changes back in 1867. I also tell him they will continue with my plans for the farmers and the gift shop. He seems surprised, looks off into the distance and then he says, "I'm glad that my parents will be able to continue with their plans to buy the property."

We ride back to the manor house in a fast gallop. The wind is blowing through my hair and I feel free again, as if I'm shedding all the responsibilities of Rivers Run.

That night during dinner with his mom and dad, I share the recent changes in my inheritance story.

They are very surprised, and Larry says, "Will the Waller's want to sell the property to us now?"

I say, "Yes, Larry. They are going to continue everything I have planned for Rivers Run. I feel very good about them taking charge. I never wanted that responsibility."

All three of them look relieved but then they seem saddened, and Martha says, "But what about you. Will you leave?"

"Oh no, the inheritance provides for me and the stipulation is that all of the heirs should live there if they wish." I see relief on their faces and a good change in attitudes.

When Roger and I are alone he says, "Jenny, this has certainly settled everything about the dreams you were having, and that's a relief, isn't it?"

"Well, I hope so, Roger." We snuggle together, watch a love story on television, and have after-dinner wine. At this time in my life it is exactly what I need.

Days go by and things are getting settled around me as Bill and Gracie take charge. Bob Humphrey comes at the request of the law firm to have everything transferred, and we meet with him.

The Waller's and I have several documents to sign for banking purposes, and Bob tells us that the bills are being paid for all the repair and maintenance projects on the manor house.

Then Bob gives me a big smile. "Jenny, I have good news for you. The law firm has awarded you compensation for the disruption in your life." The amount is more than I expect.

Bob also explains the percentages George and I will get monthly in our bank accounts from the estate. Bill and Gracie will assume responsibility for the balance that is in the estate account.

Following the meeting with the accountant, Bill meets with all the farmers, and he asks me to attend. He explains the inheritance changes and assures them that what I had arranged for the property will be honored. Things seem to be going just as planned.

CHAPTER THIRTY-ONE

One night Ward invites Amy to a movie in Richmond. After they leave, George asks me to take a walk with him on the grounds. We leave by the kitchen door.

Bill has hired several people to take care of the outside work in the gardens and the cemetery, and as we walk along I admire what has been done.

George says, "You know the gardens look a lot like the ones from the parlor window in my dream last night."

I am astounded. "George, what do you mean your dream?"

"Well, I didn't mean to say anything, but let's sit for a minute," and we go over to one of the new benches that has replaced an old wooden one.

He shakes his head as if to clear his thinking. "I had a dream last night, I think, with Helen and Donald Rivers in it, and it showed me what happened here long ago. I know it must sound strange but I learned a lot about the place and saw the parlor just as it appears today. It reminded me of the letter I found in my grandfather's chest in Richmond that had Helen's name on it as a sister to my great-great-grandfather, George Patrick Waller. That letter is what started me on my journey to find out about Rivers Run and my ancestors—her name wasn't the same."

While George describes having a dream, I sit there shaking, and not from the cool breeze. I look at him in awe! "George, I have to tell you something."

I hesitate and sigh, knowing I must tell him. He looks at me with anticipation.

I clear my throat and look around at all the new things on the grounds. "Since I have been here at Rivers Run I have had dreams too, and when I was a little girl in the orphanage I even communicated with the first little girl, Kathleen, and the little boy, Junior, in a dream. I played with them then—while now I just stand in the dream with the older ancestors and they don't see me. The ancestors have led me to believe that I have to find all the heirs of Helen's Irish bloodline or those ancestors will not rest in peace."

George has a look that resembles my feelings—surprise and anguish. "Jenny, I got that same message, but now I think the problem has been solved. Since we have been found, there can't possibly be more of the Irish heirs."

George closes his eyes in thought. "My dream mentioned diamonds. Do you think there are diamonds here somewhere?"

I know I should be serious, but I have to laugh out loud. "Oh George, I had a similar dream. Donald Rivers Senior had a thing about the sparkling water in the river in the back of the manor house. He talked about those lights in the water and called them "diamonds." He said in one of my dreams that the diamonds were blessings of good days and the dark, ugly water with no diamonds represented the bad days."

I don't think I'll tell him about the Richmond connection and my thoughts about that.

"Oh, I didn't get that message out of that dream," and he laughs with me. "It sure sounded like he was talking about diamonds being a part of Rivers Run."

"George, maybe your father has had dreams too. You should tell him about the dreams you've had and ask him. He has the same Irish bloodline."

The wind starts blowing harder and it's getting cool. He says, "Jenny, we'll talk more about this but let's go in now and get comfortable."

When we go in, Bill and Gracie are in the big parlor discussing their meeting with Jessie and Bessie Gray, who had worked for us during the New Year's celebration. We find out that they are coming to work for us and will live here in the manor house as household servants. I am pleased because they are very gracious and helpful.

In the days after my discussion with George about dreams, it is difficult to talk with him alone. He is working with his father on a few projects and with the horses, and Jessie is helping. George tells me they may set up a riding stable for customers in order to bring money to Rivers Run since there are already trails on the property. They even talk about getting more horses since there are stalls for them.

One evening Amy and Ward go to dinner in Richmond. As George and I sit in the parlor having wine, I finally have an opportunity to tell him about the other dreams I have had with John Matthew Rivers and his "affairs" with women and the servant, Lia. I disclose everything I know and suspect about those women, even Margaret and Angela. "George, that's why I think there may be other heirs that we need to find."

"Jenny, I think that is going to be very difficult. In the first place it would be hard to prove if all we have are dreams."

"It probably would be, but in one of my dreams with John Rivers, he was going to write down something about the ladies. If he did, I think it might reveal his actions that will lead us to a conclusion. That piece of information is what we need to find."

"What about the books in the library? Do you think he might have tucked it in one of those?"

"I really haven't looked, although that is a possibility. But George, there are so many books there and it will take time to find out, and neither of us have the time right now. You are working with your dad and I'm working with Amy."

George looks determined. "Well, we'll just have to find the time somehow."

That night I decide to eat dinner in my room since Amy is out with Ward. The afternoon has been exhausting in the gift shop and I go to bed reading a magazine but my eyes decide for me what I'm going to do…

I am now standing behind John Rivers who is sitting at a desk that looks like the one in the library. He is very old and seems to be in pain. He is leaning over writing something. I try to see it but I can't make out the words as I look over his shoulder.

He says, "Okay, perhaps this will stop all those dreams I'm having and will also reveal my Grandfather's exploits that I must resolve after all these years. If an heir is found after I'm gone, I don't want them to have to deal with this problem." Then I see him pick up a small cotton bag and shake his head. "I must explain my actions so it will be understood." Then he writes more on the paper in front of him, folds the letter, putting it in his breast pocket.

He talks to the bag as if it is a person and says, "You will have to go as soon as I find a way to eliminate you," and he flops it back down on the desk.

He then gets up and I move back as he walks back and forth, rubbing his chin. He goes to the window and I follow him. Before I get to see what he is doing, Boots moves on the bed, and the dream fades...

I sit up in bed fully aware that I have seen John Rivers write the information to leave for an heir. I get out of bed and write the dream in my journal, describing what I saw and heard. I still don't know where to look for his letter, but the library might be a good start. He also held a small bag and said he had to get rid of it.

The next day I tell George about the dream. I also describe the bag and his idea to get rid of the problem. I tell him that we should continue looking for the letter he wrote.

George says we should look in the library and I agree, but I tell him it will take a long time to check all the books.

George says, "Well, I'll check the desk and we can check the books every day when we have time," and I agree.

One night after dinner I see George and Bill go outside with Boots. George has said that he wanted to tell his dad about his dreams, because he says he is still having them. Gracie and I stay in the small parlor having a glass of orange liqueur while Amy goes out to the shop to order a few new things.

Alone with Gracie, I ask, "How are you and Bill doing since the change of ownership? Is everything working out like you planned for the farmers, the accountant, and Bessie and Jessie?"

Gracie leans back in the chair and sighs. "I think everything is working out fine, Jenny, but Bill isn't sleeping well. He gets up frequently during the night. He doesn't know I am watching him but he goes to the windows and looks out at the river. I pray he is not stressed over the responsibilities."

I think perhaps Bill is having dreams. Apparently he isn't sharing them with Gracie. Maybe George will help the situation by talking to his dad.

"Gracie, I wouldn't worry too much. George will help all he can and so will I whenever I am needed. Bill knows that." Then I suggest to Gracie that we go into the big parlor to watch television.

When Bill and George come in, I sense that there is a different attitude between them, and George clears his throat and says, "Jenny, I have discussed my problem with my father and we have to confess to mom. Since you are involved I thought it would be proper that we talk this over with each other—and now."

I'm sure George and his father will now reveal the dreams to Gracie and I'm glad.

Gracie looks at us strangely, as Bill goes over and turns the television off and starts apologizing to Gracie.

He says, "Honey, I'm sorry, but I was afraid if I told you about this, you would think I was getting old with a loss of my senses."

Gracie says, "What's going on—does someone have a birthday coming up? You'd better tell me so I can bake a cake."

Bill holds her hand and slowly explains the dreams he has had while here at Rivers Run, the ancestors he has seen in the dreams, and what their concerns have been about heirs. He also tells her that George and I have also had dreams.

Gracie doesn't look like she understands him at all.

I say, "Gracie, I have had dreams since the first day I came here. They all have pointed to more heirs. Now that you, Bill, and George have claimed your heritage, I thought the dreams would end—but they haven't, and I don't understand why."

Then I tell about my dream with John Rivers and that he wrote something about his past with the ladies in his life that could possibly lead to more heirs. I describe the dream and the bag that he had, and the fact that he said he would get rid of it. I mention two people named Marco and Bruno that apparently had something to do with Donald Andrew Rivers Senior.

I explain, "The room was dark and I couldn't see over John's shoulders to read the letter. He walked over to the window in the library. I tried to walk over to him in the dream, but I awoke. I never saw what he did with the letter. Now, George and I will make it our project to find it."

Gracie has had her mouth open in surprise through all our dream disclosures and says, "This is more than I imagined. I was thinking something was wrong with Bill, not you two. I just knew this inheritance would lead to trouble."

Apparently Gracie's words don't change any of our enthusiasm about our dreams and the three of us continue to talk about the ones we are having. Each of us decide that maybe in the dreams they just want to tell us about their lives back then, and it no longer may be about finding the heirs.

CHAPTER THIRTY-TWO

The dream confessions to Gracie have diminished my anxieties a great deal and I think it has helped the others as well. I retire with better thoughts about the future. I say prayers that all the Irish ancestors are resting in peace now. As I drift off to sleep I am thinking that I still want to find the letter that John Matthew left for us…

Suddenly I am approaching the cemetery with Helen. It doesn't look like the one I went to—it is very small and doesn't have a big gate. *I'm sure it is the old one before John improved it. There are* no other family graves except Robert Andrew Rivers, who died in childbirth. She walks further into the cemetery to Kathleen's memorial stone. Helen sits there on a bench and holds her hands to her heart as she prays.

She says, "Kathleen, I am so sorry you did not return. They never sent your remains back, reporting it was not possible, and for a time I had prayed and hoped. I pray you did not suffer. I'm sure the fighting was much worse than you had expected."

She dabs at her eyes with a handkerchief. "We met a wonderful gentleman who had met you years ago and wanted to see you again. I had to tell him the news about you, and he was heartbroken. Your father had plans to give you a wonderful wedding and a large dowry." She leans over and puts flowers on the stone, stands up, goes past me, and walks back toward the house…

I awaken from the dream with my heart hurting and tears in my eyes.

Poor Helen! She probably never recovered from losing Kathleen. It was so devastating for her and Donald, because she had such wonderful plans upon her return.

That morning Amy is already in the gift shop and I tell George about my dream with Helen. He doesn't comment but says, "Jenny, let's go look for that letter that John Matthew wrote about his lady friends. I have time this morning. It's still early and the gift shop isn't opened yet."

Both of us go to the library, even though I really didn't see John Matthew put it there. To look in all those books will take a bit of time but George is anxious to try. He goes first to the desk and tries all the drawers.

He says, "You know, Jenny, some desks have a little button you push that will reveal a secret compartment." Then he is very diligent and takes out papers, ledgers that my accountant works with, also large pamphlets that have very old dates on them stuck down in the side drawers.

I go over to the shelves and start looking through large books on the top shelves. We search for a time and then we look at each other in disgust. We have found nothing.

It is time now for both of us to attend to our chores and go our separate ways, but I know I am determined to continue the search.

"George, let's look again tomorrow. I think Allen is coming with another painting. He'll probably help out in the shop and I can get away."

"That's a good idea, Jenny. That letter has to be found."

After dinner one night, Bill, Gracie, George and I are sitting in the parlor. Amy is busy in the gift shop with last minute orders. Looking at the three of them I say, "I want to tell you of a news article about what happened to Kathleen that I found in my parents' things. I think it might be of interest to you."

It only takes me a minute to read it to them, and the three of them react with surprised looks when I pass it to them to see.

When I get it back, I fold the paper, and say, "Well, this article tells us what happened to her at the time. I'm wondering how my father got a copy of the news article. Did someone in the family send him a copy? It also tells me he knew we had relatives living at Rivers Run." They all agree.

Then I remember something else, "Oh, I need to tell you about Angela Morris. She has mentioned that John Rivers was so close and cared about her so much. She told me she called him 'Uncle John.' Without actually saying it, she had a questioning way about her that expressed the notion that he could be her father."

I continue with the story and mention Allen approaching me concerning his possible heritage. "He is concerned that John Rivers and his great-grandmother may have shared time together."

I see everyone's eyes open wide at that possibility.

I quickly add, "He did bring up the thought that he could be an heir, but left the thought hanging there."

That really gets a response from all three of them talking at once about those possibilities.

Bill speaks up then. "Well, I'm still having dreams. It was with Helen the other night. She was holding the notice from the government about Kathleen's death. She was crying with Donald. It was very sad and left me breathless."

Gracie puts down her fork noisily, and says, "Bill, I hope these dreams end soon. You were up walking back and forth for a time after that dream. I could tell it had upset you."

George says, "I think they upset each of us. I had a dream about Kathleen too. Her father was discussing her joining a nursing unit that was going overseas. She spoke to her father and reminded him of his trip to England where he met her mother. Donald Senior agreed that he had made the right decision and he turned to his wife, Helen, saying that it could be a good thing for Kathleen."

I remember my recent dream about Helen at Kathleen's gravesite but I don't say anything about it. I can see the subject is upsetting for each of us.

We all look at each other and sigh. The dreams are continuing. Does that mean there are more heirs to think about?

It goes without a comment but I am sure everyone is thinking about it.

George starts a different idea when he asks, "Should we tell Amy about our dreams? She is part of the household and I personally think she should know. If she knows, we won't have to constantly dodge her to talk about it."

This is new—George thinking about Amy?

I say, "I really don't mind." The others think its okay too, so George decides we should tell her when she comes in from the gift shop.

When Amy joins us in the parlor for wine, George is all ready to let her in on our secrets and he says, "Amy, the family and I want to tell you something that has been happening here. We hope you will find it of interest and perhaps helpful to you as you deal with each of us every day." Then he sits next to her.

Amy looks around at us, sits back in the chair, and says, "Hmm, that sounds intriguing." She then takes a sip of wine and sighs, "I'm ready."

I start telling her about my early dreams and the fun I had with the young Kathleen and Junior and then, in detail, the dreams I have had since arriving at Rivers Run. She doesn't say anything but, through her eye movements and deep frown, it is easy to see she is trying to make sense of it.

Then George and Bill each describe their dreams in detail.

Amy shakes her head back and forth and says, "I think I need a stronger drink." The laughter from us, I think, is a sign that confession is good for the soul.

Amy is shown the news article I found in my parents' things concerning Kathleen, the daughter who was killed in England.

I also tell her about Allen and his thoughts that imply an inheritance for him, and the recent remarks from Angela hinting that she and her daughter could be heirs.

Amy just shakes her head in disgust at their nonsense, but I tell her they have every reason to suspect such things because it is a possibility.

She is also told about the letter we are looking for that John Matthew said he would write about his lady friends, and the business his grandfather had been involved in causing them grief.

I feel relieved that Amy knows about our secrets, and Bill makes a toast to the future of Rivers Run. Amy sits back from the edge of her chair, sighs, and raises her glass with us.

One day when I'm not needed in the gift shop I take the time to go through my mother and father's other things very carefully, hoping to find more information that may link my family with the Rivers.

In among their trinkets and souvenirs I unwrap something that makes me gasp! It's a picture of Rivers Run manor house! I can't imagine it, but my father must have known about the place. Maybe it was handed down from my great-great-grandfather, Harrison, who also changed his name from Waller to Walters when he left Ireland.

From Helen's writings and dreams I know she was afraid that Donald, her husband, would find out about their unlawful deed and so was Harrison.

This is just more proof that our part of the family was basically cut off from them because of fear of her lie being discovered. Sadness comes over me for my family—and for me. Here, at Rivers Run, was a lonely old man, John Matthew Rivers, who endured being alone, not knowing about me—and me, an orphan, not knowing I had family.

I realize that it doesn't matter now, and the Waller's really don't need to add this to their frustrations. I decide not to say anything about this—what will it change now anyway? I sorrowfully tuck the little picture of the manor house back in the box.

Everything on the property seemed to go well all through the summer months and now it's late August. The gift shop has done very well, with new consignment work coming in from the wives of the farmers and a few people from town. Ward's books are selling and so are Allen's paintings. Amy is finding that with those items, she hardly has to order other merchandise.

Amy is dating Ward, Allen, and to my surprise, also George. She has a way of dealing with all three of them that makes me envious.

I never would have guessed it but George and Amy seem to be getting very close. Allen has been busy with his art gallery connections in Richmond, and Ward with his history program, leaving George, who hasn't missed the opportunity to pick up the momentum where they left off.

Roger hasn't called me for weeks. I assume he is concentrating on ownership of the farm and helping his family.

People from town are asking if there are manor house tours and Amy looks at me for an answer. I say, "No, not at this time, but perhaps in the future."

Opening the house for tours has been a topic of discussion between Bill, George, Gracie and I, with Amy putting in her suggestions. It is thought that we could do occasional tours on special days and show only certain rooms—such as the library, the big parlor, and the ballroom—that are now being planned for revamping. Money is beginning to be available for such things from the sale of the rented properties to the farmers.

In the evenings we all gather around the warm fireplace in the parlor when nights get cooler. Certain problems are discussed and resolved and it is a joy for me to see us as family. At those times I know what my father must have missed not being included with the Rivers' family.

Of course the missing letter with information from John Rivers is still on our minds and we continually discuss it and search for it, even in the attic.

One evening Bill tells us he had another dream but it was all about John Rivers talking about never having time or money to paint the ballroom. From that dream, Bill thinks perhaps the ballroom should be done next. After much discussion it is decided that the library, and the small and large parlors, need to be improved before the ballroom because we use them more.

CHAPTER THIRTY-THREE

In late September the work in the library and both parlors has been completed. New paint, rugs, furniture, shelving for the books, and new drapes change everything about the rooms to everyone's joy.

The workmen are now working in the big ballroom, the kitchen, and dining room, and they will be completed in November. It will be interesting to see the results when we are allowed in those areas again. Bill and Gracie are planning to have the bedrooms done after the work downstairs is finished. Amy thinks that will be great and she recommends new furniture and beds as well. She never has stopped complaining about her mattress even after Gracie had it changed several times.

One day, Gracie comes running into the shop with a big smile on her face. She says, "Jenny, you and Amy must come into the parlor and see what one of the workmen found!"

Allen is there behind the counter and the shop is not busy, so Amy and I rush out with Gracie. When we get to the parlor George and Bill are standing there holding a painting from the ballroom.

George says, "Jenny, I think we have found the letter." He holds up a painting done by Allen and hands me an envelope. "It was tucked in the frame on the back of this painting."

It is the painting that I saw him and Allen hang in one of my dreams. Now I remember that I saw him remove something from his pocket before he hung the painting. I had assumed it was money for the painting and woke up before I saw what he did with it. I remember Allen was turned from him and probably did not see him put it there either.

We all sit down. I look around at the faces that show looks of anticipation and anxiety, and start reading it aloud to them.

As I slowly read the words to the family, I can see they are written with a shaky hand. I hope to finally hear from John Rivers about his relationships with the ladies and also answers I need about the Richmond connections.

Dear Ancestors,

I hope this will satisfy everyone about my love affairs. First let me say that the one and only love of my life, Lia Moretti, left this world after giving birth to a beautiful baby girl in my bedroom. I never loved another, but her baby girl was not mine.

One evening, Lia left Rivers Run and went to Richmond because her last living relative, her aunt, was dying. One night while there she encountered someone on a dark street who grabbed her, shoved her into an alley, and forced her to do the act.

I was devastated when she returned and told me about it. She was in terrible shape and I consoled her as best I could. Months later she found out she was with child. I did all I could to cover up for her, even making up a story that she was married to a man that had died. I even bought a wedding band for her to wear.

I wanted to marry her myself and we had planned to marry, but she wouldn't have me after that happened. Her refusal gave me such anguish and pain, but I understood her anxiety. She was very hurt and traumatized by the experience, and would not have continued working for us, but I convinced her it was the best thing to do. I don't think she ever recovered and that may be the reason she died in childbirth.

After that part of the letter I sit there stunned with tears falling. Everyone is taking deep breaths and wiping their eyes. Then I clear my throat and begin again…

I never loved another woman in my life, although my dreams told me that I should. I did want a companion and met with many young ladies and took them to dinner. I even had them visit Rivers Run and several stayed overnight after the parties. I know many people probably think badly of me; however, I never acted on my manly instincts because I kept seeing Lia in every bedroom I was invited into. You can rest assured that there are no living heirs from my seemingly strange relationships.

Margaret was one I could not shake loose. She had a previous relationship and even had a child by him. His name is Stewart Worthington. She tried everything to get him to marry her before Angela was born, and even asked me, but I just couldn't. I paid for everything and even bought her a house to live in. Several years after, Worthington stepped up as a gentleman and married Margaret, and all was well there. This should clear up any questions about heirs to Rivers Run from me; however, there is still Grandmother Helen's life, about heirs, that could reveal more.

There is one more sheet of writings but I sigh and sit back with the information about heirs. I fold the paper and look around at the others. They are just sitting back and staring into the fireplace flames as if mesmerized.

What is it about fireplaces?

With no reactions from them, I read the words again to myself, completely astounded. Now we know there can't be any more heirs—definitely not Marvin Allen Mahon or Margaret's daughter and granddaughter, Angela and Pamela.

I say, "Well, it looks like this explains those questions, and I am so glad."

I look at George, "John Rivers mentioned Helen's life for heirs could reveal more, and now that you and your parents have been discovered, I don't see any reason we should be concerned for the Irish ancestors who have gone before. They should be rejoicing and resting in peace."

Then I take the other sheet of paper and begin to read, loudly, the rest of his writings, lacking comments from the others.

My grandfather, Donald Rivers, Senior, was a scoundrel. He played cards in Richmond often, having connections with rich mob leaders. However, I have a feeling that my great-grandfather, being a banker, could also have been responsible for that connection to the mob.

The story goes that my grandfather lost his property to an Italian mob boss, even before the manor house was finished. The mob boss didn't want the place but made my grandfather an offer. He could keep the property and build his house but he had to go to England and do a deed for the mob.

Grandfather loved his property and had no choice but to agree. After the manor house was built he went to England and fell in love with Helen Walters, but the job he had to do was necessary to complete. I learned from my father that he was to meet certain people in England and smuggle out, in his baggage, a load of goods worth millions.

Grandfather married Helen and she had bundles of personal things to bring with her to America, so it wasn't hard for him to hide the stuff, and he returned with the goods for the mob.

Through the years he had connections with a jeweler in Richmond where he would take pieces of the goods, only in small amounts, when the jeweler requested it. I was told that getting one or two items gave the jeweler and the banker ability to hide the transactions. Often, depending on the value, Grandfather would get paid and that helped him to support many causes in Opal at the time. After he died, the job was left to my father, Donald Junior, and now to me.

I must say that through the years I have met with mob bosses, meeting their requirements. Specifically, one was Marco in the bank and Bruno in the Jewelry store on Main Avenue. They have died, but Bruno had a son named Romano, and recently I have found he is deceased as well. I believe there may be cousins; however, I doubt they know anything about this.

Tomorrow I am getting rid of what is left. I am not going to leave this problem for another heir. I must tell you, my Grandfather never wanted to say what he smuggled out of England but often explained what the items were when he said there were diamonds in the river, he was also referring to the stolen sparkly diamonds he had at Rivers Run.

I don't think my grandmother ever knew there was an extra meaning when he described the diamonds in the water to her, and I believe she was totally unaware of his transgressions.

After my actions at the river tomorrow, if an heir is found, they can truly say there are diamonds in the water, and no one will ever be the wiser about what grandfather had to do for those evil people to save his land.

I am shocked, and I can look around and see the other faces must be still trying to understand what the family of Rivers had to deal with all those years. It is appalling. My great-grandfather, Donald Andrew Rivers Senior, left a strange legacy for his son and grandson, and the knowledge of it has left me speechless at the moment too.

I looked at Amy and she is shaking her head back and forth. The others start talking at the same time and saying how terrible it had to be for each of the sons, especially trying to keep the information from getting out.

After considerable time to digest the awful facts, all of us decide it is a time to celebrate the fact that we found what we were looking for in regard to the heirs, and we hug each other with joy and relief about everything in the past.

Bill says, "Jenny, I will keep the letter in our official papers and if someone makes a claim about being an heir we will have it for proof."

Bill scratches his head, "I'm thinking that this is the reason I was told in my dream that the ballroom should be painted—just so we could find the letter."

I feel very good that we now have something that will take the pressure off of us regarding the inheritance. Bill assures us that from now on when each of us say goodnight we can be confident there will be no more dreams, and that night it happened to be true.

CHAPTER THIRTY-FOUR

One night the following week, Roger calls to say hello and tells me he has been very busy. I wait for Roger to ask me to dinner but he says, "Jenny, I have to run. I'll call you sometime."

I get a strange feeling about him. He has been very absent lately, but then I've been busy and haven't been available for him either.

That night, with a good feeling that I can sleep without any dreams disturbing me, I go off to sleep quickly…

I suddenly see a light and I'm in the parlor with an old John Rivers and a woman who looks like a servant. She tells him there is a man by the name of William Jones to see him.

John says, "Show him in, Martha."

The man comes in and shakes hands with John. He says, "Sir, I'm from England, touring places in the U.S. and am staying in Richmond for several days."

"Why come here? We don't give tours."

"Well, when I was growing up, Rivers Run was constantly talked about in my home town of Weymouth because of a bracelet."

John tells William to sit down and enjoy tea with him. He says, "Why do you think Rivers Run was mentioned?"

"All I know is my father told me that my great-grandfather was in a war in Southern England many years ago and came back with stories about people who died. He had a bracelet that apparently had belonged to a nurse that had been killed in the war. The bracelet was damaged and only the name of Rivers Run showed up on it. He said that after the war there was a woman that lived in our town for a while. He said she did not remember anything—not even her name."

William sips his tea and says, "My great-grandfather had the opportunity to show her the bracelet one day, and she started crying and holding it to her chest, so he gave it to her. He asked her if it was hers and she said no, but it made her cry and she didn't know why."

John says, "Well, what happened to her?"

"She apparently left the town with a man who had befriended her, and great-grandfather never saw her again, but he did say he read an article later about the nurses who had died and where they were from—and found that one of them from America was from an estate called Rivers Run in Virginia."

John Rivers gasps and seems distressed, and walks back and forth. He is wiping his eyes.

"Well, thank you, William. You must stay for dinner, enjoy my hospitality and tell me more." The two of them walk out of the parlor and I try to walk with them...

I awaken in shock. I sit straight up in bed... The dream has told me about the bracelet that Kathleen wore when she left for her assignment. I get up, open my drapes, look out at the view that is lit with the bright moon, and pace back and forth, the details of the dream swirling in my mind. The moon is shining over the hills in the distance and the sky is very bright, changing my shadows on the floor, as I walk back and forth with remorse. Later I doze off in my lounge chair.

The next morning I try to remember my dream.

The man's name was William Jones from a town called Weymouth in England. He said the name "Rivers Run" had been mentioned by his great-grandfather and apparently there had been a woman to whom he gave the bracelet because she had cried when she saw it. Could it have been Kathleen, or maybe someone who had known her?

At breakfast I tell about my dream and everyone is amazed that I had a dream. Bill and George slept very well.

I guess I just have all that stuff about Kathleen still on my mind.

George says, "Do you think it could be Kathleen's bracelet? They never sent anything back of hers."

I explain, "In that dream William said the bracelet was damaged and only the name of 'Rivers Run' was on it. It had to be Kathleen's. I wonder if William Jones is still living in that town."

Amy says, "I think you should forget these dreams. Everyone has dreams of one type or another. Sometimes I have dreams with strange people in them but I don't sit and think about what they mean all the time—it's just ridiculous to try and make sense of them."

I don't comment—maybe she is right.

The subject is dropped.

Amy continues to date Allen, Ward, and George, but I can see Ward is getting anxious about her actions. He is not visiting the gift shop as often and seems to be getting the message from Amy.

Roger finally calls me one Sunday to go with him for the day, and we visit a museum in Richmond. I happen to see a few relics of old things from the old town of Opal. There are pictures of Rivers Run, and one picture in particular stands out as I recognize several people. They are Kathleen, Donald Junior, Helen, and Donald Senior, sitting on the porch, dressed in fine clothes, surrounded by guests of all ages. I can see in the photograph that the windows of the manor house were all open and rose bushes were blooming around the house.

The caption on the picture says it is Kathleen Rivers' tenth birthday, and I remember I was there with Kathleen before the party. She was putting on a very frilly white dress and she wanted me to dress up too. With Kathleen's help I tried to get into a pretty pink dress with ruffles but it would just fall to the floor and I was left with my shabby attire, a gray uniform dress I wore in the orphanage. Kathleen was very upset about it and so was I. Kathleen cried, and said I couldn't be in the picture if I couldn't change my clothes—that's when I woke up. I believe that is the last time I joined them in a dream.

I tell Roger about it as I continue to stare at the members of the first family and point them out to him. He makes a face at me and says, "You should forget about those dreams."

That's when I realize that I can't forget because they have been a big part of my life. I vow not to say any more to him about them. I definitely don't tell him about the letter we found from John Rivers. I think it is something I can't reveal to anyone else but the family. At that moment I wonder about my feelings for Roger. He seems to have changed, but maybe he wants to protect me from all that.

That night when I get back from Richmond it's late and the house is quiet. I guess everyone has retired for the night. I go to the big parlor with Boots and sit looking at the picture of Helen for a long time.

I say, "Helen, I'm here for a reason I know. There is something you want me to know, and I want to know what it is." I stare up at the beautiful lady and her two lovely children. It's very quiet in the house and my eyes are very tired...

Instantly I am with a woman about my age that looks like me—it must be Kathleen. She is running to get on a dirty brown truck with a brownish covering over the top and I run along. She holds her hand out for someone to help her up into the back of the truck as it moves forward. I hear loud noises like gunfire and explosions all around us and it is terrifying. Another lady is trying desperately to pull her into the vehicle but a bracelet slips off Kathleen's hand and she is left in the muddy road watching the truck advance slowly with the other lady holding her bracelet.

I hear more noises and another explosion. Suddenly Kathleen falls to the ground, hitting her head on a large rock, and rolls off the road into the bushes. She's there in the ditch covered with leaves and sticks with a deep wound on her face and head and she's bleeding. I hear myself yelling loudly for her to get up and it wakes me...

Boots jumps down, looks at me and turns her head to the side as if to say, "What's wrong." I sit there astonished and frightened from the excitement and terror that I have just experienced!

That was Kathleen in a battle, and I was there with her! She doesn't make it onto the truck, but her bracelet is pulled off. Is that what happened to her? That must be what Helen is trying to tell me!

Then I remember the other dream with William. He told about a bracelet his great-grandfather had found, but gave away. Did he find it in the debris from the exploded truck? If so, it was Kathleen's!

I stare up at the painting again and think about that scenario.

The next morning I am very quiet at the table. The dream is racing through my brain again.

I'm visualizing Kathleen trying to get onto the truck. I have the story that was in the news about the incident where the truck exploded, killing all on the truck—but what if the dream is correct and she didn't get on!

Then I remember that William said the woman in Weymouth did not know who she was. Was it Kathleen? Did she live from her fall into the bushes? Where did she go after she took the bracelet from William's great-grandfather? What if Kathleen lived and had children? Could there be heirs in England? I want to know more! The others are talking so I decide not to tell them. It always seems to upset them to hear about the dreams. I think they are convinced there will not be any more.

I start listening to what is being said, and they are talking about the tours that are going to be given in the house. Their plan is to allow the tours only certain times of the day on a few days a week. They think Ward might be able to do a good job as the Rivers Run Tour Guide, and Bill decides to ask him. He thinks it will be a good way for Ward to also sell his books. Bill says if Ward will agree to do it, he will do the tours when Ward isn't available. He will put a sign in the gift shop about the tours.

That day in the shop I walk around very upset and in a daze, still thinking about the dream and Kathleen. How can I prove what happened, and that Kathleen may have lived? I decide to drop it for now unless I hear of more dreams from the other members of the family.

Months go by with everything going well except for Roger and me. The gift shop has been taking my time so I really haven't thought much about it, but one day I realize that his absence is unusual. Maybe something has happened to his family and I decide to call him on my break for lunch.

His father answers the phone and tells me Roger has gone to Richmond. I tell Larry that I just wondered if things were going according to plans with the sale of the property.

Larry says, "Well, Jenny, we go to settlement soon, and Bill Waller will be notified."

"That's good, Larry. I'm very glad for you. Tell Roger to call me when he returns."

Larry clears his throat and says, "Jenny, ah—Roger's old girlfriend, Tammy, has been keeping him occupied. He met her in college, you know. I'll have him call you when he returns but it might be late."

This is rather earthshaking to me.

"Oh thanks, Larry. I'll call Roger tomorrow." Then I hang up the phone abruptly.

I sit there and visualize Roger with a girl named Tammy. He has never mentioned her in all the times we have been together, and it suddenly dawns on me that since I haven't been the major owner of Rivers Run, he has acted indifferent about my dreams and problems. Then I remember Miss Brewster from the county orphanage program telling me to be vigilant about people taking advantage of my sudden wealth.

Could Roger have been using that to his advantage—and then I think about the rental properties being turned over to the farmers because of my conversations with Roger. Actually, I think that has been a good decision for everyone though.

What else was he up to that didn't pan out for him? Could it have been ownership of Rivers Run when he thought I was the only owner? Maybe George was right about his character.

CHAPTER THIRTY-FIVE

After my talk with Roger's father, Amy finds me wiping my eyes after a flash flood of tears. "Oh, Amy, I think I just needed a good cry."

"Well, you can't fool me. I've noticed that Roger hasn't been calling. What's up with that?"

"Amy, he has a girlfriend from college in his life again. His father just told me he's in Richmond with her. I have a feeling that my ownership of Rivers Run was attracting him, until he found out I was no longer the sole owner."

Amy pats me on the back. "That may not be true—give him a chance, but let him be the one to call you and explain. That way you'll know what he's up to with this girl. In the meantime keep busy and see what happens. You know what I say though, you might be happier with the one who will come along next," she laughs, and it makes me laugh too.

Amy's comments have reminded me that things happen for the best. I dry my eyes and fix my face. "Okay, Amy. Let's go take care of the shop with Allen and George."

Back in the shop, Gracie brings trays of several kinds of cookies to sell to customers that she and Bessie have prepared. She sets them on one of the counters and Amy thanks her for them.

Their bakery goods have been selling very well, and I have noticed that Amy is being generous, paying Bessie half of the money from them.

Gracie says, "Jenny, Thanksgiving is next week and Bill and I want to have a nice dinner party again like last year. Are you and Amy up for that?"

Amy and I think it is a great idea.

The next day I want to call Roger but I don't, and he doesn't call me. I am sure his father told him I called, so I have made up my mind to just close that door in my life with something like "good riddance," even though I still care.

Thanksgiving goes very well, just like before. We invite all the farmers and their children and we begin to celebrate joyously. Most of the children come, even Roger, and I am surprised to see him.

Roger approaches me as I am talking to George about the trays of food and where to put them.

He says, "Good evening, Jenny. It's been a while—how are you?"

I turn from George and look at him. "Hi, Roger. I've been very busy and I guess you have too."

"Yes, I have. Dad has settled on the property and we are planning to build. It is very exciting, but there's hard work involved. We are trying to get Mike, your builder, to agree to work with us on dad's house."

I say, "Mike is very good. He did a great job on the manor house and the gift shop." Then George offers him a glass of wine and I go toward Bessie to help her with several trays of appetizers.

When the buffet dinner is ready I say a prayer of thanksgiving and everyone begins to enjoy the meal. George and I sit with Amy and Ward. I notice Roger sits with his family. Allen is busy in Richmond at an Art Gallery that is giving him an exhibit of his paintings the next day, and is not able to be with us.

As the families leave, Roger starts to leave with his parents but turns to me and says, "I'll call you, Jenny."

I respond with a wave as he goes out the door.

Well, you got the property you wanted, but I'm not up for grabs and neither is Rivers Run.

When Gracie and Bill join Amy, Ward, George, and I in the parlor after the company leaves, we sit and relax. Jessie and Bessie come in serving glasses of liqueur, and Bill invites them to relax with us. The day has been busy for all of us and it is very nice to have the fireplace lit and friends around.

Amy says, "I noticed Roger was a bit quiet around us tonight."

I do the best I can and give her a grin that has disgust in it.

George, sitting next to me, puts his arm around my shoulder and doesn't say anything.

I say, "What's done is done," and lift my glass as in a toast.

The conversation turns to things at Rivers Run and how we have progressed with plans. The place looks very stately and rooms have all been refurbished. It is very rewarding as they talk about our accomplishments. I just lean back on the beautiful, new, tan sectional sofa and soft, bright-colored pillows, thinking of Kathleen and my dreams with her.

The days leading up to Christmas bring happy memories of my time with Roger. I'll always have those moments and feel good about them. As for George, I see him making progress with Amy and think I have finally convinced him that he is a close relative.

Life at the manor house is busy these days, especially for me. Between working in the gift shop and getting together to plan things with Gracie, Bill, and George, I am exhausted, and look forward to nights in my room alone.

It's Saturday night and Amy has gone out with George. I find myself sitting in my lounge chair by the window even after the sun has disappeared. I have had my dinner delivered to my room and it sits there on a cart, but I don't feel like eating. My thoughts of this Christmas and the New Year's Eve party give me too many past memories. I really don't feel like participating in all of that this year. I close my eyes and think about John Rivers and his love for Lia. I am sure he was heartbroken...

When I open my eyes I'm with John Rivers. He is holding his head in his hands.

He must be talking to himself because I don't see anyone around him.

He says, "Kathleen, what happened to you? William Jones talked about a woman his great-grandfather had seen in his town after the battle in England. The lady couldn't remember anything, was that you?"

Then he rubs his eyes. "Kathleen, where did you go? Why didn't someone bring you home? It's been so many years—how can I find out what happened over there now? I need to contact the people who might know if you had children. Maybe I should send someone over to the little town of Weymouth, England."

Then he rubs his face again and looks up as if in doubt. "My life is ending and I have no time—what am I thinking?"

A strong wind outside shakes the shutters on the windows and the dream fades as I sit there half awake thinking about what I saw...

John Rivers had the same questions about Kathleen as I do, and he said exactly what I'm thinking. Did Kathleen live, and did she have children? John Rivers, being very old, questioned if he had time to find out anything about Kathleen in England.

I quickly eat my cold supper and go to bed. I try to sleep but all the details in the dreams seem to jell together and I can't fall asleep. I decide to go down to the library and get a book to read. When I get there I look all through the romance novels but no title interests me.

Wishing I had put on my soft, warm slippers instead of just my thin socks, I sit at the desk. This desk is one piece of furniture that we kept when we renovated the library because I thought it looked sturdy and something to keep that was used by my ancestors.

When I look down at my socks I see what looks like a long mark in the wood on the desk near my feet. I rub across the scratch with my foot, and the wood seems to move. I discover it is not a scratch but a definite line in the wood.

I get down on my knees and exam it closer. It takes some effort but finally a panel slides across, leaving an opening. There appears to be something stuffed in the enclosure. I pull the object toward me and it comes out.

It's a cloth bag! I carefully put it on my lap and feel small bulges like marbles in the bottom of it, and suddenly I suspect what they are! I untie the drawstring from around the neck of the bag. I reach in and bring out two glistening round uncut diamonds, and hold them in my hand, thinking that there must be at least fifteen more in this bag! They look uncut but still beautiful, and I realize that is probably why the jeweler was involved, in order to prepare the diamonds making them available for sale in his store.

I thought John Rivers was going to toss them into the river—he said he would in his letter!

I sit there stunned, and look around to make sure I'm alone.

John Rivers must have died before he could get rid of them! If I tell the others that I found them, there is bound to be someone greedy enough to want to sell the diamonds—George perhaps—and that would not be good. If the story ever was revealed that the senior Donald Andrew Rivers was involved with the smuggling of these out of England, Rivers Run would never live it down and others in the family, even me, could be blamed for keeping them and possibly prosecuted for this crime!

It dawns on me that everyone here thinks, from the letter we found, that John Matthew Rivers threw the diamonds into the river. Another stunning thing comes to mind, making me tremble—now it is up to me to get rid of them once and for all—but how, and when? I always have someone around me, especially George!

I carefully slide shut the opening in the desk and close the bag. My robe has a large pocket and I tie the bag and stuff it down into that pocket. I go upstairs to my room, being thankful that no one has interrupted my return from the library, and I am relieved when I close my door and lock it.

The only place I think will be a safe place for the diamonds, at the moment, is under my mattress tonight. Boots wakes up and looks at me, as I lift the mattress and push the bag toward the middle. I sit down on the bed remembering my dream when Kathleen and I, as children, disturbed her father in the library.

The bag I have stuffed under my mattress looks identical to the one he tried to hide from us. Once again it's clear—those dreams were real!

I'm exhausted from the stress and turn off the light.

I will worry about all this in the morning…

When I awaken it only takes me a second and I'm right back into my alarming experience from last night.

What am I going to do with these diamonds? When will I be able to toss them and let the river claim them, just as John Matthew planned to do?

I get dressed and go down for breakfast and find out from Bessie that Amy has had breakfast and left with Ward for the day to attend a birthday party with his family for his eighty-year-old great aunt.

I realize that Amy didn't tell me but then she is not including me in many things anymore.

No one else is having breakfast but me, and Bessie says that the Waller's have gone to a special Sunday breakfast at church.

I sigh and finish my breakfast quickly, knowing what must be done before anyone gets back.

From that moment on I have a plan and begin to feel joy that comes from a final decision, as I put on my winter coat, hiding the bag of diamonds in a large woolen tunic pocket underneath.

I tell Bessie that I'm going for a walk with Boots.

I know it will be a long walk because I plan on going beyond the stable down to the river that flows from the high banks of the property into a larger, deeper body of water.

I feel the diamonds nestled in the tunic pocket under my coat. It will be a good feeling to finally dispose of these and shed the problem that has haunted this household for many years. I know it will give me a feeling of peace and freedom.

CHAPTER THIRTY-SIX

With the diamonds hidden securely beneath my winter coat, I go out the door and down the walkway, with my obligation clearly in my thoughts. I'm thinking about the long walk to the water when I hear someone calling me.

"Jenny, what are you doing out here so early?"

I turn around, annoyed. "George, I thought you went to church with your mom and dad."

"Oh, you know me by now." Then he laughs. "I had breakfast, but I can't be bothered with those old people. There is nothing there in that church for me, and God knows I would rather be here."

I put my hand on the small bulge under my coat.

Now all I want to do is go back to the house and hide these things. I guess I'll have to get rid of them another time.

"George, I just wanted a breath of air. It seemed stuffy in the house." Then I walk toward the back, planning to go into the kitchen.

He walks along with me and says, "Well I'm glad to meet up with you. I had a dream last night about Kathleen, and I believe she lived through that war. If she did, I don't think she ever wanted to come back here. I never tell anyone but I've had more dreams, so there must be more heirs. What do you think?"

"George, I honestly don't know. Perhaps Kathleen did live through the war, but I don't think we will ever know for sure, and we just have to go on and let it be. If she did live and got her memory back, don't you think she would have come home?"

He shakes his head and says, "You're probably right. I suppose the ancestors just want me to know what happened in their lives, but I wish they would be satisfied about the heirs and rest in peace—and let me

211

rest too." ~~He laughs to himself and says, "At least we now know~~ that John Rivers had no heirs from his lady friends."

I turn to go back inside through the kitchen, hoping George will stay outdoors so I can put these diamonds back.

"Jenny, what do you think about that smuggling deal that Donald Senior made with someone back in 1867? It's sure interesting about the diamonds. I'm sorry that John Rivers threw them in the river—it would be wonderful to have them!"

Now I know I have to get rid of them—George would want to keep them and things will get ugly for sure if they are traced back to Rivers Run. I'll just have to keep this secret until I can dispose of them!

I hurry into the kitchen and meet Bessie, but George is close behind. I say, "Oh Bessie, now I need another cup of coffee. It's very chilly out there. I'm going to my room but I'll be back in a minute. Just put the coffee in the small parlor and I'll return shortly."

George says, "Jenny, I'll have coffee and I'll wait for you."

I feel lucky he's not following as I hurry upstairs. Boots is getting fed, so she doesn't come along.

When I get to my room I lock the door. I really don't want to leave the diamonds under the mattress because Bessie may decide to wash the sheets and discover them.

I look around for a place for them where they won't be discovered if Bessie cleans the room. I sit down on the cedar chest and it gives me an answer—*this will be a good place for a while.*

Under the quilts in the chest I find the satin box from the attic that I left there. It has the diary from Helen and all her mementos. I quickly place the bag of diamonds in the box, flatten the bag as much as possible, and cover it with those embroidered handkerchiefs and trinkets. I no sooner close the chest and someone is knocking on my door.

"Hey, Jenny, I thought we could sit in your room and have our coffee, so I brought the coffee up here. I love your view."

"Just a minute, George," and I cover the cedar chest with the silken material that adorns it, and open the door. He comes in with Boots following.

For a good hour we sit by the windows and discuss our dreams and how George is trying to feel comfortable in the manor house. He also discusses his new feelings for Amy, and I tell him that I'm glad.

I sit back in my lounge chair and breathe a sigh of relief for the moment, but there is still stress with those diamonds so close to us in the chest.

The weeks before the holidays keep everyone busy with the decorations for Christmas, and plans for the New Year's Eve Party. With everyone scurrying around and the other things I have to do to decorate the gift shop, I have no time to worry about the diamonds. I think they are in a safe place for now.

George seems to be right behind me every time I turn around and it makes me crazy. He always has a dream or something to discuss with me, and I try to find reasons to go in an opposite direction or make some excuse to get away from him.

The gift shop is doing tremendously well. Amy ordered many Christmas-type gifts that go off the shelves quickly. It's a busy time and often we have to ask Gracie to give us a few hours of her time to keep up with the customers. The farmers' wives have brought jars of peach, grape, and blackberry jams for sale and those items have been very popular. They are even decorated with red and green ribbons.

More people have come for the tours of the house since we have decorated. Bill and Jessie cut more trees from the woods and decorate them with painted pinecones and lights, putting them in all the rooms. The entrance, large parlor, the ballroom, and dining room look especially lovely.

Each night, after dinner, we all usually gather in the big parlor to rest and discuss the holiday excitement that has brought people to the gift shop and for the manor house tours.

I will be glad when January comes and all of us get back to a normal life, so I can concentrate on my obligation that is waiting for me in the cedar chest.

Christmas is finally here and the household is quiet as everyone meets for breakfast and gathers in the big parlor to open presents. Allen has come over this year to spend time on Christmas Eve. Amy says Ward has met another history buff in Richmond by the name of Sally and has plans with her for Christmas. George and Allen are friends and both are working with Amy in the gift shop. Amy is amazing the way she handles herself, and I just enjoy how she copes with her admirers.

I get a call from Roger to wish me a very Merry Christmas, but other than that he stammers about how I am and how things are going here. He tells me that the building of the house on the property is coming along better than expected and his mom and dad are very happy. He thanks me again for my actions to make this possible for them.

I wish him a Merry Christmas as well, and the conversation ends there in a rather awkward way. It's like neither of us have anything to say to each other anymore. I would have liked an invitation to go and see the house they are building—but it never happened.

After the call I don't feel much like continuing my Christmas celebration. I sit in the corner watching the others enjoy their wassail punch and talk about their gifts. I receive many lovely presents but it almost makes me feel out of place like I did as an orphan. I eventually perk up as we share the joy of the birth of a Savior and sing Christmas recordings from the old record player.

New Year's Eve comes quickly and the preparations have been stressful but also fun. The guests that came last year have been invited again and many of them have arrived and are having a great time. Amy is busy with Allen when Ward arrives with his date.

Ward introduces her as Sally Burch. She is a lovely woman, a bit heavier than Amy, about his age, with a beautiful smile and long dark brown hair that hangs in curls, swept back from her face. She is wearing a gorgeous gown of light green silk.

This year Amy and I decided to wear evening gowns. Mine is dark blue satin with lace trim that has sequins around the low neck and waist. Amy looks lovely in a formfitting, red satin gown that has a low neckline and a lacy stiff collar that stands up around her neck.

I see Amy go over to greet Ward and Sally with a nice smile. She ushers them over to her table where Allen is sitting and it looks like all is well with the four of them together.

I have been busy greeting the guests. There is much talk about how successful the gift store has been and many have great things to say about the manor house and the tours. I am very pleased that all is well.

So much has changed for me since last year and I reflect on those changes as I stand there with Bill, Gracie, and George as more people arrive. I was the sole heir last year and looked forward to all the new things that were going to happen in the years to come. Life has its changes and people must adjust. I have done some major adjusting that's for sure.

Most of the guests have arrived when George and I have a drink from the Champagne fountain. While making small talk, I see Larry and Marsha Jackson arrive. Behind them is Roger, looking very sharp in a nice dark blue suit. He is looking around as he greets Gracie and Bill, and suddenly I catch his eye. He begins to walk over to my side of the room and meets Amy in the middle of the dance floor. She says something to him and he shakes his head in an agreeable way, smiles, and continues over to the band, talking to the leader before walking to George and me.

"The Pop-tops" start to play a slow ballad and Roger comes close, holds out his hand, and says, "Jenny, would you like to dance?"

I take his hand and we go out to the dance floor. He doesn't say anything as we dance to the music, but he is holding me very close and says, "Jenny, I've missed you. How are you doing with all the changes here?"

"I'm okay, Roger."

"I guess George is taking over your time now."

"Not really." Thinking of the dreams, I say, "He and I do have something in common these days."

He looks down at me and says, "Yes, I thought so."

I look up into his gorgeous eyes. "How are you and Tammy doing?"

"She's fine. It was nice seeing her again. She's working on her doctorate now and is very busy with her studies. She will be a very accomplished woman."

"Oh, that's nice."

How will I compete with her, I have only a high school education and a certificate for passing college preparatory classes in night school.

The music stops but Roger continues slowly dancing with me until the band starts another song.

It's one I remember from last New Year's Eve—"True Love."

He says, "Jenny, this is one I requested." He loosens his grip on my back and looks down into my eyes. "It reminds me of our time together last year. I have thought of you so much lately. I know you have been distracted with things besides me—and I have been temporarily distracted as well, but I hope…" We dance close and his lips touch my face with a kiss.

I remember the days when I wanted him to call…and he was with Tammy.

"It's okay, Roger. I understand we both have different lives and different goals now. I realize you have other ideas for your future. Besides that, I'm not the sole heir anymore. Time goes by and things change you know."

He doesn't comment.

When the song is over he hugs me before taking me back to where George stands and says, "Thank you, Jenny."

I watch him go over to his mother at the Champagne fountain.

I think it is strange. He seems like his old self, holding me close and kissing my cheek during the dancing. Is he like Amy—happy with two loves in his life, or what?

CHAPTER THIRTY-SEVEN

George dances with me several times, but especially with Alice Bogart, Tim and Barbara's daughter, and she seems to enjoy his company. I'm really happy about that and also his interest in Amy.

I dance with Roger again several times through the night, but he doesn't say very much, holding me close as if he enjoys the moments.

I also dance with Joe Hoffman, the son of Jeff and Betsy. He is very handsome and I've noticed he has been watching me several times during the night, finally asking me to dance. He has a great dance step and talks about how nice I look. He is tall with dark hair and blue eyes, a lovely smile, and is fun to be around, making me laugh about little things that are happening on the dance floor, especially couples getting together, like Lydia Bogart and his brother, Jeff.

Joe laughs about how the two of them use to run through the cornfields together. He tells me that Jeff, working and living in Richmond, is a problem for them, but he thinks they may challenge that obstacle when Lydia gets out of college. We laugh about that possibility.

When it's time for the last dance before the clock strikes Midnight, Roger starts walking toward me but I notice Joe starting my way as well.

Right now it's strange but I don't care which one gets here first.

Roger is faster and takes my hand and we walk to the dance floor. As Roger looks into my eyes and holds me close there is no way my heart can go in a different direction. The song, "Feelings," is playing, and at the moment it is appropriate.

The "Pop-tops" start calling out the minutes and when it's Midnight Roger kisses me, and it's as I remember. We are as one, overwhelmed with emotion. He says, "I love you, Jenny," and we kiss again before turning to leave the dance floor.

I am completely without words. I don't understand what has kept him away these last months.

There is joy in the place as the guests go around kissing and hugging each other and the band plays on with "Auld Lang Syne." Suddenly I am jerked away from Roger by George who kisses and hugs me intensely, turning from me to continue greeting others similarly. I turn around and am hugged and kissed by Joe Hoffman and then several others. When I'm free from the kissing crowd, I am near the band. I look for Roger and see him putting on his coat and going out the door with his mother and father. By the time I reach the ballroom door, they are walking down the hall to the front door.

There are several people at the ballroom door saying goodbye and thanking us for the party. Then Barbara Bogart stops me and is talking about how many things she has sold in the gift shop for Christmas on consignment and goes on about the opportunities there. I thank her for all she has contributed, especially her time. When I get a chance to look down the hall again, Roger has left.

Others are leaving now and I get caught up in all of the goodbyes. My feelings for Roger have never changed, and he said that he loved me.

Why didn't he stay until we had some private moments together? I wanted to hear him say more about how he felt about Tammy.

When the festivities are over and stillness engulfs the house, Bill, Gracie and George invite Amy, Allen, and me to join them in the parlor with Jessie and Bessie.

Bill says, "Well, that was wonderful. I hope all of you enjoyed it too."

We all agree that everything was marvelous and worth all the hard work.

Bill opens a bottle of expensive wine he bought and we toast to the New Year's happiness and blessings at Rivers Run and to future parties.

George follows me to my room to end the night, and I say, "Goodnight, George. I'll see you in the morning perhaps."

He says, "Is Roger going to call you tomorrow?"

"I'm not sure, why?"

"Just wondering. I saw you on the dance floor with him."

I just glance at him and say, "Goodnight, George."

When I enter my room I close and lock my door and walk over to the bed. Boots changes her position on the bed and curls up comfortably. She has been taken care of by Jessie for the night, and I sit and pet her, thinking about how she comforts me at times like this.

I think about what happened. Roger seemed close with me, then all of a sudden he left, and without saying goodbye!

I look over at the cedar chest and that problem comes to the surface again, causing me to realize that I have other things to think about besides Roger and Tammy.

I dress for bed and soon all those things are left for another day.

The next morning when I go down for breakfast George is still asleep and everyone else has had breakfast but me.

Since the gift shop will be closed today, Allen and Amy are out there cleaning and getting things back in shape from all the crowds that the holidays brought. Bill and Gracie are in the big parlor watching television.

I know I don't have a chance to do anything today with the diamonds, so I just relax and take my time enjoying my meal while Jessie takes care of Boots. I take another cup of coffee into the parlor where Bill and Gracie are watching the news.

Gracie says, "I thought Roger looked very nice last night and you two looked wonderful together."

I say, "Yes, he did look nice, Gracie."

Then she looks at me and says, "I noticed you didn't go to say goodbye when he left. Is something wrong?"

I sigh, "Gracie, he has another girlfriend, I think. Her name is Tammy."

She gets a funny expression on her face and says, "Well, when I talked to Marsha about you two, she said just the opposite. She said that Tammy is just a good friend he has known for years but they never got serious."

I just shake my head and say, "Well, he was the one who left me on the dance floor and left for the night without saying goodbye. I just think he is mixed up and doesn't know what he wants."

Bill says, "Just give him time—he'll come running back," and he laughs.

Just then on television there is news about the new owner in Richmond at Romano's Restaurant. It makes me sit up and listen. His name is Russ DeLuca. I also wonder if he'll find out about the agreement that was made with Donald Rivers Senior. I can see by the concerned look on Bill's face that he noticed as well.

Bill says, "Jenny, I'm sure glad those diamonds were thrown away. If the Italians are back in town, we don't need that problem again. We do have the letter, though, from John Matthew, if anything needs proving."

I say, "Bill, that was so long ago. I would think there is no record of it."

Bill pats Gracie's hand. "I hope you're right."

The next week in the shop requires less work because business has slacked off. We make notes of what needs to be ordered to replace the things that were popular. Allen is working on more paintings, since his successful gallery reception in Richmond. Between the gift shop and the gallery sales, he has become very popular.

One day while I'm in the shop without Amy, I notice three men, in black suits, come into the gift shop. They are new to me but perhaps Amy would have seen them before.

Right away I don't get good feelings about these men.

I'm behind the counter and I notice one of them is a rather tall, broad shouldered man with dark hair and dark eyes. He comes over, his mouth busy chewing gum, and says, "This is nice in here. Who is the owner?"

I say, "Well, it is the River's Run Gift Shop, and Mr. and Mrs. Waller own Rivers Run. May I help you? We have some wonderful gifts, some are provided by the farmers on consignment and are very well made."

"Actually I would like to talk with Mr. Waller."

I'm noticing the other two picking up little things from off the shelves and examining them. Turning them over and over.

"May I say who you are, Sir?"

"Just say Russ DeLuca from Richmond. I'm a cousin of Romano DeLuca who recently passed. His father, Bruno DeLuca, was very familiar with Rivers Run and the late John Rivers. Bruno was a jeweler in Richmond."

I suddenly remember the name, Russ DeLuca, from the television news....

Just then Amy comes into the shop. She looks surprised when I introduce her to Russ DeLuca. I quickly tell her what he explained to me, and that Russ wants to speak to the owner, Mr. Waller.

Amy is quick on her feet, and very calmly with no outward looks of distress says, "I'm sorry but Mr. Waller is not available to speak to anyone today. I will leave him a note and he will call you later. What is your telephone number?"

Russ looks at Amy with his eyes squinted, pulls out a notebook, writes something on a page, tears it out, and gives it to Amy. Without another word the three men walk out of the shop.

Amy gives me the note, shaking her head with a look of concern. It has his name, phone number, and a note that says "Very Important." I take it to Bill right away.

Bill is in the kitchen with Gracie and Bessie. I get his attention and ask him to come to the parlor with me. There, I tell him about the three men who approached me in the gift shop. I hand him the note, telling him that Russ DeLuca said he is the cousin of Romano DeLuca, a restaurant owner in Richmond, who has passed. I also mention that Romano was the son of Bruno, the jeweler in Richmond.

When I explain about that to Bill, he says, "Jenny, what can we do? If he questions me about the deal that was made in 1897, all I can really do is tell him I know nothing about it. I am just a new owner. He doesn't need to know I am an heir. What do you think? Will that be enough for him?"

"It's worth a try. Really that is all we know anyway, except for the information we have from the dreams and John Matthew Rivers' letter."

Bill tucks the phone number in his pocket. "Jenny, I'll call him tomorrow and give it a try. I guess I'll find out what he knows about this, and if he tries to explain the situation, I'll definitely try to get the message across that I don't know anything about it."

That night I put this problem in my prayers and pray for a chance to get rid of the diamonds so that Donald Rivers Senior, Rivers Run, and now Bill, will never be connected to that fiasco in any way.

The next evening when the household is sitting around the fireplace watching television, Bill says, "Well, I called Mr. Russ DeLuca today."

I look around when George shuts off the television and we all stare at Bill for more explanation. George knows nothing about the visit by Russ DeLuca, and I take a minute to explain.

Bill takes a sip of his drink and says, "When I called him, he wanted to know how I was handling the deal that was made years ago. I told him I did not know what deal he was referring to. He did know, apparently from the newspapers, that I was an heir, so I did not deny that."

Bill shakes his head back and forth. "At first, Russ didn't seem to believe me that I knew nothing about the deal; however, I went on about the timeframe he was talking about and I was totally unaware of anything that had been going on before I was born. I said if there was something that bothered him, he should go to the police or a lawyer about it as soon as possible."

I say, "Bill, I think that was handled very well. I hope Mr. DeLuca was satisfied."

Bill rubs his chin. "I think he was, because he thanked me and we hung up; however, it was all I could think to say at the time. To me, it has been too long to matter now!" Bill slams his hand down on his leg, signifying closure.

After that show of determination from Bill, the room takes on a different atmosphere, everyone settling down.

I breathe a sigh of relief, but as we watch a comedy, I realize Bill's handling of the situation has only brought me stress and a new obsession—the disposal of the diamonds!

Weeks go by but I have no chance to eliminate the problem that is tucked away in my cedar chest. The house is too full of people and it has given me no time to go out on my own to the river.

With no more visits from Russ DeLuca, I assume he is satisfied with Bill's explanation and it is settled. I am very thankful that we have not had to deal with this problem any further. The newspaper stories tell me that many of the problems with the Italian mobs have been eliminated, and I understand many of those people have been under police surveillance and prosecuted. This is music to my ears and I try to relax over the deal made with them by Donald Senior so long ago.

CHAPTER THIRTY-EIGHT

One night in early March around 11:00 o'clock I'm in bed thinking about the diamonds, and how and when I will be able to dispose of them. My eyes are very heavy and I doze off several times, but then I get up and look outside my window. The moon is very bright and I can see into the property very well.

Perhaps I can do it now while everyone is asleep.

I put on some warm clothes, get the diamonds, tucking the bag into the large pocket of my winter coat, open my door and listen for anyone who might be up. I look at Boots who is still asleep on the bed. I don't hear anything in the house, close my door, and go down the stairs. At the back door I take a last look around and step out into the strong wind.

I continue down the walkway, getting almost to the grass next to the stables when I hear the kitchen door open behind me. I turn around in despair—I must have alerted someone in the house.

I dread looking to see whom I have to lie to about being out tonight. What if it's George? What am I going to say?

"Jenny?"

Thank heavens it's Bill!

"Oh, Bill, I'm sorry if I woke you. I couldn't sleep and decided it was a beautiful night with the moon so bright and wanted to take a walk."

"Can I walk with you, Jenny? I can't sleep either. I've had another dream."

"Oh my, Bill. Yes, tell me about it."

Now what can I do. I'll have to tell Bill about these diamonds.

We start walking and Bill says, "You know Jenny, I just don't want to tell Gracie I've been having dreams. She gets so upset about them."

"I know. I have the same trouble and don't talk about them. I have had several dreams about Kathleen. I think that maybe she lived over in England and had children who would be heirs if any are living now."

"That's right. I get those messages from Helen Rivers and Donald Junior too, but they don't say it with certainty."

I shake my head hopelessly. "Maybe we should hire a person to investigate that possibility. From my dream I know the name of the town is Weymouth, where a man named William Jones tells about his great-grandfather that had the bracelet and he gave it to a woman who cried over it. That could have been Kathleen!"

We walk along and I have my hand on the bag in my coat pocket as we talk. Then I realize this isn't getting me anywhere with the diamonds.

"Bill, I have to tell you why I am really out here." I touch his arm, "Let's sit down on the bench for a minute." I tell him all about finding the diamonds in the library desk and explain that I must throw them in the river now for the sake of us all.

Bill is very surprised and says, "Oh no, Jenny! John Rivers must not have had a chance to do it, but now I know we have to. If any of them are ever found here, they could be traced back to Donald Andrew Rivers Senior, and it will not be good for us."

"It's a long walk down to the deep water, Bill, we ought to go and get it done." He agrees, and we start down past the stables as he buttons up his coat and I pull my scarf around my head.

Just then we hear someone call from the back of the house, and it sounds like George. Bill is behind me and waves me on. I hurry around the back of the stables as he calls out to George. When I disappear from view of the house, Bill rapidly walks back. I hear him try to explain to George that he was checking the horses because he heard a noise from the stables.

I stand there while they talk for a few minutes and then they both turn toward the house.

Now I must do what I am here to do, and I continue walking toward the river from the back of the stables.

When I get close to the water, I see that there is a rocky embankment and the water is about ten feet down from me. There are large waves smashing up onto the bank but I don't feel the spray. I know I must get closer in order to throw them farther out into deeper water. I walk carefully to the very edge.

I look around to make sure I'm alone and reach into the bag. I come out with a handful of round uncut stones.

The bright moon shines on them, lighting them up in all their glory. They are radiant, and shimmer with colors that seem to come from within the heart of each stone. It is a sight to see and I hesitate to throw such beauty into the gloomy darkness before me.

Looking at the brilliant, glittering lights reflecting in my hand I'm truly mesmerized. The moon is doing all it can to change my mind as the magnificent diamonds roll around in my palm.

My mind is busy trying to figure out a way to keep them and not have to give them to the river.

Then I put the evidence of my family's past indiscretions back into the bag and sit down on the bank, while the argument within me continues.

The river is very active, the large waves smacking against the bank seem to be fighting the undercurrent that is forcefully pulling back, just as I am doing with these gemstones.

I stubbornly resist, and sit there on the bank unsure, listening to the sounds from the waves, pounding against the bank.

They seem to say, "D o n ' t D o I t!" ----- "D o n ' t D o I t!" ----- "D o n ' t D o I t!"

Suddenly, the wind and the terrible threats of disclosure make up my mind for me. Shutting out the arguments, the logic, and the voices from the waves, I suddenly stand up.

Without looking at their glorious beauty, I toss them, one handful after another, until the bag is empty.

I watch as wave after wave hits the bank, not only taking the diamonds, but also removing all traces of Donald Andrew Senior's unlawful, disturbing past, from Rivers Run and his heirs.

When I start walking from the scene, I look back at the water and say, in a loud voice, what John Rivers probably would have said, "Now there really are diamonds in the water, and the deal with gangsters has ended."

The wind is blowing harder but I don't feel the cold. As I make my way back to the house I enjoy the feelings of deliverance from distress and anxiety now that the diamonds are gone.

Suddenly I feel a strange sensation! Boots moves on the bed and I open my eyes to shockingly discover I'm in bed! I look around the room and wonder—was that a dream? Didn't I get rid of the diamonds?

I hurry to open the cedar chest and discover the diamonds nestled safely among the box of things. I am totally shocked, remembering the ordeal of tossing those beautiful diamonds into that raging dark water. It was a dream! They are still here with me!

Like a ragdoll I collapse with fear onto the floor, and tremble from the thoughts of it. With tears my mind goes over and over again the events in the dream. I was so sure the diamonds were gone! The details in the dream were so real. I know now that I must tell Bill that I have them. He will have to dispose of them.

Spring weather is beginning to show up, and so are many people to see what's new in the gift shop. Flowers are appearing in the gardens, and Amy has restocked with beautiful new things.

On days when a tour of the house is offered, many of the customers wait to get the tour after shopping in the gift shop. Ward has gotten very good with the stories of the ancestors and how they managed through the years with sharecroppers. He also has some very nice stories he has learned from the people in Helen about John Matthew Rivers' parties.

Amy and George are getting very close, going on dates more often, and I have noticed how she favors him as opposed to Allen and Ward.

My relationship with Roger has been showing signs of improvement as well. He definitely has been busy on his dad's farm and they are ready to move into their home. I have had a tour of the house and it is lovely.

One day Roger and I walk through their property. He has put a bench in the flower garden.

We sit and enjoy lemonade, and Roger says, "Jenny, I think I was mistaken about something and I want you to know I'm sorry."

"What do you mean, Roger?"

"Well, I've talked with my mom about you and my feelings. She explained what she thought was the problem. When I thought about it, I'm sure she's right."

"I don't understand."

He takes my hand and looks into my eyes. "I thought you and George were getting close, especially at the New Year's Eve party, and I didn't know how to handle it. Now I see it differently. I've been a fool and I hope you will forgive me."

"Roger, maybe, to you, it looked differently, but George was just flirting and didn't mean anything by it. He never meant anything to me and I have told him that. Now he has a real thing for Amy, I think, and she likes him too."

I wonder what Roger thinks of Tammy, but I don't mention her.

I feel very good that he has explained his actions, and we spend most of the afternoon together. Somehow, though, I don't feel as close, but it is nice to get together with him.

When I am in my room again I think about my recent dreams. In one of them I saw a woman in the distance looking at a bracelet. The vision is never clear enough for me to recognize her.

When Bill and I are alone he tells me he still has dreams too. He says he would like to hire a detective to look into Kathleen's death and the bracelet, and I think he may do that one day soon.

I'm going to tell him that I have the diamonds. Maybe he will suggest some way to get rid of them properly. I really don't like throwing them in the river.

"Bill, I need to tell you something important. Do you have time?"

"Of course, Jenny."

I tell him my story about finding the diamonds and where I have them hidden, but leave out the ungodly dream I had where I tossed them in the river.

"Oh, Jenny, they are going to haunt us until we get rid of them. You'd best give them to me and I will hide them in the garage."

"Okay, Bill."

That evening I find a way to turn them over to him after dinner when he is alone in the garage office and the others are watching television.

"Thanks, Jenny. I'll think of something to get rid of them. This will be just between us for now."

CHAPTER THIRTY-NINE

One day in May the gift shop is very busy and I get called to help out. When the day is over I am very tired and take a call from Roger before retiring. Boots and I curl up in my lounge chair together and I look out at the mountains. The view is not as pretty tonight because heavy clouds, that look ominously close, are covering up most of the scenery as I drift off…

Suddenly I'm in a room with a young woman in bed. She calls out a name, "Susan."

A door opens and a middle-aged woman comes in. "Madame."

Then they both start talking but I can't understand what they are saying. I think she's speaking with a British accent. Then Susan gets all excited and runs out of the room.

Soon more people come in, one person has a doctor's bag and following him is a young man who is all excited and calls out the name, "Catherine," as he approaches the bed and they kiss.

Catherine calls out to the young man, "Mason," and they look so happy and discuss something I can't hear.

The doctor says words too fast for me to understand, but addresses the man as Mr. Taylor, and escorts everyone out of the room before coming back near the bed. Then I see that Catherine is pregnant and now I know the reason this is happening. Catherine is having a baby.

Several women come into the room and I assume they will help the doctor as they prepare several things on a table near the bed.

I try to go close to the bed so I can see the woman better and as I get close I am very surprised. This woman looks like Kathleen except her face is a little thinner and slightly older than when I saw her as a nurse in a dream with her mother, Helen, as she was leaving Rivers Run to go to her assignment.

I sit down near the bed hoping I can find out more but a loud thundering noise puts a stop to my dream...

As the dream fades I look outside to see a heavy downpour of rain hitting my windows and Boots jumps up because of the loud thunder and lightning.

I try to think about the significance of what I just saw in my dream. If that was Kathleen then she must have had at least one child! Her name was Catherine and her husband's name was Mason Taylor. I must tell Bill about this dream. Perhaps Kathleen had a child and the names may give us a way to find answers.

The next morning Amy is in the gift shop when I meet Bill in the parlor with George and tell them the dream I had, remembering the names, Catherine and Mason Taylor.

George is amazed and Bill just shakes his head and says, "I knew it! That's why we are still having dreams about Kathleen. Well, now I have to find out if she has given us heirs. They would probably be her great-grandchildren. I will contact someone to look into this for us, and I'll do it today."

Bill wastes no time contacting a detective agency that was recommended by a friend. Mr. Bernard Stapleton arrives to talk with us two days later and Bill escorts him into the library as George and I follow.

Bessie brings in a few refreshments and we sit and invent reasons for trying to find Kathleen Rivers' heirs, giving the years involved, without mentioning our dreams. He seems surprised at the timeframe but doesn't ask why it was not pursued earlier, and I was relieved that we didn't have to explain.

Mr. Stapleton takes down all our information without saying very much. He is provided with the names Catherine and Mason Taylor, and information about the town of Weymouth, England. We tell him that we think she may have lived through the battle in Southern England, and may have suffered from Amnesia. I provide the old news article about the battle that told about the deaths of all the nurses.

He makes a few notes and then quotes a price that is agreed upon.

Then Mr. Stapleton says, "I'll need half the amount upfront to cover the cost of the airfare and other expenses. I'll leave on Monday next week."

Bill writes the check and provides Mr. Stapleton with our telephone number.

We walk him to the door and Bill says, "We are very anxious about this and will welcome any information as you research it."

He says, "Mr. Waller, before leaving I will check a few reports and information from Scotland Yard with the names you have provided. If I find out anything of interest, I will call you immediately."

The days go by as the household waits patiently for answers. It is like a nightly thing in the parlor as we get together for dessert or drinks after dinner, and we discuss many scenarios.

Each day I try to focus on other things but I continue to see Kathleen having a baby and wonder if her child lived and had children too. That is really what we are looking for—a descendant who is still alive, and I am pretty sure there may be an heir. Otherwise, why are we having dreams?

One day in the shop I find that Allen has heard about our search for an heir in England and is upset about it. He says, "Jenny, what's this I hear that a detective is searching in England for another heir to Rivers Run?"

Amy and I look at each other wondering how he found out, and I say, "Allen, some information has been forthcoming and we are just having it investigated to make sure there is no one that may have been a child of Kathleen, the daughter of Donald Rivers Senior and Helen. She went off to England and was killed in a battle over there; however, there is reason to believe that she lived. Of course, we want to make sure there are no great-grandchildren of hers that could be heirs."

He looks at both of us and shakes his head, "Well, no one investigated the possibility of *me* being an heir and from what I remember, John Matthew Rivers could be my great-grandfather because of his relationship with my great-grandmother, who was a servant here for eleven years!"

Amy's eyes make me laugh to myself because they are making all kinds of movements, blinking and rolling, and we stand there and sigh, knowing what a "can of worms" this is beginning to be.

However, both of us know the answer for him is in the letter from John Matthew that Bill will have to provide.

As Allen stands there for an explanation of some kind, I can see he is upset. This is not like him. He is usually cool and calm.

Amy pats him on the back and says, "Allen, I suggest you talk with Bill. He has a letter you need to read and it will settle this for you."

While Amy stays in the shop I take Allen to see Bill. He is in the parlor with Gracie when we walk in. They are discussing the stables and the possibility of offering horseback rides for the town.

I say, "Hi, can we interrupt for a few minutes?"

Bill says, "Come in Jenny. What can we do for you? Do you need some assistance in the gift shop?"

I sigh, "No, Bill. Allen has found out that we are investigating about Kathleen's possible life in England and if there are heirs. He has been wondering about his great-grandmother and John Matthew Rivers, and if it is possible that he is the great-grandson of John Matthew."

Then Allen speaks up, "Bill, I am not trying to make trouble, but I just heard about the man you hired to go to England to find an heir. Why hasn't my inheritance been questioned too? I had talks with John Matthew Rivers and he supported me through the years with my painting classes and bought many of my paintings. Also, my great-grandmother is buried in the Rivers cemetery."

Bill goes over to a drawer in a table and brings out a folder. He tells Allen to come and sit with him, and gives him the page of the letter that explains Lia Moretti and John Rivers' relationship.

Allen begins the letter and we watch his optimistic facial expressions change to surprise and anguish as he finishes reading John Matthew Rivers' words.

He says, "Wow! So that's what happened to her! Well, it sounds like he really loved her though. I'm glad of that!"

Bill says, "Yes, Allen, we are very glad to have found the letter and know he truly loved her."

Allen says, "I'm sorry to have bothered you about this. I feel foolish now, and heartsick about what happened to my great-grandmother. The man that attacked her was a scoundrel that I will never identify with again! I will visit her grave today."

Bill pats him on the back and says, "That's all right. It's natural that you would question John Matthew, but now we know the truth."

Allen and I go back to the gift shop and he has a discussion with Amy. I sigh with relief as I go back to work opening a few new boxes of gifts to display, very thankful that we found the letter from John Matthew.

That night in the parlor after dinner the phone rings. Bill answers it and motions to everyone that it's the detective. He listens and after a few minutes he thanks him and hangs up. George, Amy, Gracie, and I anxiously wait to hear what was said.

Bill says, "Well, he has found out a few things about a family named Durand that go back to Mason Taylor. There are about three families of them in the area. However, he says it will take him a few weeks to hunt down the ones that may be related to the family of Mason and Catherine Taylor."

Amy says, "Well, that sounds like he is making progress." We all agree.

I say, "I wonder what Jerry Whitaker will do when we tell him about another heir?" That gets a laugh from everyone.

I am working in the shop one day the next week and I see Russ DeLuca with the two men who came with him before. They step into the shop and Russ approaches. I put down the crocheted item I am refolding and greet him, because Amy is busy with several ladies.

He says, "I'm Russ DeLuca, and I have been here before."

"Yes, may I help you Mr. DeLuca?"

"I would like a meeting with Mr. Bill Waller, the owner."

Amy has joined us and says, "Mr. Waller may be busy or not here at this time. I'll have to check for you. Please wait here."

She turns to go to the house as I watch the two other men examine the pottery, rolling them around in their hands, giving me the impression that they don't care if they drop them.

I step closer to them and say, "Those pieces are very fragile and done professionally. The prices are marked on the bottoms."

Russ says, "Yeah, boys, be careful. We wouldn't want to have to pay for them now, would we?" Both of the guys put the pieces down and laugh out loud.

After many agonizing minutes Amy comes back. She says, "Mr. DeLuca, Bill Waller will meet with you in the garage office," and she points to a door to the garage from the shop.

Walking toward the garage door Amy says, "He will speak with you out there, alone." Amy opens the door, and they leave the shop through the door to the garage.

CHAPTER FORTY

Amy takes Mr. DeLuca to see Bill in the garage office, I'm left with the two rough, unpleasant guys. I watch them as they wander around, picking up crocheted pillow cases and sewing equipment, leaving them unraveled, unsorted, and in the wrong places.

I no sooner wish that George was here, and he appears with Amy when she comes back.

George says, "Jenny, how's it going?"

"Fine George. I could use a little help though, keeping things in their places."

He goes over to one of the men and says, "Good morning, I'm George Waller," and puts his hand out to shake.

The guy shakes his hand but doesn't give his name and George says, "What can we do for you today? Have you seen some of the paintings? They were painted by the famous artist, Marvin Allen Mahon." Then the man follows him, as George points out the paintings hanging on the wall. *Amy and I just watch in awe.*

The man shakes his head after looking up at them, makes a face like he could care less and says, "We're here for the boss, but thanks anyway."

George goes over to the donuts and cookies and says, "I come out here just to find out if there are any sweets left over," and then he takes a cookie and indulges. He shoves the cookies over to them and says, "Are you guys interested?"

To my surprise both of them take a cookie. He then offers them lemonade from the pitcher on the counter, and pours a few cups for them as he also enjoys a drink.

For the next ten minutes or so George talks about the weather and the traffic in Richmond. He asks about the Romano restaurant that he has heard is being remodeled. One of the men says it will be a nice place when the work is finished and tells us Russ will be the new owner.

I'm thinking Russ is never coming back when the garage door opens and Bill comes in with Russ. They are laughing and shaking hands. Russ looks at the other two men and says, "Let's go, boys. I'm finished here. Bill Waller and his family have been invited to our opening night at the restaurant." They leave and Russ gives us a wave goodbye.

I stand there completely astounded. George and Amy seem totally surprised as well.

We can hardly wait until Russ and his men are safely driving away. We look at Bill who is smiling and seems totally delighted. He puts his hand up to his face and makes a gesture of wiping his forehead in relief and says, "Wow!"

Bill looks around the shop and there are no customers so he starts to explain, "I just handled him like a gentleman, sat him down, and let him read John Matthew Rivers' letter—only the page with the information about the diamonds and the fact that John Rivers had planned to dump them in the river."

Bill says, "After he read the letter I told him that I had no knowledge of this until I found the letter and I kept it in case I needed it for proof."

Bill goes over to the lemonade and pours a glass.

I comment that it's wonderful that Russ took it so well. Amy agreed with vigor because she was actually scared of what they would do, and so was I.

Then Bill says, "You should have seen Russ's face. He was actually relieved too, and told me that he was getting pressured by the top people about the diamonds they thought were here, and were giving him grief over it. Of course, he told me he had no knowledge of the agreement in 1867 either, and had told them it was impossible to try and "dig up" those problems now."

Bill continues, "Then Russ said the big 'boss' provided a copy of the agreement that someone had found in an old safe, and that really gave him heartburn because he didn't want to come back here and make trouble. He then brought the original agreement out for me to see. I looked it over. It was hardly readable, brown from age, and I saw the signature of Donald Rivers Senior, and gave it back to him."

"Did he keep it?" George asks.

Bill wipes the sweat off his brow and gives me a wink that I interpret as something good he is holding back from the others.

Then he says, "I figured he would keep it, but I was shocked! I watched him strike a match and burn the document right there in front of me!"

Then I see everyone's face relax with relief and feel mine do the same.

Bill takes another drink from the lemonade and says, "Russ told me he would tell them that there are no more diamonds and he would refer to the letter he read. He is positive the idea will drop now because, for one thing, they won't have the original agreement document. Russ DeLuca is so pleased to get on with his plans for the restaurant—and we have an invitation for opening night."

That evening in the parlor, we toast Russ DeLuca and wish him well.

"Bill says, "You know, I like the guy. He's a little stiff at first but when you get to know him and are honest with him, he is a regular person with feelings."

When Bill gets close, he tells me that he gave DeLuca the diamonds and they are his problem now. He also said if he hadn't given him the diamonds, it might have turned out differently. We both give a sigh of relief. I have a feeling Bill will tell about those details, and the diamonds, when we all need a good laugh. I know that me, finding the diamonds, will also be a part of that story. For now the basic truth, that we are entirely free from the obligation, and off the hook, seems to be all anyone needs to know.

As we enjoy relaxing in the parlor, we get a call from England. Bill talks with the detective who is checking on the possibility of descendants from Catherine and Mason Taylor.

We learn that Mr. Stapleton is narrowing down the search and plans on visiting a couple people tomorrow who might prove to be worthwhile. He mentions another good lead—a young man who lives in Weymouth, England.

That night I close my eyes thinking about everything that has happened and I believe I have seen a good example of the "diamonds in the water" representing good times.

A week goes by with no word from Mr. Stapleton. Everything at Rivers Run seems to be progressing. Bill and Gracie are involved in buying horses to start up a nice business offering horseback riding at Rivers Run. Bill loves horses and has two new ones to add to our two, Kota and Major, and also two ponies for children to ride. Amy is thrilled with the new ones and is out there with them whenever she can get away from the gift shop, mostly in the evenings.

On June 13, the week begins with a call in the evening from Bernard Stapleton in Weymouth, England. We are all in the parlor after dinner and I go over to the desk to answer, thinking it is Roger. I give the phone to Bill, and all of us are listening.

Once again Bill is vague with information, while listening and asking questions. He writes down a few things on a piece of paper on the desk. When he hangs up he sits down as we all wait patiently to hear what Bernard discovered.

Bill looks at his notes and says, "Well, I think he has found a family that goes back to Kathleen. There is a great-great grandson, who is twenty-two years old. His name is Martin Durand, whose mother's maiden name was Marie Dubois, whose family name goes back to Mason Taylor, her great-grandfather.

"Mason Taylor married Catherine Louise Withers, and she had a daughter, Jane. Catherine's maiden name was recorded as Withers but the records were not complete on her family." Bill stops and looks at his notes again and says, "It was noted in the report by Mr. Stapleton that the name 'Withers' sounds like 'Rivers' and 'Catherine' sounds like 'Kathleen'."

I say, "Well, maybe she really did suffer from amnesia, and those names sounded good to her."

Bill continues, "Well, that sounds possible. Mr. Stapleton said that the story is that before Catherine died she mentioned Rivers Run and gave them a name of her father, Donald Rivers—and that proved he was on the right track. Tomorrow he is going to ask Martin Durand to come back with him to America and meet some of his Irish relatives at Rivers Run."

This information has all of us smiling. We hope the detective can convince him to make the trip, and we all have a toast about the news.

Two days go by before we get another call from Mr. Stapleton. He says by going through the history of the case with Mr. Martin Durand, he has convinced him to make the trip to Rivers Run, and they will arrive next Sunday. We are also told that Martin's mother died when he was young and there are no other siblings in the family. Martin's father, Claude Durand, would not be an heir with the bloodline of Helen Marie Walters Rivers. He is married again and will not be coming with his son.

Gracie prepares a Suite for Martin Durand upstairs in their wing of the manor house, and Bill contacts Mr. Whitaker.

After talking with the lawyer, Bill tells us that he is very skeptical about another heir, but will try to come next week to talk over the information with us. He says he will prepare necessary papers to include Mr. Durand, if all is found to be authentic.

I am hoping that Mr. Stapleton has all the proof that is needed. With the information he has given us, and with the dreams I have had about Kathleen in England and what happened to her in the war, I can't wait to meet Martin Durand and see the proof as well. There is excitement in the air!

Sunday morning when I go to the dining room for breakfast, I find that Bill, Gracie and George have had their breakfast and are at church. Amy is finishing her meal and says, "Oh, Jenny, I am looking forward to meeting your long, lost relative from England today."

"So am I. I hope that Mr. Whitaker will be satisfied with all the proof that Mr. Stapleton has uncovered about him and we can get on with our lives at Rivers Run with no more dreams."

Amy and I are in the large parlor when Bill, Gracie, and George arrive back from church. They happily come into the parlor and, with big smiles, are talking about the situation that will take place today.

All of us are in the parlor having tea when the phone rings. Bill answers, and after a few minutes, he tells us Mr. Stapleton will be here at 3:00 p.m.

Bill says, "Last night I couldn't sleep for thinking about Kathleen in England all those years and having a child—a little girl named Jane."

I say, "Yes Bill, and then apparently more ancestors continued from there who are also not 'Resting in Peace.' I can't wait to hear the proof of Martin's heritage." The others make comments about the situation as well.

We have a few hours to wait and I, for one, am very anxious and just want to be alone. I go upstairs and sit in my lounge chair by the window, thinking of what this day will bring. Breathing a sigh of relief I close my eyes…

Helen Rivers is lying in bed and I am standing at the foot of the bed. She doesn't look well and is very thin. She is looking toward the windows of her bedroom, and as I look I can see the front gardens. She is crying, and tossing her head back and forth, as she talks to herself. She says, "Kathleen, you were in my dream last night and you had a little girl you called 'Jane.' Was I just dreaming, or did that really happen? Did you not die in that war? Am I just hoping you are alive? Can I believe you have an heir for us? My dream was over before I knew for sure. I must tell your father, but he won't understand. I hope he will search for you! He's very sweet about my dreams, but I'm sure he thinks those dreams I have are just nonsense. Oh, I wish I didn't feel so tired all the time," and she blots her eyes with a part of her sheet…

The dream fades. Someone is knocking on my door. "Come in."

I can't believe that Helen had a dream and Kathleen was showing her that she had a baby girl named Jane. That is wonderful to know—and it also substantiates the heritage of Martin coming from that lineage. I know that Donald Rivers Senior never searched for Kathleen. Perhaps Helen died shortly after and he never thought of it again.

"Jenny, they are here and waiting for you to come down," Amy says, as she opens my door. I quickly get up, still thinking about the dream with Helen, but I know I must hurry down with Amy to the parlor. I splash some water on my face and check my appearance in the mirror and we rush out together.

CHAPTER FORTY-ONE

Amy goes in first to meet our guest, Martin Durand, and I follow. Everyone is chatting in the center of the room. I go over to Mr. Stapleton who is talking with Bill, Gracie, George, and a tall man who is wearing an unfamiliar style of clothing. His brown hair has a touch of gold in it and is very wavy. The ends touch the top of his suit coat in the back. He comes forth to shake my hand as Bill introduces us. His eyes are dark blue and he has a very handsome face with full lips, and he gives me a smile.

I look up at him, "So glad to meet you, Martin."

He smiles in a strange way and says, "Jenny, is it possible for me to know you and this place from my dreams with Kathleen and Junior long ago?"

I notice his accent, but his question really surprises me, and I quickly try to get control of the situation. He is remembering dreams with me, Kathleen and Junior? Could he be Marty, the little boy that was here in my dreams? I am stunned and can hardly speak!

I manage to say, "Martin, what are you saying? Are you Marty?"

He let's out a very loud chuckle and tries to explain the dreams we were in together. Everyone else is looking at us like we have lost our senses, but we are both laughing by this time and he surprises me with a tight hug.

Marty says, "Mr. Stapleton told me that he found out, on his search to find me, that my great-great-grandmother was Kathleen Rivers from a place in Virginia called Rivers Run. He read that she began to mumble on her dying bed about life at Rivers Run. She even called out to her mother before she took her last breath; however, those around her thought she was not rational."

I say, "That is wonderful that she remembered!"

The others in the room are standing there shaking their heads and looking at one another and back at us in confusion, and I am sure we will have to explain in detail.

Marty says, "The name, 'Jennette,' was significant to my mind as soon as Mr. Stapleton gave me the details about the people in this place, but it wasn't until I stepped into this house, that the name 'Jenny' connected. I have been wondering about this place all my life."

He looks directly at me and says, "After my mother passed away, I had the dreams with you Jenny, along with Kathleen and Junior in this very house. I was so lost and lonely, but then the dreams came and I never forgot being here."

He hugs me again and says, "I loved it and always looked forward to those dreams that brought me here, but when I was older, my father put me in a boarding school and I never had another dream. I loved Kathleen and Junior, but it was you who was always there for me and seemed to know my sorrow."

The others are still looking at us and taking it all in with sighs and gasps—watching us as if we are performing a play. I'm not so sure I like his take-charge attitude, as if I am suppose to like him, but I go along with him.

Then Marty turns to the rest of the household, and talks with Bill, Gracie, George, and Amy, trying to explain the circumstances to them.

I can see understanding in Bill and George, because they have had dreams with ancestors too, but Amy and Gracie look perplexed. Eventually, after many explanations about our dreams, everyone seems to get a little more comfortable with the situation.

Bill and Gracie talk about what is planned for our dinner to honor our guest, and Amy wants to show him the gift shop later. I am sure every moment will be well spent.

The moment Mr. Whitaker arrives the room becomes ghostly quiet. I can feel the importance of it. It's as if breathing has stopped and won't continue until he speaks. He walks in and is introduced to the detective, Mr. Stapleton, and Martin.

"Bill says, "Well now, let's sit down and sort all this out, please."

Mr. Whitaker opens his briefcase and Mr. Stapleton sits next to him on the big sofa. We all find a seat around them, Martin conveniently finding a place next to me.

Everyone is staring at the lawyer and the detective, and waiting for them to begin. Mr. Stapleton gives papers to the lawyer and he begins to review the people named. He names people in the family of Mason Taylor and Catherine Withers Taylor that led to Martin Durand. Catherine and Mason Taylor had a girl, Jane, who married a Jean-Paul Laurent. Then we hear the others, all through the years and marriages until Marie Dubois married Claude Durand, Martin's father; leaving Martin, the only living relative from Catherine and Mason Taylor.

Hearing the dates of birth I focus on Martin's birth—*it was in 1964, and that made him about eight, the same age as me, when we had those dreams with Kathleen and Junior.*

I sit back next to Martin, convinced now that this is for real—and that includes all the dreams I've had.

Martin seems to be content with the obvious outcome, and we sit there waiting for all the others to be convinced as well.

He says, "Jenny, I know that many years ago Kathleen went to England, and I am sorry she didn't come back here, but if she had, I wouldn't be here, and I wouldn't have been in those dreams with you either."

We laugh but realize that the others don't think this is very funny, and we get a few looks that tell us to be quiet. It makes me feel like I am a child again in a dream that won't quit this time, and that makes it funnier to me.

Jerry Whitaker continues shuffling through stacks of papers for a good half hour. Then he stands and gives us his long analogy of the situation. He finally says all the papers seem to be complete and prove the ancestry of Martin Durand. He discusses with Martin his heritage benefits and has paperwork for Martin to sign. After Marty signs, he passes the papers for the rest of us to sign.

After the signing is finished, Martin stands up and says, "This is very strange for me. I plan to eventually go back to England. That's my home, I have a job, and I know many people there."

He looks around at all of us and says, "I hope you will understand that's why I have signed the paper to leave Rivers Run; however, for a while I would love to stay here and get to know all of you."

Bill says, "I am happy with that and welcome you for as long as you wish to stay."

Everyone gets up to welcome Martin with hugs, passing the signed papers to Mr. Whitaker. The lawyer shows remarkable patience with all of this, gathers up the documents, wishes us well, and Gracie shows him out.

Gracie has Bessie bring refreshments and we enjoy talking and being together as family. During this time Bill, Gracie, and George explain to Marty how they became heirs and took their places in my life at the manor house.

Marty can't believe how that came about or how George discovered the papers from his grandfather that revealed the name change. We told him about our dreams with long ago family members and how they insisted there were more heirs. He says that he never had any dreams with older family members. That brings on comments that perhaps it is because he wasn't at Rivers Run, and I agree—I never had those dreams until I came to the manor house, and neither did George or his father, Bill.

This makes me wonder if, not only the ancestors, but also the house had something to do with all of our dreams.

After a special dinner, the family spends most of the night hours with Marty, showing him the ballroom and Allen's paintings, explaining the things that took place there, and how the windows open to the porch area.

The next day after a large family breakfast, Marty is interested to know all about the late John Matthew Rivers.

I explain how we found a letter from him revealing things that took away our fears about the people who could be heirs.

When Bill explains Donald Senior's agreement with the Italian mobster boss that left his children obligated to them, Marty is very surprised.

In the days that follow, we give him tours of the house, and Marty continues to go along close to me, very interested in all of the dreams that Bill, George and I had, and the challenges trying to find heirs.

As we go through different rooms, he and I banter back and forth about the things we did together when we played with Kathleen and

Junior. Some of our talks bring sadness as we remember our dreams with them. He remembers things that I have forgotten, and it is a joy to talk with him about how we couldn't hold on to cookies and other things that Kathleen and Junior would give us.

One day the following week, everyone at Rivers Run is busy continuing the household tours with the people from town and gift shop responsibilities, except Marty and me.

The weather is a typical hot summer day, but Bill tells me there is a nice breeze to help keep the heat tolerable.

After breakfast when we are sitting in the parlor having coffee I ask Marty if he would like to visit the cemetery.

"Oh yes, Jenny. I would like that."

We walk to the gardens, pick flowers for the graves, and Gracie gives me a container for them.

Marty spends a few minutes at the cemetery gate, looking at the beautiful ornate fencing that John Matthew had built years ago, just as I had done on my first visit.

We walk through the cemetery and place flowers on many of the graves as I tell him about our ancestors. Marty stays at Kathleen's memorial stone for a good while and tears come to my eyes. I guess he is remembering her, and I notice he is very emotional, looking off in the distance and bowing his head.

"Jenny, it is so sad that her mother and father thought she had not survived that war. Of course, now they may know since she is with them in Heaven."

"You're right, Marty." The mood seems to lighten up a bit, and we walk to the gravesite of John Matthew Rivers, where we place flowers. Marty comments that he wishes he had known him.

I say, "I wish he had known about me, because I could have been at Rivers Run a lot sooner and would not have had to spend time in the orphanage."

Marty seems surprised. "What happened?"

I guess he doesn't know about my circumstances. We sit down on a bench and I explain everything to him.

He puts his arm around my shoulders and hugs me. It is very sweet of him to show concern, but I don't want him to get that familiar. I notice, since he has been here, he tries to be with me a great deal. I still think he is a bit too familiar—after all, we were children when he knew me in the dreams.

We start back to the house after going to all the graves, even Lia Moretti's, where I spend time explaining that story and how Allen Mahon, the artist, is related to her.

CHAPTER FORTY-TWO

On the way back from the cemetery, Marty and I get to the stream in the back of the house. I take him to the branch that hangs close to the water and we sit down.

"Marty, see the lights on the water?"

"Yes, they are beautiful."

"Well, in a dream I had with Donald Senior and Helen, he referred to them as 'diamonds in the water' and how they represent the good times in life and the muddy, dark water representing the bad times. These lights are what he referred to—however, I think he also was thinking of the real diamonds that he was hiding from everyone."

Marty is amazed at that part of the story, and also thinks it is a wonderful explanation of how the water sparkles.

Then he says, "You know, when I think about it, they are my grandparents, very far removed, and it makes me crazy that I am in their house."

"Oh, Marty, I never thought about that! For me it is different—I go back to Aunt Helen's era with her brother, Harrison, who was my great-great grandfather."

He says, "Think of this—When I was in a dream with you and Kathleen, it was back in time, and I was playing with my "to be" grandparent in the years to come! I have to laugh thinking about what that makes Junior to me."

That is a comical thought, and I laugh thinking about it.

We sit there a long time enjoying the breeze off the water and Marty looks over and says, "I am so glad I came to Rivers Run. This is such a delightful place, and to meet you, and know you are real, and my dreams were real, has given me a reason to live again."

I am stunned and look at him with surprise.

He hesitates, and tries to explain, "Jenny, I was ready to get married last year and my bride-to-be never showed up at the wedding. I dearly loved her with all my heart."

His face shows pain and he says, "I have been trying to get my life back where I feel good about myself again, but it has been a struggle. I almost lost my job and still think they will get rid of me if I don't make a better effort when I go back. When Mr. Stapleton came to me with the story about Rivers Run—it was a godsend and got me moving again."

"Oh, I'm so sorry, Marty, but glad you're here."

The breeze whips up around us as we stare out at the ripples on the water and I say, "I know you are worried about the job, but you should stay here with us—even for longer than you planned. It may change you—this place has changed me."

We get up and he says, "Jenny, it has meant so much to confess to you that terrible truth about me, and I feel better. You have made this time very special, making me aware of what matters."

I hope I have helped him.

Then he comes close. He holds my face in his hands and says, "Jenny, you are beautiful and have taken my sorrow away again, just like you did when I came here in my dreams after my mother died."

I think he is going to kiss me and I'm startled and stiffen up. He hesitates and gives me a hug. Then I turn away and we start up the hill. I really don't want him to think of me as more than a friend. I am not so sure I like him yet. He has approached me in a way I'm not used to, even more than George did, and I feel strange about it.

When we are back in the parlor, we have lemonade and snacks that Jessie serves everyone. I think seriously about that moment with him by the river. I think he would have kissed me. It has put a different spin on the situation.

When I happen to look over at him, he is looking at me. I hear the conversation that is going on in the parlor but I can't concentrate on it.

Bill and Gracie seem to be discussing the people taking part in the horse activities and Bill says, "Gosh, I think I had five children taking turns riding the ponies today."

Then Allen comes in. He says, "Bill, I just talked to Amy about your new guest from England. I thought I would come in and meet him."

Bill is happy to introduce Marty and tells Allen the circumstances that brought Marty to Rivers Run.

Allen says, "Welcome. It's good to meet a new heir to this place," and they talk for several minutes about England, and the town that Marty lives in.

Then Allen says, "Marty, I have to go back to the gift shop to help Amy. Would you like to go and visit? It will get you out of here for a while."

Marty looks at me as if to ask me to go with him. I say, "You two go and enjoy. I think I will go freshen up and I might be out there later."

When I'm in my room I sit in my lounge chair. I don't know what I'm doing or what I feel about Marty. He has completely confused me. I feel very vulnerable. I wash my face and put on another summer outfit before going out to the gift shop.

When I go in, Marty comes over to me. He says, "Gee, the gift shop is nice. Amy has been telling me about the way you got the idea to build it, and I'll have to meet Ward. The history of Virginia sounds fascinating, especially with the Civil War episodes." Then he goes on about Allen's paintings and wants to see those paintings in the ballroom again.

I listen as we walk around in the gift shop and he points out all the things that he wants to buy for his place in England. That immediately makes me think of him going back. Strangely, I'm not sure I want him to go, which gives me questions about my feelings for him. I believe it's too soon for him to go back into those circumstances with his job and his distressing relationship.

That evening we are all sitting around in the parlor. George and Amy are talking together about new things for the shop, and Bill and Gracie are discussing the new ideas for the manor house.

Marty says, "Jenny, will you go with me to the ballroom?"

"Of course, Marty, I'll go with you."

At first we walk around and comment about the nice arrangement of paintings and Allen's talent. I show him my favorite, the one behind which John Rivers hid his letter, and I explain that scenario to him.

Then we walk over to the windows. He opens them and we walk out. The glow from the sunset is superb causing everything to change color. There is a soft breeze as we walk off the porch.

Bill and Jessie have done a marvelous job in the gardens out there, and Marty comments about how lovely it is.

He takes my hand and we walk among the Willow Trees and he motions for me to sit with him on a bench.

He says, "Jenny, I thought I was in love with Julie back in England, but I know now that my heart has been for someone in my past all this time. I have not thought of Julie since being here with you. I know it seems outrageously sudden, but I want to ask you if there is someone else in your life. If so, I will do my best to convince you to see me in your future."

What is he talking about? I've gotten over being aggravated with his attitude toward me, but this is beyond my thinking. I like him but there seems to be no "love" attraction with him.

My heart is beating beyond control at this moment, and I'm thinking of Roger. I look at this unknown creature from the past and try to talk.

"Marty, I don't know what to say. I feel like I have known you all my life—but only in dreams. I can't explain it and I'm questioning my feelings because they seem to be coming from another time."

He doesn't answer me. Instead, he instantly puts his left arm around my shoulder, leans over and puts his right arm around my upper body in a close embrace while advancing for a kiss.

Why I lean toward him is beyond me, and right away he takes charge. Seductively his mouth claims mine. After the kiss, his dark eyes capture me as his hands tend to roam, and we kiss again. I am spellbound and totally lost in the moment, forgetting all about discretion.

I know my heart has never felt this way before. I've heard that people know when love is real, but this—even though amazingly wonderful—is too soon and too quick, and it is disturbing because I know it is not a dream, but it's like I am in someone else's body allowing it to happen.

Then we hear George and Amy coming out onto the porch and it stops progression of Marty's impulses. He quickly sits up straight but holds onto my hand.

I am thankful because at that moment I need the support, and Marty and I need to stop and consider what we are doing.

252

Amy says, "Gee, it is a lovely evening." They see us across from them and come over.

George says, "This is lovely out here now that my father and I have fixed it up and made it comfortable."

I'm shaking, but sit up straight, and Marty puts his hand through his hair. I say, "Yes, George, it looks so much better now. Two years ago when Amy and I arrived it was terrible. It had weeds everywhere, the benches were old, and the gardens were non-existent. You and your dad have done wonders."

Amy and George continue walking past us into the willow trees. George and Amy are beginning to show their love for each other and I am very glad. George is perfect for Amy, and I think they make a great pair.

The night is progressing and I'm wondering about Marty and me. *All I can think of now is him, but what about when he goes back to England? My mind doesn't want to go there. I need time to think about this.*

I make an effort to get up from the bench and Marty follows. He and I go back to the ballroom and he takes my hand and leads me to the middle of the room. He starts humming a beautiful melody and we dance around the floor, with him holding me very close, kissing my neck and my ear, and taking liberties that I never experienced before.

I have never been like this—not even with Roger! It is very strange how that kiss changed my attitude about him completely—but at the same time I am surprised and confused that I have let him touch me in such a manner.

Marty stops humming and stands there on the ballroom floor, holding me tightly. He looks down into my eyes and says, "Jenny, I love you," and he kisses me with a kiss I may never forget. I feel like it represents all the years we haven't been together since I was eight years old.

Suddenly, I think about how strange this is, and I pull away and tell him it's getting late. We start up the stairs with his arm around me and he stops halfway up, and we kiss again. My mind says no, but I don't resist.

Jessie has just come in with Boots, and the dog follows us the rest of the way.

Marty kisses me again at my door with his hands rubbing my back and pulling me close. Then he says goodnight, and stands there until I go in. I watch him as I close my door, and then lean against it, overwhelmed and unable to move.

I think of Roger, and wonder what happened. I think about the person who left this room this morning, laugh and think of the song, "What a difference a day makes."

Over the next few weeks I don't hear from Roger. I try to keep busy while Marty gets acquainted with everyone. George has been getting Marty familiar with the town and all the different roads and back roads that lead to Richmond. He thinks that it is important that men should know exactly where things are and how to get to other places. He has been driving Marty around using Bill and Gracie's car and also the Buick in the garage left there for Amy and me.

I'm wondering what Marty is discussing with George while they are together.

One night in late July, Marty wants to take me to dinner. He says George and Amy are going to the newly renovated Romano's Restaurant and they want us to go with them. I remember the Rivers Run household was invited for the Grand Opening but we didn't go at the time. It used to be Romano's, and Russ DeLuca said he was remodeling it. The name is Russ's Restaurant now.

George is driving and we take the Buick. George is dressed in a brown suit and Amy has on her yellow and brown pantsuit.

Marty and I sit in the back. Marty is wearing a dark blue suit and he compliments me on how I look. I'm dressed in a calf-length print dress with teal and dark blue flowers. It has a flowing bodice overlay, with a tiered skirt, and is very comfortable.

Russ's Restaurant is lovely. Colors of violet and blue accents on the tables, walls, and candles give a luxurious showing. They have a band that is playing slow tempo songs for evening dancing.

We order our meals and the four of us go to the lovely dance floor where we enjoy several musical numbers before our drinks are served.

CHAPTER FORTY-THREE

At the restaurant when Amy and I go to the ladies room, she says, "Wow, Marty looks at you in a way that tells me you had better watch out."

I laugh, not wanting to tell her just how I feel because I'm not sure. "He is a very good dancer and I like him."

"I see more than that coming from you, and it's more than I ever saw with you and Roger."

"But he's going back to his country, Amy."

"Oh, I think he could change his mind with a very small nudge from you," and then she laughs.

Right now I am afraid it is just a fantasy from dreams. Is it possible that he would stay here? What about George and Amy?

"I've noticed how George looks at you also. He is falling—and hard too!"

"Well, I am beginning to see all his good qualities and it might be love this time for me as well. Maybe I will find true love again."

My discussion with Amy is interesting and we return to the table. We have a nice meal and enjoy a few more dances before we return to Rivers Run.

In the back of the car, Marty and I share a time together with kisses and caresses. This is all new to me, and my reactions soon give him the message to slow his desires but I can see that upsets him.

When we get back to the manor house, Marty walks me to my room. George and Amy are across the hall saying goodnight and we say goodnight to them, then Marty gives me a kiss goodnight and I go in and close my door, with him standing there not moving away, just as he did the last time he walked me to my room.

It gives me the feeling that he wants me to invite him in—and I just can't do that, because I don't think my willpower is good when it comes to him. I am so distraught that I have let myself get so attached. When he kissed me the very first time, I felt as if my body and soul were destined to be with him. Those feelings are ridiculous and unreal—or are they?

The next day I get a telephone call from Roger, and reality starts setting in. He wants me to have dinner with him tonight. I knew this time might come and I can't think of what to say, and stammer, thinking twice.

Roger notices my hesitation, and he says, "I guess you've been busy with your new relative, Martin, from England. I've heard about him from Bill."

"Well, I have been busy getting him acquainted with the house and the others here. Perhaps another time, Roger."

"Sure, Jenny. Give me a call when you're free from your obligations."

Gosh, I do like Roger. That wasn't nice. He is a special person in my life—why is my heart leaning toward Marty all of a sudden?

The rest of the day I work in the gift shop. I understand that Marty and George are going to help Jessie and Bill with the children who come to ride the horses.

Bessie cooks a great meal that evening and I see Marty and the others are really tired. Everyone congregates in the large parlor and we relax on the new sectional. It's not really a talkative crowd but Marty starts a conversation about his country.

He tells us about the Second World War that his grandfather endured and lived through some frightening times while the region was being bombed by Germany.

Bill and Gracie then talk about their time during the war as children and what Americans also went through, mentioning the rations of things.

The next day Marty wants to take a drive to Richmond and asks me to go along. We arrive in Richmond with no problem. He parks the car, and we decide to go for a walk in the business district. There are many clothing shops, restaurants, and a jewelry store. We go into the jewelry store and Marty asks to see diamond rings.

I hope he is just looking.

While we wait I look around the store and realize that the people behind the counters look Italian. It makes me wonder if this could be the store where Donald Rivers Senior did business. I am getting looks as if I am recognized.

I know the newspapers had my story in them. Could they know who I am?

A man comes over to Marty and says, "Good afternoon. I am the new owner, Lorenzo Giovanni. My great-grandfather was the first owner and we have been in business for many years and we have quality merchandise."

I wonder if his great-grandfather was Bruno. Maybe I'm just getting paranoid!

Marty says, "Glad to meet you, Sir. I am Martin Durand. We are just looking today. I would like to see your diamond rings."

I go back over to them and Marty introduces me to Mr. Giovanni. He doesn't react as if he recognizes me, but I wonder about him, the owner, approaching us for a sale.

Mr. Giovanni brings several rings out for us to see, and I look at Marty, shaking my head questioningly, and say, "Marty, what are you doing?"

"Jenny, let's just look at them, okay, and then he proceeds to hold them up one at a time. There is one I really like but it isn't the one he is holding. It is a very beautiful solitaire diamond, set in an intricate yellow gold setting, and as I look at it with the lights shining on it, I see the same inner glow and sparkles that I saw in those uncut diamonds. It stuns me for a moment and I quickly shake my head "no."

Could that diamond have come from the collection we had at Rivers Run when John Rivers had to work with the mob years ago, or is it one from the collection Bill gave Russ DeLuca recently? I don't feel comfortable any longer with these thoughts about Rivers Run involvement.

Marty finally senses my disturbing looks, puts the beautiful rings back and tells Lorenzo Giovanni that it will have to be another day. I grab his arm and we walk out without another word.

When we get outside I take Marty over to a nice outside area of a café and we sit at a table. A waiter comes over and I order ice tea and Marty orders a soda.

I start reminding Marty about the long horrible agreement in which the late Donald Rivers Senior obligated Rivers Run and his sons.

Marty holds my hand and says, "I understand, Jenny. I have been told all about that connection thing in Richmond."

"But Marty, it all started involving a jeweler here in Richmond and a banker. I think that jewelry store could be the one involved and Mr. Giovanni could be a great-grandson. Did you see the looks I got? I think they recognized me from Rivers Run. I don't want to start up anything with these people."

Marty says, "I'm sorry, Jenny. I didn't realize it would matter now. I've heard about it, and assumed it is over, now that the original culprits are all dead and the original agreement has been burned."

"Marty, it is just better we don't stir up anything again."

From there we visit the museum. He is very interested in all the pictures of Rivers Run and the people. I show him the one that was taken on Kathleen's tenth Birthday and tell him that was my last dream with her. Marty sits there for a long time looking at those pictures of Kathleen and the people around her and I feel a special connection with him.

There is a walkway down by the river near the museum, and before we go back to Rivers Run we walk among the trees. He holds my hand as we walk along and enjoy watching the ducks that are out on the water. I feel like I could do this for the rest of my life.

The next day I get a call from Roger. I try to be more gracious and agree to go with him to lunch. He drives me to the Riverside Landing Restaurant where we sit on a bench. He puts his arm around me and we watch the diamonds in the water and look over to Rivers Run.

I am now feeling close to Roger again—what is happening? Am I enjoying two people at the same time—just like Amy?

"Jenny, I have been very anxious to see you again. I know it has been difficult for you being obligated to familiarize your guest, Martin, with Rivers Run and places like Richmond. I have heard that you have been with him quite a lot. How does he like Rivers Run?"

"Oh, he seems to enjoy everything about it. I'm not sure he will go back to England. We have gotten very close and, in a way, I hope he stays."

Roger removes his arm from around my shoulders and looks at me directly. I know he has more questions but I hope he doesn't ask the ones I can't answer just now.

He says, "Let's go in and have lunch."

I know he has given me time to think, but I know the questions will rise again, just as surely as the tide.

We go in and order lunch, and while we wait, Roger reaches across the table to hold my hand.

I do feel the same about him as I did before but is it enough? Does it compare to my feelings about Marty? I try to know what to say to Roger, but I just sit there and look across the river at the place that has given me peace but has also caused a lot of complications in my life.

Roger sits back and looks at me intensely and says, "Jenny, I want you in my life. Now, with our property I can plan on a place of my own and I would like to think you might want that too. What did you mean about Martin when you said you two are close?"

I knew Roger would pursue my words about Marty but I had to tell him something that sounded like I felt. I just don't know now what to say.

"Roger, you have to know that those dreams were real. Marty and I shared time together at Rivers Run when we were only about eight years old. We were sent back in time to be with Kathleen and Junior, I think because both of us were traumatized because of our losses. He lost a mother and I lost my parents."

Roger puts his hand up to move his escaping blonde curl that I admire. "What you are saying is very strange! Do you believe it happened just like that?"

"I do, Roger, and it is hard to understand, I know! However, because of those dreams that put us together in a different time, we have a connection that I can't explain. Please believe me when I say that I love him because of those days spent together. I can't understand my feelings right now. We are related, that's true, far-reaching for sure."

Roger shakes his head in disbelief and looks at me as if he is trying very hard to believe my story—for the sake of his feelings for me—I think.

"Jenny, I love you with all my heart. I think I can look beyond this stuff you are saying and just hope you love me enough to give me time to digest this."

I look out at the water and see the diamonds, wondering if they are telling me that this is good. Then I say, "Roger, I think I love you too, but what the future brings for Marty and me remains to be seen. I think that our connections are drawing us closer, and I have to figure this out."

"Well, Jenny, let me say that I am determined, after hearing all this, that I will be strong about it. I do need your support. Suppose I meet him and explain my love for you. Perhaps he will realize that his love for you is just a fantasy from long ago, or something like sister love." He reaches across the table and holds my hand.

Sister love is not what I would call it, but it could be just a thing from the past that is drawing us together.

"Okay, Roger, I'll introduce you."

After our meal we sit outside on the bench and Roger holds me close and we kiss. I do get that excitement again from his kisses and am more confused than ever.

When we return to Rivers Run we sit in the car before going in to meet Marty. I am breathing deeply trying to get control of the situation. Roger reaches over and kisses me and his kiss is breathtaking, putting a feeling of joy and permanence in my life. I also know Roger is respectful about my feelings and not overly anxious to see how far he can go with his advances.

He reaches for his door handle. I don't want to go into the manor house, but realize it's time.

He gets out of the Bronco and comes around to open my door. I step out thinking about how I will introduce him to Marty and be with both of them at the same time. It makes me feel dizzy and nauseous.

CHAPTER FORTY-FOUR

The minute Roger and I step into the house to see Marty, I sit down on the little double seat by the door and hold my head. Roger wants to know if I am okay. I tell him to give me a minute and begin to take deep breaths, as he sits with me.

I finally stand and tell him that perhaps Marty is in the parlor, and we walk slowly there as I try to control my feelings of anxiety.

When we go into the parlor, Amy, George, Bill and Gracie are having a discussion with Marty about the gift shop and how the tours were started.

They all look up and Marty stands to meet Roger. I introduce them and I tell Marty how Roger and I met. They shake hands.

Bill asks us to enjoy ice tea with them and we sit down on the other end of the sectional, Roger not hesitating to put his arm around my shoulders.

Bill relates the story about how Marty was found and I can see that Roger is interested. I notice Marty is paying close attention to Roger and me.

Marty says, "Yes, and, believe it or not, Jenny and I go way back years ago when we came here in our dreams to meet with the first children living here. Their names were Kathleen and Junior." Then he tells about the support and love he got from me in those dreams while missing his mother who had died.

"Oh yes, I heard about that from Jenny at lunch," Roger says, as he shakes his head back and forth as if it is hard to believe.

The conversations go on in the parlor including the horseback riding offered for children and their parents on the trails at Rivers Run.

Roger contributes his stories about building on their property and his plans for building his own house someday.

After several hours Bessie comes in to ask if she should prepare another place at the dinner table for Roger.

Roger looks at me, and somehow senses my hesitation, and says, "Thank you, but I've got to be going. My mother is probably expecting me for dinner there."

I get up then to see him to the door and Marty shakes his hand and says, "It's been very nice meeting you." Roger agrees.

When we get to the door, Roger gives me a quick kiss and says, "He's a nice guy, Jenny, I'll call you," and walks out without looking back.

I stand there admiring his thoughtfulness about dinner, but noticing his attitude with me was different. He probably won't call me—I'll have to call him if I want to see him again.

There are many things discussed with Marty over the next few weeks, especially the dreams all of us with the Irish bloodline have had since we have been in the manor house. Marty is interested and hopes he has a dream or two while here. We tell him that since all the heirs are accounted for, there should not be dreams because the ancestors will finally be resting in peace.

I have noticed that since Marty met Roger he has not been around me very much and my feelings for Roger have kept me from being with Marty as well. I am still confused and one day when I am with Amy in the gift shop I approach her.

"Amy, can we talk?"

"Sure, Jenny. I think I know what you want to ask me. Is it about Roger and Marty?"

"Yes. I feel totally unable to know what to do about the situation. Both of them seem to want to love me and I can't make up my mind about them!"

"Well Jenny, it's like this. I would just hang out with both of them as much as possible. If one asks you to spend time with him—do it. Then when the other one asks to take you out—go then. One day when you least expect it, you will know without a doubt. Right now you can enjoy both of them."

Why didn't I know that's what she would recommend?

The very next day Marty wants to take me to lunch. He hasn't seen the town and the shops and he drives the Buick. I recommend Helen's Café and before we go in I tell him about it being named after the owner. I introduce him to Helen and we have a very nice lunch. From there he parks the Buick on the street and we visit several shops. He buys me a lovely scarf that actually adds a nice look to the outfit I'm wearing. Marty gives me a hug, telling me I am beautiful.

We take a drive and he parks under some trees. We sit and talk and Marty puts his arms around me, brings me close and gives me a kiss.

"Jenny, I am thinking about staying at Rivers Run and not going back to England. I feel there is nothing there for me anymore. I know I can find work in Richmond and I love it here. What do you think about that, Jenny?"

"Marty. I'm very glad, and hope you can find work."

"I mean, can you and I find our way together in this life? If I stay I want you to be my wife, Jenny." He doesn't wait for my response but kisses me while his hands caress, telling me there is no doubt what he wants. I turn away and open the car door, because unless I do, discretion will not be a word I'll use. I can see he is very disturbed.

Roger has been so much more respectful and he has plans for the future, while Marty just rushes ahead and has so much love to give. I'm afraid I could easily go along with his needs, but is it really what I want?

What about my college plans and how I love biology, or future plans with Roger and his farm someday?

When Marty follows me for an answer I try to explain. "Marty, you need to give me time. I don't know how to react. I have never experienced these feelings before and I must tell you it is hard for me. I like both you and Roger, but I need more time to decide what is best. I have other plans that don't include marriage. I hope you understand."

"Jenny, perhaps those feelings are telling you to accept my proposal and get on with your life just as I want to do."

"I still have feelings for Roger and I can't give you an answer yet. It is too soon for us, Marty. We need to slow down and consider everything. I can't tell you 'no' just yet and I can't tell you 'yes.' I'm sorry. Please take me home." He just shakes his head and I don't think I convinced him in any way.

When Marty and I return to the house I go to my room to think. I see Marty going to his room down the hall from mine. He didn't wait at my door this time. I know I can never invite him into my room—I can just imagine what might happen and it's best if I don't rely on my control.

The next day I call Roger and ask him to take me to lunch at our favorite restaurant, Riverside Landing. When he arrives I am ready to go.

At the Restaurant I sit with him on a bench that he cleans off for me with his hanky, and we watch the tide come in. The diamonds are on the water and I feel at peace and very happy. I lean against his shoulder and he holds my hand. I look up at him and he leans down and kisses me. We don't say anything. We just sit and enjoy our time together in the quiet. That tells me he cares for my feelings and is happy to just be with me. I know he has future plans for us but I sense it will be when I'm ready.

We finally go in to have lunch and enjoy our Seafood Platters. I reach across the table and stroke his hand and he holds onto mine.

"Jenny, I love you and whenever you want me, I'll be here."

"I love you too, Roger. I love the way you treat me and look out for me."

After lunch we spend time by the water and then he takes me home. I realize he is not quick to satisfy his needs, and at all times thinks of me, giving me a feeling of security.

I feel good when I'm with him because it seems that just being with me is all he requires.

The following week everything continues in the house as usual. We all gather around in the parlor and discuss the sales, the tours, the horses and things that need work.

I call Amy aside in the gift shop when she's not busy and try to explain my feelings about Marty and Roger. I tell her about Marty's aggressive lovemaking and how it makes me crazy because I feel like I can easily be persuaded. Then I try to explain my love for Roger and the fact that he cares for me differently and I feel protected.

"Well, honey, you love them both, I think, for different reasons, and it should be what is best for you. I have found that a love like Marty's may not be what is long-lasting. Those types of men sometimes look elsewhere after they are married. I don't know that he will. I'm just telling you what I know about men. I knew a young lady once who went along with the desires and once her boyfriend got what he wanted, he left her."

I pace back and forth until customers come in and later I go to my room to think about what Amy said. While there, Marty knocks on my door.

"Yes, Marty?"

"May I come in? I have helped with the horses and now that I've cleaned up I would like to see you."

I know that I just can't open the door and spend time with him here in my room. It will mean more than opening my door to him—and I hesitate.

"Marty, the weather is nice, let's walk in the gardens."

"But Jenny, I'd like to talk with you about my plans for our future."

"We can do that outside—I need to take Boots out anyway."

When I open my door he is standing there leaning on the door jam and looking downhearted. I have Boots on her leash and I march out before he can step into my room. *At that moment I think that my feelings for him are based on passion and not on a true relationship.*

Marty and I walk Boots out to the gardens a little farther from the house among the trees. He turns me around, guiding me to sit on the soft ground there. We sit and he whispers in my ear that he needs me and wants me in his life forever, while gently making advances, and I lean back in his arms. The feelings are marvelous that someone is so in love with me. I realize I am temporarily letting things begin, as if I have someone else's body. Then I wake up to what is happening and know this is the wrong place and the wrong time. Marty's emotions seem out of control at this point with actions from his hands and his kisses, repeating how much he loves me.

I start thinking about Roger. He is a loving person and has plans for us but will wait until I am ready. I turn away and get up from the ground with Amy's words repeating in my thoughts.

"Marty, I need to go in now," and I quickly get up and start walking back, adjusting my clothes with Boots following.

Marty gets up and follows me into the house and wants to talk. We go into the small parlor and I know we will be alone there, but it is safer.

"Jenny, I'm sorry. I felt sure you enjoyed the love from me—now you're not responding. You've never said 'no' before or turned away. Maybe I have misunderstood and moved too fast, but I react that way because I love you and need you."

"Yes, Marty, I'm sorry. Forgive me but I need time."

I leave him there and go back to my room more convinced of my love for Roger. Sitting in my lounge chair I think of the two of them. I love Roger's caring ways, and feel protected when I am with him. Marty's love gives me a different feeling that I think could be dangerous, just like Amy suggested.

Each evening as we gather in the large parlor we are all anxious to know if any of us have had dreams with the ancestors.

Bill says, "Now be truthful because if there is another heir, I'm sure we will start having those dreams again."

He looks around and we are shaking our heads "no," and holding our glasses up in a toast.

I look up at the painting above the mantle of Helen Rivers sitting there with Kathleen and Junior, and I hope peace is what they have now. I can just imagine Helen, enjoying the company of Kathleen and Junior again. As I look closely, maybe it's me, but I think I can see a new smile on Helen's face. I hope she is pleased with all our efforts to bring some kind of a closure for her and the others in her Irish bloodline.

It has been a real adventure for me!

Marty looks at me and winks, "Well, what about the heirs who will come from all the remaining heirs, like children from me and Jenny, and even George when he marries?"

I notice how he words that—me and Jenny—and I shiver. He's at it again, but I hope I have discouraged him.

It is obvious that none of us had thought of those heirs, and we all have a good laugh because we suddenly realize it is not over yet. What comes in the future will have to be dealt with accordingly, and dealing with heirs may go on indefinitely to the end of time.

Bill says, "I think it all has to do with this property. I think this old house has a lot to do with it. It will go on because of Rivers Run perhaps—and will depend, I'm thinking, on how the heirs and future heirs take care of it."

I say, "Perhaps the house does have something to do with it since we had to be here to have our dreams, but I believe it goes back farther than Rivers Run."

I look at Marty and I say, "I think the Irish ancestors want us to always be together in this world, and always recognize our Irish heritage. Their loving concerns for me and Marty, bringing us here in dreams when we had a family loss in our younger years, seem to prove this point."

I stand there together with Bill, Gracie, George, Amy, and Marty. We hold up our glasses in a toast to our Irish ancestors for their concerns for our happiness in our manor house at Rivers Run.

I continue, "Like Marty suggested, I believe the heirs, just like the 'diamonds in the water' at Rivers Run, will happily go on forever. That's what Donald Andrew Rivers Senior told Helen in my first dream with them."

I look around at the raised glasses and happy faces, and feel peace, love, and joy.

I think Bill feels that way too when he holds up his glass, smiles, and as we drink he says, "May it be so!"

The End

ACKNOWLEDGEMENTS

I believe that God's love and His gifts of fellowship and encouragement from many people have given me the courage to pursue this endeavor. I am deeply grateful.

My books usually start with an idea, or something that triggers my imagination and that is what happened when I was visiting my lifelong friend, Deloris Lewis, who lives near the water in Virginia. We were looking out of her windows at the water that had tiny beautiful sparkles of light from the sun as the water moved gracefully along. I mentioned to Deloris that the lights on the water looked like diamonds, and she agreed with me. I then thought about that and said that *"Diamonds in the Water"* would be a good title for a book. The titles of my books usually come *after* my stories, but this time I started with the title and built a story around it.

I received support and encouragement from members of my watercolor painting classes held at the JC Hall in Waldorf and I am very grateful to all of them.

When I completed the first draft, Mary Kercher, my good friend in the art class, and wonderful artist, who read the first draft of *The Journal Reopened,* also volunteered to read this one. Mary gave me suggestions that I believe made a difference in the overall outcome, and I am grateful and consider her a blessing.

I am also grateful for encouragement from family members that helped to keep me focused on a "first person" dialogue for this book—a real challenge.

This novel touches on historical remembrances, but not specifics, of the civil war, the strife in Ireland, and a battle in England territory.

My books have either a cat or a dog in them in honor of Mary Anne Enslow. She made sure our book, *The Cardboard Box*, had a dog in it because she loved animals and supported the local Humane Society. She made an untimely departure to Heaven in 2010. It was a great loss to everyone who knew her, and I still miss her friendship, humor and creativity.

I hope you enjoyed my story and all the characters in it that have tried to keep you involved by their actions. If it inspires you to find out why the dreams return, look into the Sequel, *"Dreams Return to Rivers Run."*

Mary Ann Jenkins
majenkins@earthlink.net

www.ingramcontent.com/pod-product-compliance
Lightning Source LLC
Chambersburg PA
CBHW072207170626
46813CB00003B/831